Forbidden Addiction

(Claimed #3)

Alaina Drake

Published by Accent Press Ltd

ISBN 9781910939673

Published by Accent Press Ltd – 2016

To E for all your love.

To SK. I'm so happy we've reconnected.

Chapter One

The smell of the lilac blossoms planted near the outfield wall drifted into the suite as I swallowed the last bite of salty hot dog. Their perfume was always my favorite sign that winter had thawed to spring; a sweet promise of a new beginning.

I chuckled at the irony. Both of us knew we were sitting here to end something.

Tanner's serious gaze burned the side of my face as he cleared his throat. 'I've met someone, Nina.'

I kept my feet propped on the railing in front of me as I turned my head to meet his stare. 'I figured as much. I'm happy for you.' I smiled while he measured the sincerity of my reaction. I decided to fill the silence. 'No, seriously. I really am happy for you. Tell me about her.'

'I … I … met her … um …'

I reached my hand across the metal armrest separating us. Taking his warm hand in mine, I reassured him without words.

His brow furrowed as he glanced down at our joined hands. His confused eyes returned to mine before he whispered, 'Her name is Emily. I met her in New York on my last business trip. She's amazing … and …'

'You can see yourself falling in love with her.'

'Yes.' His agreement was swift and absolute. "And I don't want to jeopardize what I could have with her by …"

"Being involved with me," I finished when his voice trailed off

I squeezed his hand before releasing it. I turned my attention back to the baseball game that was still in warm-ups. 'Then, by all means, I want you to have that.'

I could still feel his scrutiny burning holes in my cheek seconds later, so I turned back to him. He was looking at me like I was some puzzle that he couldn't figure out.

'What?' I asked.

He blinked twice before answering. 'It's just not how I expected this conversation to go.'

I scoffed. 'You expected me to rant and rave? Or, even worse, cry? Come on, Tanner. Just because we've been having amazing sex for the last six months doesn't mean I'm going to sob myself to sleep tonight. You know me better than that.'

His head tilted to the side as he studied me. 'I also know you well enough to know that you say the most outrageous thing that comes to your mind when you're hiding your true emotions.'

'Oh? And what true emotions am I hiding now?'

His voice was barely audible. 'That's what I'm trying to figure out.'

'Sorry to disappoint, Sherlock. There's nothing to figure out. Come on, Tanner, we had some great nights, but you're looking for more. I respect that, but I'm not going to follow you down that road.'

He scowled. 'You're happy with the casual fuck?'

Why was that concept so hard to understand? 'Yes.'

His next question belied the intimacy of our friendship. 'Are you being honest right now?'

I stared into the outfield, unseeing. 'I never lie to anyone other than myself.'

'That's what I worry about,' he murmured as the PA announcer's voice boomed from the loud speakers, 'Welcome to the sellout crowd here tonight to see your Denver Raptors take on the Memphis Redbirds.'

I looked around the stadium, realizing for the first time that there wasn't an empty seat. The Raptors were doing well this year, but I'd never seen a crowd this huge for a

2

minor league baseball game. And Lord knows; I'd been to a lot of games.

I broke open a peanut shell and threw the peanuts into my mouth. 'Why are there so many people here?'

Tanner took another sip of beer before he answered. He propped his feet along the railing next to mine, pointing to the bullpen out in left field where the starting pitchers were warming up. 'They're all here to see him.'

'Who is "him"? You gotta remember I've been to fewer games this year. This dissertation is kicking my ass and it's a forty-mile drive from Boulder.'

'Oh. I thought for sure you'd heard. Landon Griesen is the starting pitcher for the Raptors tonight.'

I stopped mid chew. 'Are you shittin' me?'

Tanner's eyes lit when he smiled. 'Nope. Not shittin' you at all. I was sure you knew.'

'No. I didn't, but you just made my night. Hell, you made my weekend.'

'I can tell from your response that you aren't entirely sequestered in your dissertation cave. You know who Griesen is, then?'

'Hell yes. Landon Griesen is nothing less than a prodigy.'

Tanner nodded. 'This is what he was born to do. Hell, at thirteen years old, he led his Little League team to the World Series title by pitching a no-hitter in the finals.'

I added, 'Wasn't he taken in the first round of the Major League draft right out of high school?'

'Yep. He signed a multi-million dollar contract with the Dallas Stars and quickly made it into their starting pitching rotation. His curveball was damn near unhittable, and his fastball could top 100 miles per hour. He was even voted an All-Star. He was living the dream.'

Tanner's tone turned solemn.

I finished what I knew. "But we all knew what was coming. The team leaned on him for too many innings. His arm couldn't take the stress. His tendons snapped on some random pitch, his career threatened as he underwent reconstructive surgery. I heard on the news that it was one of those injuries that some pitchers never recover from." That was the extent of my knowledge, so I asked, "How long ago was his injury?"

Tanner swallowed a mouthful of beer. His tongue darted out to lick the foam from his top lip. 'About a year, I think.'

'I still remember how all the sports channels replayed the footage of his injury.' It was gruesome. It was some early season home game. He'd pitched seven strong innings and, without warning, something in his elbow snapped. After he threw a pitch, his body simply crumbled into the dirt. The team trainers rushed to help him from the field, holding his right arm immobile while the audience stared, stunned and silent. All of it had been caught on camera, and it was replayed hundreds of times on TV. Maybe the worst part was the pitying tone of the play by play announcers. 'Oh, no,' they'd say grimly. 'This could be the end of his career.'

Every time I watched that footage, pangs of sympathy ricocheted through my chest. No one wanted their lowest moment broadcast on a national stage.

'Yuck. Me too. It was brutal. The way his elbow just hung made me want to throw up.'

'Same here.' I gestured towards the outfield bullpen, where I could barely make out a figure moving through the fine screen of a fence. 'But he's starting tonight. That's a pretty impressive recovery.'

'Yep. But it's his first rehab start, which means he might not be anywhere near what he used to be.' After an injury, Major League Baseball players usually play in the minor leagues for a few games to test their abilities and their bodies' limits. Most begin in Single-A or Double-A baseball and then work up to Triple-A. After a few

4

successful starts in Triple-A, most are called back up to the Major Leagues, but with this severe injury, no one really knew the recovery timetable. 'I bet he doesn't even know what kind of arm he has anymore.'

I sat forward in my seat. 'We'll know soon.'

On cue, the PA began announcing the names of the starting infield and outfield players as they ran out on to the field. After a pause, he continued, 'And welcome back to the field for his first start in just under a year, former All-Star pitcher ... Landon Griesen.'

My heart stuttered and fluttered back to life as the audience stood and clapped. I stood along with them, peanut shells crunching under my nervously shifting feet. Goosebumps shot up my spine as dramatic music thudded over the stadium speakers.

Soon, the door to the bullpen opened and out trotted six foot of hard, lean muscle wrapped in tight pants and a loose, button-down uniform. He didn't sprint, nor did he walk. His casual gait betrayed no nervousness, as if thousands of people weren't staring at his every movement. His face was shadowed under the baseball cap, but I could see his jaw working on a piece of gum as he ran. Blond tendrils of hair escaped from under his hat where they curled at the nape of his neck. As he jogged past second base, a few of his teammates welcomed him with a lift of their chins. He acknowledged each with a small, warm smile.

He slowed as he reached the mound. His chest expanded with a big breath before he walked the half dozen steps to the top of the mound. He raised his right hand in acknowledgement to the crowd that was still cheering his entrance. His catcher trotted out and shook Landon's hand before he handed him the game ball. The gesture was reverent as if the catcher knew he was in the presence of greatness. Landon was a man among boys here, destined to return to the big stage.

5

The catcher walked back to home plate and crouched down, ready to catch the first pitch Landon had thrown in the public eye in nearly a year. The crowd around us hushed in anticipation. Would his arm look anything like the All-Star pitcher he once was? How hard would he throw? My heart beat against my ribs as I held my breath. Why I was so affected by this moment, I wasn't sure. I guess a huge part of me rooted for him to come back even stronger after the injury, to conquer the doubters who said he'd never be the same. The athlete in me respected all the grueling work he must have put in to recover, not to mention the mental hurdles he had to overcome.

Landon twirled the ball in his right hand a few times while he blew a small bubble of pink gum. The bubble snapped against his lips, and his tongue darted out to bring it back to his mouth where he chewed it again.

'Earth to Nina,' Tanner said.

I startled. 'What? Did you ask me something?'

Tanner chuckled. 'You were laughing, so I asked what you were laughing at.'

'Oh.' I pointed to the mound. 'It's just so funny that thousands of eyes are on him and he acts as casual as he pleases. He's popping gum, for heaven's sake. I'd be so nervous I'd probably pee myself.'

Tanner's chuckle turned into a belly laugh before he said, 'This is nothing for him, I bet. One small blip on his radar before moving back to the Bigs.'

'Maybe,' I whispered, but I wasn't buying it. No one could go through that much work, that much pain, that much heartache to simply blow off his first start in nearly a year. No matter how good he once was, he had to have some doubt.

Landon's torso leaned towards home plate, then straightened and came set for his first warm-up pitch. The second before his entire body worked in unison to propel the ball forward lasted an eternity.

I couldn't blink.

I couldn't breathe.

The silence turned deafening as his right arm bent at an extreme angle, and flung the ball to home plate where it popped loudly against the leather of the pitcher's mitt. My eyes quickly scanned to the digital read-out of the radar gun.

89 mph.

I let out the breath I hadn't realized I was holding. 89 mph was great for any pitcher, but especially good for a warm-up. And a rehabbing pitcher, nonetheless. The crowd murmured now the bubble of anticipation had been popped.

'Nice. His motion looks good,' Tanner said through a mouthful of sunflower seeds.

'Nice speed, too.' Landon threw a second and third warm-up pitch. I checked the radar for each one.

Tanner laughed. 'Only a handful of people in this crowd would even know to check that.'

I smirked at him out of the corner of my eye. 'You know I was basically raised at the ballpark. Dad and I spent our summers here.'

Tanner's look sobered. 'How is your dad?' He asked softly.

I sighed, unable to meet his worried look. 'The doctors say he's fully recovered, but I still worry about him.'

My dad, the only parent I'd ever known, suffered a heart attack a few months ago. To say I'm a daddy's girl is an understatement; so, of course, my life stopped for the few minutes between hearing the news of his collapse and being reassured he was alive. Even now, I never felt comfortable; I was always waiting for the next heart attack to take him from me. 'Thanks for asking, though.'

Tanner's heavy sigh made me shift uncomfortably in my seat. 'Nina. Look at me. Please.' He waited me out, damn him. I turned my shoulders towards him and stalled as long as I possibly could to lift my eyes to his. I knew the emotional crap he intended to say, and I didn't want to hear it.

'No matter what happens with Emily, I want to still be friends.'

'I'd like that, too, Tanner.' I let Tanner sense my sincerity before I finished, 'But I'm not sure Emily would.' I playfully bumped my shoulder into his. 'There's something about being a recent fuck buddy that makes pesky girlfriends bring out their claws.'

Tanner glanced down with a furrowed brow. His weak smile looked pained. 'I know you'll hate me for saying this, but you were, and *are*, more than a fuck buddy, Nina.'

I looked away from the sincerity swimming inhis eyes. I really did want to tell him I counted him as a friend as well, but the thought stuck in my throat. I took the road most traveled, at least for me, anyway. I tried to make the casual tone not seem forced when I began, 'Now you're leaving me high and dry, I'm going to have to find myself a new fuck buddy. Maybe a good old one night stand is on the menu. Have any candidates for me?'

Tanner's long stare was both exasperated and exhausted; resigned, even. After a breath where it appeared he gave up some battle, he painted a smile on his face. 'Well, now that you mention it I do have someone in mind.'

'Ooooh. Let me guess, one of those hot, young lawyers you work with?'

'No.'

'Damn.' I tapped my finger against my bottom lip. While I thought, I watched Landon finish his last warm-up pitch. Before the first batter came to the plate, he circled the mound. He stopped to rub rosin on his pitching hand at the back of the mound, and before he walked back up, he did a small sign of the cross from his head, to his chest, and both shoulders. He then lifted his chin and pointed at the sky. I felt like a voyeur, although he had knowingly completed what looked like a ritual in front of thousands of people.

I desperately wanted to know who he was thinking about as his first footfalls took him up to the top of the mound. He dug in with his cleats and looked to the catcher for the sign to tell him what pitch to throw. His ass stretched his pants as he leaned forward and his muscled right arm hung loosely as he waited for the pitcher's sign. I could see the network of veins that pumped blood into his strong arm. I watched his face for any signs of stress as he threw the first pitch, and I prayed that he wouldn't shake out his elbow.

Strike one.

No wince.

Strike two.

Then the third.

He struck the first batter out in three straight pitches. His delivery to the plate was so graceful, so smooth that it didn't look like he'd thrown three pitches over 90 mph. Every movement was purposeful, calculated. No extra energy was expended in his flawless, well-rehearsed delivery.

The batter walked away shaking his head. Tanner offered his commentary. 'That didn't even look fair.'

'It wasn't,' I murmured as I sat back in the seat. The metal back dug into my spine, but it didn't distract me from studying every movement of the man on the mound. So confident. So in control.

'Any other guesses?' Tanner's prompt pulled me back from the game. What were we talking about? Oh, yeah. I was guessing who he was going to hook me up with.

'I know. How about Jake?'

He shook his head.

'Michael?'

He scoffed and shook his head. 'I wouldn't do that to you.'

'OK. Hmm … what about –'

Tanner interrupted my list of potential matches. 'You'll never guess.'

'Your smirk tells me I'm going to like your answer. How long have you been planning this?'

'Just tonight, actually. When I saw your reaction earlier, it gave me an idea.'

'My reaction? What the hell are you talking about?'

Tanner gestured towards the field.

'Oh, hell no. You know I can't fuck one of the players. Dad would not approve.'

'What if the player is only here for a few more starts?'

The reality of his proposal slammed into me. 'You mean Landon Griesen?'

Tanner laughed. 'Sure. Why not?'

'You think I should fuck Landon Griesen?' I asked again. Surely, I was misunderstanding him.

Tanner chuckled. 'Hell yes, you should. Why not?'

'I could think of a billion reasons why not. Dad –'

'Wouldn't have to know,' Tanner finished, although that wasn't what I was going to say.

'Even if that is true, I can't just go up to Landon Griesen after the game and say, 'Hey, I know you're on every magazine's list of hottest athletes and you can have any girl you want, but do you want me? I'm ready and willing if you are.' I'd get laughed out of the locker room.'

'What if I told you where the team is partying after the game tonight? You could simply show up. And you're hot. You know that. What guy wouldn't want you for the night? Landon is just like any other guy.'

I felt the idea take root and blossom in my chest. Just one night. 'How do you know where the party is?'

'I work for the law firm that represents the Raptors in their contract negotiations. I was dropping off some paperwork today, and as I was leaving Landon was coming in. We made eye contact and I stopped to introduce myself. I wondered what he would do. He could definitely blow me off like many of the other big leaguers we get in here. But he didn't. He took out his earphones and shook my hand. We chatted for a few minutes. He was really down-to-earth, easy to talk to. He invited me to their *exclusive, invitation-only* party tonight.' He emphasized the words like he was a spy.

I moved forward on my seat. 'What did you tell him?'

Faking nonchalance since he knew he had my interest, Tanner said, 'I told him I might be able to make it.'

'And you could introduce me to him?'

'Sure. Go with me, and I'll introduce you. The rest will be up to you.'

'But look at me. I'm in jeans and a T-shirt. It's hardly something to wear to an after-party, and my apartment and all my clothes are forty miles away. We don't have time to drive back.'

Tanner shrugged. 'Wear what you wore last night.' I considered his suggestion. We'd gone out with friends to some clubs the night before in Denver, so I did have my tight black skirt and heels to wear. I spent last night at my dad's house that was literally across the street from the ballpark, so the outfit, while probably wrinkled on the floor of my old bedroom, was definitely a practical option. 'We can leave in the seventh inning so you can shower and get ready. Then we'll go.'

I let the simplicity of the plan stew in me, willing myself to believe that it could work. 'But what if some of the other guys recognize me? They'll surely tell Landon who I am, and then he'll want nothing to do with me.'

Tanner dismissed my worry with a wave of his hand. 'You haven't been to a game in a while. Many of the players you knew have been traded or have moved on to a different league. Most probably won't recognize you.'

'And if they do?'

Tanner smirked. 'You'll just need to get him out of the party before anyone notices.'

Silence stretched between us. I considered the man walking off the mound at the end of the first inning. 'He looked good. But some of his pitches aren't back yet.'

Tanner nodded. 'The curveball.'

'I thought so. It creates the most torque on the elbow.'

'I bet they haven't allowed him to throw it much at all.'

Landon jogged down the dug-out steps. He took off his glove, placed it on the back of the bench, and filled a small paper cone with water from a cooler. He brought the cup to his lips and swallowed the liquid. His hand crunched the cup before he threw it in the trash can. He sat down next to his catcher and started looking at statistics about the batters he'd face in the next inning.

One night with Landon Griesen. I let the thought swirl through me. As I finished two more beers, Tanner's proposal gained momentum until it was a tsunami of hope I couldn't ignore. I had at least a few more innings to think about what I'd do to seduce him.

As day turned to twilight, a light breeze from the outfield blew a fresh wave of lilac into the suite.

Chapter Two

It turned out that Landon only pitched three innings, which was actually long for his first rehab start. He gave up a few hits but no runs, and he left the field to a standing ovation from the crowd.

Tanner and I left halfway through the game, as did most of the crowd who had really only paid to see Landon pitch. Tanner watched TV in the living room of my dad's empty house while I showered and changed. The silky black shirt caressed my skin as it slid over my large chest. The black mini skirt rode above mid-thigh when I leaned over the sink to apply my favorite smoky eyeshadow. The final touch was the peep-toe black high heels with bows on the heels. My feet, weary from all the dancing the night before, protested when I slipped my fire engine red toes into the heels.

'Let's go, Nina,' Tanner yelled, coming down the hallway.

He leaned against the doorway to study me as I finished straightening my hair. Unable to read his expression, I asked, 'What are you thinking about?'

His contemplative look surprised me. 'It feels weird to try to set you up with another guy. I know you're not mine, but ...' He shook his head when he struggled to finish the thought.

I knew what he was trying to say. It *was* weird to see him perched in the doorway when only weeks earlier he would have wrapped his arms around my waist and kissed my neck. He would have whispered the dirtiest of words in my ear as he made promises he almost always kept. His erection would have pressed into me from behind with the intimacy of a lover who no longer bothered to hide his lust. In the past six months, we'd explored every inch of our bodies. The current distance between us was awkward, uncharacteristic for a relationship built on nothing more than mutual lust.

I met his eyes in the mirror to tell him I understood. A single corner of his mouth lifted in a wistful smile. 'Let's go get you laid,' he said, breaking the moment by slapping my ass.

I yelped and rubbed the stinging skin. 'Damn you! You know that turns me on,' I yelled as he walked down the hall.

'I'll be sure to relay the message to Landon,' he yelled back.

I met him in the small, outdated kitchen my father rarely used. I grabbed my purse and applied a thin coat of lip gloss. Pointing a finger at him, I scolded. 'You'll do no such thing. No prepping. No coaching. I want to see what kind of fire this boy has all on his own.'

Tanner opened the door and gestured for me to leave first. 'I'm almost scared for the guy. He hasn't a clue what's coming.'

I smirked. 'I wouldn't have it any other way.'

Fifteen minutes later, Tanner parallel parked along a busy street in downtown Denver. 'What's the name of the club?' I asked.

'Ascent.'

'Wow. Nice place. I've only been in the front half of the bar, but I've heard the VIP section is spectacular.'

'I've been there once, but it was a while ago. Here, come this way.' Tanner took my hand and led me past the front door. The bouncer, dressed in a tight, black T-shirt and ripped jeans, eyed us wearily as we skirted around the side of the building. The alley's cobble stones made me teeter on my heels and slowed our pace. We rounded the corner to the back of the club and arrived at another entrance I didn't know existed. A single bouncer, this time dressed in a pressed white tuxedo shirt, stood guard next to an unmarked door.

'Name please.'

'Tanner Marks. Guests of Landon Griesen.'

The bouncer's face registered no reaction to the famous name. He spoke into a microphone perched on his shoulder, and minutes later, the bouncer nodded.

'Enjoy your evening,' he said as he opened the door. We stepped into a small room where another employee stood guard next to an elevator. We stepped in, the man pushed a button without a label, and the doors closed, only to open seconds later to a wide foyer that was sectioned off from the rest of the open space by teal-tinted glass. Tanner's hand pressed on my lower back as we rounded the corner into the massive main room. Large, clear glass tiles lined the room and the bar that was situated along one long wall. Behind the bar was a large plate of suspended glass. A sheet of water cascaded down it, the surface tension of the water making it cling to the smooth surface. Soft lights were embedded throughout the clear walls, lighting the room with a muted vibrancy. There were no seedy dark corners in this bar that looked like it was dipped in ice.

An equal balance of men and women talked in small groups around the room that was noticeably absent of thumping techno music. Everyone held thick crystal tumblers full of amber liquid. A waiter brushed by us with a tray full of glasses. He stopped in front of us. 'The house special,' he offered, and we both took a glass. When Tanner moved to his back pocket for his wallet, the waiter stilled him. 'It's on the house.' The waiter winked before returning to his place behind the bar.

'Fucking spectacular,' I said in bliss after the first sip of whatever the house special was. 'This goes down easier than Coke.'

'I'm sure that's the aim. Cheers,' Tanner said. I clinked my glass with his and took another cool sip as we walked further into the room.

I scanned the expanse, recognizing a few familiar faces here and there, but Tanner was right when he said that most of the guys I'd known were gone in favor of fresher talent. A few sets of eyes seemed to pause when they looked at me, like they were trying to place me from somewhere. I moved on quickly in search of the guy I'd come for.

Of course, it didn't take long to spot him. He was standing with one other player near the bar. His blond hair shined in the bright room. The loose curls around the nape of his neck were darker, while the strands around his forehead and ears were more sun-kissed. The endless shades of sand on a beach – that was what his hair reminded me of. Although I could see only half of him from my vantage point, his plain, V-neck T-shirt and fitted, light-washed jeans hugged each bulge of his lithe body. He nodded in agreement with something his companion said. His smile came and went as he talked, and his entire attention remained focused on the conversation. Everything about him told me he was a man comfortable in who he was. The ultimate turn-on.

'There's Landon,' Tanner said, guiding me towards the bar. My normally confident stride faltered when a player moved out of my line of sight, allowing me to get a better look at his entire body.

His right arm was wrapped in translucent plastic, which held a large bag of ice on his right elbow. I paused, worried that maybe he'd done too much for his first outing. Had he reaggravated the injury? It couldn't be very serious if he was at the after-party, right?

Tanner pulled me closer until Landon's eyes met

Tanner's. Landon's face lit with an easy smile. He excused himself from his teammate and walked with a purposeful gait towards us.

Landon held out his right hand. 'Tanner, right? We met earlier. Glad you could come.'

The two men exchanged a firm handshake. 'Good memory, man. Thanks for inviting us. I brought a friend. This is Nina.'

I stepped forward and held out my hand. Landon's slightly cold right hand gripped mine as our eyes made contact for the first time. They were ocean blue, the color of water I'd choose to drown in.

'Nice to meet you.'

'Nice to meet you, too,' I echoed. He let go of my hand and let his right arm hang loosely at his side. 'We were at the game tonight. You looked great.'

'Thank you. It was a long time coming, but it felt good to be out there again,' Landon said.

Tanner patted me on the shoulder. 'I'm going to catch up with someone, Nina. You mind if I leave for a minute?'

A shot of adrenaline raced through my chest at the prospect of being left alone with Landon. 'Not at all.'

Tanner's knowing smirk told me he had known the answer before he'd even asked it.

I watched as Tanner headed towards the bar, then I turned my attention back to the man in front of me. When I lifted my eyes to his, the flirty smile I had plastered on my face sobered. His penetrating gaze was studying me with an intensity, a heat that wasn't there seconds ago. I'd been in too many bars, met too many single men, not to know what that gaze meant.

His eyes advertised his interest, mirroring the attraction I felt deep in my belly.

Game on.

And this was a game I was good at.

I decided on small talk first. No need to get personal.

'So how do you feel after the start? Sore?' I glanced at the ice pack on his right elbow. His eyes followed mine.

'A little sore, but that's to be expected. It's all precautionary.' He shrugged. 'I've lived the last year with ice around my arm, so I don't even realize it's on anymore.'

His eyes returned to mine when I took the last sip of liquid in the glass. When had I drunk all that?

His gaze paused at my lips for a split second before he waved over a waiter, who quickly exchanged my empty glass for a full one.

So attentive, this one. 'Thank you, Landon.'

He tipped the waiter twenty dollars. His eyes darkened to a deep sea blue as his left hand slid into his pocket. 'You looked thirsty.'

For more than scotch, my look over the top of the glass told him. His lips tipped in a sly smile. *Message received*, it said.

But now was the time for subtlety. Slow but sure. 'I can't imagine the work you've been through to get back so quickly. And for your first three innings, allowing no runs and only a few hits is a victory, I'd think.'

His grin dimmed as his eyebrows furrowed. 'Yeah, but I would have been slaughtered had I been going against Major League hitters. But compared to a month ago when I couldn't even throw off a mound, I'll take it.'

The depressed look on his face made me want to console him. My hand lifted and squeezed his left elbow, and before I had a chance to check myself, I blurted, 'Don't worry. The curveball's the last thing to come back.' I instantly knew I had a made a mistake. No. No. If he figured out who I was, what my experience with baseball was, all my plans for the night would be ruined. I tried to distract him by taking a step forward so less than a foot separated our chests. I could feel the heat radiating off his body before he took a step back and leaned down so our eyes met on the same level.

His arm bent so that his hand cupped my elbow. His fingers traced lazy circles on the back of my arm. The sensitive skin there prickled as the hairs on my arm stood. Even if I wanted to, I couldn't have pulled away from the intimate touch, the first we had allowed ourselves. Wordlessly, his fingers continued up and down my arm as he studied me pensively.

Finally, he said, 'You know the game.' It was an observation, not a question.

I shrugged one shoulder, feigning nonchalance. 'I grew up around it.' It wasn't a total lie. More like a half-truth.

With a tilt of his head, he studied me. Seconds later, his fingers stilled, and he pulled his arm away. He leaned his back against the bar and rested his elbows on its marbled top. He bent one knee and propped his foot against the bar's wooden base. Casual in his repose, he looked like he was settling in for an inquisition. 'Are you a doctor?'

'No. Definitely not.'

'A physical therapist?'

It would be really fun to stretch him out and rub out all his kinks. 'No. Unfortunately.'

He bit the corner of his lip in thought. How I wanted him to nip me. 'Are you an athlete? Do you play? Like softball or something?'

This was a much safer topic. I took a long drink to regain my composure. 'I run. I'm training for a half marathon right now.'

I didn't miss when his eyes scanned from my heels, past my skirt, along the low-cut neckline of my shirt, and back to my eyes like he was cataloguing every piece of me. 'Impressive. We run to stay in shape, but nothing like training for a half marathon. Have you run one before?'

'No. I have trained before, but I had to stop because I got terrible shin splints. I had to take time off, so I can identify somewhat with what you went through, although

I'm sure yours was much worse.'

'Sorry to hear that, but you're back at it now, which is what counts.'

The unexpected compliment warmed me in a surprising way. The praise was offered sincerely. And the humble way in which he offered it by taking the focus away from his own struggles made him even more attractive.

'Hey, Griesen. Looked good tonight, buddy,' a teammate said as he passed by. Landon smiled and lifted his chin in acknowledgement, but, undeterred, his attention quickly returned to me.

His expression turned serious. The intensity of his scrutiny, solely concentrated on me, made me feel sorry for any batter who attempted to stare him down. This man, when completely focused and in control, was intimidating. When he was going after something he wanted, he was relentless. In that moment, I got a glimpse at the type of determination, the drive that made him so successful at such a young age.

'But that still doesn't explain how you somehow knew I couldn't get my curveball over the plate tonight.'

Damn. I thought I might have distracted him. I took a gulp of alcohol, emptying it like I'd find a way out of this mess through the bottom of the glass. My head swam as my stomach heated with the potent liquid. 'I think Tanner might have said something about it,' I said. Another half-truth. Tanner *had* said something about the curveball, but I'd already known.

Landon frowned at my empty glass, but he quickly schooled his reaction to a polite smile as he placed the glass on a passing waiter's tray, but didn't grab another.

How I missed it earlier, I don't know, but I instantly realized Landon clutched a bottle of water in his left hand. And he had been all night.

I pointed to the bottle. 'Don't you drink?'

He unscrewed the bottle and brought it to his lips. His

throat worked on a few heavy swallows before he screwed back on the cap and narrowed his gaze on me – a gaze that said he was uncomfortable with my question. I knew that gaze – I'd perfected it.

His reply was curt. The confident man so comfortable in his skin had vanished. 'Not during training, and definitely not during rehab.'

I could tell instantly that I wasn't the only one in the business of selling half-truths. No problem. Honesty was something a one night fuck didn't require. Heck, I didn't even require it of myself.

The lights dimmed throughout the bar; pulling me out of the cocoon we'd been absorbed in. My focus was so intense on our conversation that my brain had chosen to disregard the world around me. The smells, the sounds, had been judged as inconsequential. All of it came rushing back like I'd reached the end of a tunnel. 'Are they closing? Why did the lights dim?'

His scowl morphed into a grin that for the first time displayed the most playful dimple on his left cheek. Good Lord, the tingles. I wasn't prepared for that. 'You've never been back here, have you?'

'No.'

His near-empty bottle clinked as he placed it on the bar behind him. He reached into his back pocket for a small knife. He exposed the blade with a click and slid it along what looked like Saran wrap that held the ice pack to his arm. The thin plastic tore easily, and he caught the pack with his right arm before it hit the ground. He reached over the bar to place the ice pack in the sink and tucked the closed knife back into his pocket.

I couldn't take my eyes away from the man, even when he was performing such a mundane routine. My feet were motionless as he stalked towards me. His large hands circled my hip bones gently. He kept an arm's length of space between us. 'You with Tanner?'

21

'No.' Another half-truth. I wasn't now, but I surely didn't offer up that I had been for quite a while.

He nodded and stepped closer so he could lay his forehead against mine. He even smelled like the ocean – a little salty, mixed with a fresh breeze, and the hint of something untamable. I could feel the puff of his breath when he spoke. 'Now's when the real party begins. Do you like to dance?'

Maybe it was the wave of lust I felt with his body so near to mine. Or maybe it was the alcohol racing through my veins. Regardless, I was ready to finally cash in the chips I'd been holding all night. I placed one hand on each of his elbows. One was hot, the other so cold, the skin was flushed a bright red. 'Only if it's considered foreplay.'

I lifted my chin an inch, so our noses brushed and then our lips. The feather-light caress was charged with electricity like lightning building up the energy to strike. His fingertips dug into the skin at my hips, the only warning I got before the delicate gave way. In a flash, his firm lips pressed against mine just before the velvet of his tongue stroked against mine. The kiss pulsed and ebbed, turned, and twisted, until I felt him pull away. His nostrils flared to take in a deep breath. His eyelids hooded as he stared down my halter top.

Somewhere in the periphery, my mind registered that the lights had been dimmed to near darkness, and the lights that once glowed pure white now blazed a deep red. A song with a heavy, thumping bassline boomed over the speakers. The time for pleasant, casual conversations was over. Hips, arms, lips, all became glued together like they'd waited patiently all night for this moment.

His right hand left my hip and drew a line on my sweaty skin from my throat to the top of my cleavage. My breasts hardened as my nipples puckered against my bra.

'Get a room, Griesen,' a drunken teammate offered as he whizzed by.

Landon didn't bother to move his eyes from my chest as he used his left hand to flip the guy off. 'Planning on it,' he yelled over the music.

A devious grin rolled across his face.

Fuck. That dimple was going to end me.

His fingers laced with mine as he tugged me towards the darker side of the room, through the single door in the floor-to-ceiling wall of windows, and onto the secluded balcony that overlooked downtown Denver. The sparkling lights dimmed whatever stars there were in the clear night sky. We stepped around the corner into a darker alcove.

His front to my back, he wrapped his arms around my waist and his chin rested on my shoulder. I could feel him take long breaths against the oversensitive skin on my chest. His erection pressed against my back. My chest lifted with labored breaths as the simmering lust I felt all night boiled over. I pressed back against him. He groaned in response and slipped his fingers between the top of my skirt and bottom of my shirt. His finger drew circles below my belly button.

I thought about making some comment about the view, the skyline, something. But all my thoughts centered on the heat, the fever burning me up.

Landon broke the silence. 'You don't mind dark corners, do you?'

In ways you'll never know. 'No, I don't.'

'Because you're just one dark corner yourself, aren't you? I know because I've got 'em too. There are places I don't let people see. I guard them like you do. And because we're so similar like that, it makes me want to explore them.' His fingers drew lower and slid under the top of my thong. He passed the small patch of hair and paused, waiting for a response.

'Please,' I begged, pressing my ass against him more firmly.

His fingers continued their journey. Down. Down.

Until he rubbed circles around my clit. He pressed gently then more firmly so I bucked against him. His teeth grazed my ear as I tilted my head back.

With my eyes closed and my entire body focused on what he was doing between my legs, I could speak the truth. 'You can try exploring all you want, but I have no need to shine a light into the dark corners. They don't scare me.'

'Of course. You like the thrill of them.' Two of his fingers entered me with a firm thrust.

'Fuck. Yes.'

Landon's lips skimmed my collarbone on their way to my shoulder, where his teeth left dozens of love bites. 'I can tell you like the thrill of the dark corners. But you also like that you can hide stuff in there, too. There's plenty you haven't told me.'

A third finger entered me. One of his feet nudged mine so that I had to widen my stance, allowing him more access. When the palm of his hand rubbed against my sensitive nub, I whimpered. 'I'm close. I'm close.'

He continued like I hadn't said a word. 'Like the truth about why you know so much about baseball. You can hide it tonight, that's fine. But you won't be able to hide from me when you fall apart in my arms. You're going to, aren't you?'

He pumped his fingers twice more before he pressed the heel of his hand against my clit. I pulsed around his fingers and flew apart in an instant. Lightning bolts charged with pent-up energy exploded in my core. 'Yes. Yes. I am. I am.' His fingers continued to pump me through my orgasm until white bursts that looked like exploding stars sparkled behind my eyelids. My legs started to shake when he pulled his hand away.

I swallowed, trying to wet my dry throat. I reached my hand behind me to my lower back, where his rock-hard erection was pressing against the zipper of his jeans. 'Your

24

turn, or do you want to get out of here?'

He hummed while he thought. 'Here. I don't think I can wait.'

I started to turn around to unbutton his jeans and pull down his fly, but his hands stilled me. 'No, stay like that. I've wanted to touch these all night.' He unbuttoned the top two buttons of my shirt and unhooked the front clasp of my bra. If anyone happened to walk by, I was technically still covered, but the silky caress of my shirt against my pebbled nipples told me I was very much exposed.

His arms snaked below mine so he could access my breasts from below. He groaned in my ear when both his hands squeezed and pressed upwards. His hands were strong as each tendon flexed and extended, bent and straightened. 'Such a handful.'

Yes, I am.

He smiled against my jaw.

'Go ahead and lean against me, Nina.' I relaxed my head against his shoulder. I could feel his chest muscles flex as he kneaded my chest. 'Yeah. Just like that.'

Beads of sweat gathered at my lower back as his heated skin burned behind me. A moment later, he continued. 'So you know a curveball from a fastball, but do you know how to throw one?'

'What?' I stammered. 'Of course not.'

In a voice drizzled with playful sarcasm, he said, 'Well, since you seem to be *such* a student of the game, I thought I'd give you a little education.'

I opened my eyes to study his face in the darkness. Shadows danced here and there across his cheekbones, but there was enough light to see the flush of his skin, the heat pooled in his eyes. 'Do I need one?'

'You're going to get one.' He paused, then continued. 'You see, this here is a fastball.' The fingers on his right hand separated, grazing my nipple as they spread out.

'Your fingers should be firm.'

He squeezed so tightly that I felt the muscles between my legs clench and re-clench, begging for another release. 'But you don't want it to be too stiff. You want a little space between your palm and the ball so that the ball can rotate out of your hand. Do it right, and the ball looks like it's a rocket taking off out of your hand.'

He twisted his wrist just enough so I could feel the pressure against my nipple. He squeezed and kneaded twice more with his right hand while his left slipped beneath my panties.

'Now, this here's a changeup. You hold the seams of the ball the same way so it appears like a fastball to the hitter, but you actually take away your index finger, which takes away your power. The changeup requires a really light touch. Loose is key.'

His right-hand grip turned feather light as the pads of his fingers circled around my hardened nipple. His index finger pressed downward as his palm skimmed the pebbled peak. At the same time, two fingers on his other hand entered me and curled to press against the spot that spiraled me close to another release.

I closed my eyes as a whimper bubbled from my chest. He trailed a line of kisses on the side of my throat and pressed his lips against my pulse point. I felt his lips curve into a smile against my skin. 'Now, here's the one I really need to practice. The curveball. Everyone teaches it differently, but usually you put this middle finger inside a seam.' His finger pressed firmly to the point of discomfort just to the inside of my nipple. Every time he pressed and released, using the same rhythm for both hands, need zinged to my core. 'Now, you want to throw it like a fastball to fool the hitter, but then you turn your hand in.' I squeaked when he gripped so firmly that my heels lifted off the ground. My chest lifted in rapid pants, enjoying the edge of pain and pleasure. 'Now, pull down on the front of the ball to get the best rate of rotation.' His voice broke on the last word. 'Fuck. I'm so hard it hurts.'

I reached around to rub my palm against his length through his jeans. 'Please. Let's get out of here. I need you in me.'

His breath left him in a rush. 'Yes. Let's –'

A woman's voice behind us popped our bubble. 'Landon. Sorry to interrupt, but Laura says you're late and you really need –'

It was Landon's turn to interrupt. 'Tell her I'm busy. It can wait.'

'Yes, Mr Griesen,' the woman replied before her clicking heels signaled her retreat. My blood ran cold. The electricity zapping through my body had been extinguished in an instant.

Landon grabbed my hand that was trying to get the last of the buttons on my shirt righted. 'Where were we? Let's get out of here.' His forehead creased in confusion when I turned to walk away. 'What? What are you doing?'

He grabbed for my arm and lightly circled his fingers around my elbow. I yanked my elbow back from his grasp and turned on him.

'I'm an adventurous woman, but the one thing I will *never* do is be the other woman.'

His jaw ticked. 'You mean Laura? She's just –'

I stilled him with an open palm. 'I don't want to hear it.'

He ran his hand through his hair. 'Please. Let me explain.'

'There's no explanation needed. It was stupid for me to assume that you, the baseball superstar, wouldn't have a girl waiting for you at home. Hell, your diamonds are probably wrapped around her left hand.'

He leaned forward, almost desperately. 'No, it's not like that.'

Sure it isn't. 'No? All that travel has to be hell on a

relationship. And there are gorgeous women in each city ready and begging for one night with Landon Griesen.'

Anger crept into his voice now, matching mine. 'Where is this coming from? You know nothing about me.'

'That's what you're banking on, right?'

His wide eyes stared at me in response.

'You know the game.' I echoed what he'd said to me earlier in the night. His had been an observation, a compliment. Mine was just a sad realization. 'And congratulations. You played it well.'

Chapter Three

My feet pounded the concrete in a familiar rhythm. The sun rose twenty minutes into my run, warming my back enough that I had to strip off my long-sleeve T-shirt and tuck it into my shorts. I always loved this ninety minute run on Sunday mornings before church, and despite the alcohol I'd consumed last night, my body welcomed the stress of a challenging run around Coot Lake and Boulder Reservoir, my favorite Sunday morning routine.

The weight of the previous night diminished with each stride, although it provided excellent fuel for both my body and my thoughts.

After I'd learned about Laura, I had quickly called a cab and left Ascent. Sitting alone in the back seat, I texted Tanner to let him know I'd left. Ten minutes later, I crawled into my old bedroom at my father's house and set my alarm for 5 a.m. I woke groggy but eager to take on my Sunday morning run. I slipped on my running clothes and kissed my dad goodbye as he sipped his coffee at his kitchen table. He looked up from the sports section of the newspaper long enough to wish me a good morning, warmly.

'Take it easy, baby girl,' he said as I closed the front door behind me.

A forty-five minute drive later, I stretched out in the parking lot near Coot Lake. As always, my legs protested the first quarter mile, but they soon gave up their futile complaints and settled into a natural stride. Dew shined its rainbow colors on the tips of the grass when the sun shined just right. Birds welcomed the morning light with their twitters and chirps. A few passing joggers huffed quick hellos as they passed, but mostly I was alone with my thoughts. Despite multiple attempts to focus on the beauty of the dawn, my mind wouldn't let go of Landon Griesen.

I couldn't forget his easy, comfortable smile. Or his expressive eyes that hid little. Or his dimple that made me want to glue his lips to mine. And his strong grip squeezing my chest. The way his teeth grazed the top of my shoulder as his fingertips toyed with my nipple. But with each of those memories came the sinking feeling in the pit of my stomach when I'd learned I was the other woman.

There's too many fish in the sea to get involved with one already taken, I told myself when I turned the corner to finish the last mile of the run. It was always my favorite along this route. Running west with the rising sun on my back, I could see my shadow trot along ahead of me. The shadow showed no signs of the stress I was sure were etched across my face in deep lines. My shadow's arms pumped effortlessly while my stride showed no signs of the cramp I'd fought in my right calf for the last two miles. Most of all, my shadow's lungs weren't burning with the final push up the hill to the parking lot. By concentrating on the shadow, I could pretend the run was effortless. That's why running was a perfect fit for me: I'd perfected pretending a long time ago.

My right calf was still sore as I sat in the pew in front of the pulpit. The minister delivered the homily and I sang along to the hymns, although my voice wasn't choir-worthy. After the service, I chatted with a few other twenty-somethings over a plate of pot-luck meats and salads. But the part I looked forward to the most was playing pinochle with Betty, Carol, and Mary, three grey-haired widows with arthritic hands and stories that made me roll on the ground with laughter. These three were what I imagined Hannah, Jenn, and I would be like in fifty years.

Two hours later, I drifted out of the large, wooden church doors to my car, relaxed and happy, with thoughts of the night before purged away. My Sunday morning ritual complete, I was reenergized to take on the week ahead. My heels clicked against the concrete as I walked to my car and a rush of heat escaped when I opened the driver's door. The sun-soaked leather seat warmed the back of my thighs as I sat down and started the engine.

When I turned on my phone, it beeped to signal missed texts. Many, in fact. First, was Tanner's: *What happened last night? Call me.*

An hour later, he texted again: *You'll want to hear it. Trust me.*

'Want to hear what?' I asked the empty car. But my question was answered with the next missed text from a number I didn't recognize. It simply read, *Call me.*

I had a sinking suspicion I knew who sent the mysterious text. It was confirmed with the last text from Tanner: *Sorry. Don't hate me.*

I closed my eyes as I exhaled heavily. Deciding to get this over quickly, I called the number I knew would connect me to the man I'd spent the last two hours forcing myself to forget.

His deep voice answered on the first ring. 'Nina. Hi.'

'How did you get my number?'

'Hello to you too.' He paused, waiting for a pleasantry. Too bad – he'd be waiting a while. Within seconds, he gave up with a huff. 'After you left, I at least wanted to make sure you had a ride home, so I found Tanner at the bar. I told him there was a misunderstanding, and I needed to talk to you.'

'There was no misunderstanding,' I interrupted.

Landon continued like I hadn't spoken. 'Tanner wouldn't give it to me last night, but when I tracked him down this morning, he relented. Reluctantly, I might add. He's a good friend to you, Nina. He cares about you.'

A knot formed in my chest. 'He's in the doghouse now.'

'Don't be mad at him. I was pretty persuasive.' Landon's voice wavered before he grunted in pain.

'Still hungover past noon, huh? You must have closed the place down last night.'

'No.' His breaths panted into the phone. 'I'm in physical therapy right now. Laura, *my therapist*, always stretches me after a workout, but today she's just being brutal.'

'Ow! Mercy, woman!' He yelled to someone on his side of the phone. Most likely, Laura.

He turned his focus back to the phone. 'She's torturing me for missing the session I was *supposed* to have last night. I always have one after a start these days'

'Oh, shit.' The silence lengthened and unfolded as my breath whooshed from my lungs.

'Yeah. Oh, shit,' he repeated sarcastically. 'Now you know there's no ring-wrapped wife waiting for me at home.'

'I'm sorry,' I whispered. 'That one's on me. One of the dark corners, I guess.'

My perception of him righted, I waited for him to cut off the call with a pleasant goodbye. And he'd have every right.

He blew out another breath into his phone speaker. Here it comes, I thought. 'Now you have to make it up to me. You owe me a date.'

'Oh, no way. I'm not that sorry,' I joked.

'Just for that comment, I'm not even going to tell you where we're going. Not knowing is going to kill you, isn't it?'

'The worst kind of torture.'

He groaned in pain again, and I heard the effort it took

in his voice to remain playful. 'Nope. Pretty sure that's what I'm going through right now. Your torture will end on Saturday, when I pick you up for our date at 10 a.m. Sorry. I'd end your suffering sooner, but we're on the road for the next week. That's my first day off.'

'As much as I would love for you to put me out of my misery, I'm not sure that's going to work.' Sarcasm sprinkled my every word.

'Man, you're gonna fight me at every turn, aren't you? Don't worry. I like a challenge. Saturday, 10 a.m.,' he reiterated.

'Well, if you insist. Every other Saturday morning is an important training run. I skipped it last Saturday as I was down in Denver, so, lucky for you, you get to come with me.'

'How far do you run?'

'This Saturday? Seven miles.'

'You're killing me.' Although it was possible he was talking to Laura, I was pretty sure he was talking to me.

A satisfied smirk slid across my face. 'I thought you said you liked a challenge?'

'Difficult woman,' he huffed under a frustrated breath, so low I doubt he knew I'd heard. 'OK. I'll see you at 10 a.m. We'll go for a run. Then we'll shower and change at your house because, of course, you're going to text me your address. Then *I* get to call the shots the rest of the day.'

'If you insist, you difficult man.'

Chapter Four

'How did your start go in Milwaukee?' I asked as we sat on the front stoop of my house in Boulder and laced up our running shoes.

He took a bite of a protein power bar before he answered. 'Good. The pitches have more action with each start, but I was pretty sore for two days afterward. We're going to push back my next start as a precaution.'

I chugged the last of my water. 'Does that worry you?'

Both of us stood up to stretch the backs of our legs against the concrete steps. 'Sometimes. But Laura and my pitching coach, Trevor Raines, don't seem to be too worried.'

'Trevor Raines ... isn't he ...?' I pretended to only recognize the famous name even though I knew him well.

'You probably recognize the name because he was voted Most Valuable Player in 2004 before he shredded the tendons in his pitching arm and had to have Tommy John's surgery –'

'Which is what you had done, right?' I interrupted.

'Yep, so he knows what it's like to basically learn how to pitch again. How difficult it is to trust your arm, to trust that the next pitch won't make it tear again. But he came back and pitched even better after his surgery, so he's the perfect person to have in my corner.'

Fully stretched, we strolled down my front walkway past his car. I pointed at his sleek, black Mercedes. 'Nice car.'

'Thanks. I don't spend my money on a lot of big purchases, but this baby was my one weakness.' He stroked the front fender like it was a beloved pet.

Picking up the pace of the walk, I said, 'Maybe you'll let me drive it sometime.' I wanted to test how close he'd let me to his baby.

'Sure, but do you know how to drive manual?'

'Damn. No.'

'Maybe I'll teach you sometime.'

The promise of future dates, of future lessons, sparked embers of hope in my chest. 'I'm always up for more education.' His knowing smile caught mine before I continued. 'Speaking of lessons, I'm glad you're getting good guidance. I'd think that not having a support system in place for your recovery would make getting back to the majors more difficult.'

He scoffed, which confused me. Then he added, 'There are a few people in the organization who need to be replaced, though.'

Damn my curiosity, but I felt the need to ask specifics. 'Oh? Who?'

'Well Dave, the general manager, has been there since the dawn of time and Craig, the head coach, isn't much younger.'

I pointed to the trail head that marked the beginning of the run and stopped. I squared my shoulders to look at him directly. 'So they should be replaced because they're old? Maybe that just means they're experienced.'

'Both are definitely experienced, especially Craig. He played for years in the majors, but he's very old-school. We younger players do things differently now, and no one has the guts to tell him his ways died with the dinosaurs.'

My heart thudded at the criticism, and I attempted to school the displeasure in my eyes, thankful they were hidden behind dark sunglasses. Ready to run, I decided to change the subject. I placed an ear bud into one ear. Landon took the cue and inserted his as well. I set down my water bottle next to the entrance sign. 'This is where we start.'

Landon's eyes scanned the horizon as he settled his water next to mine. 'Pretty place.'

'This is one of my favorites. It's an old rock quarry that was closed and filled with water. They made it into a recreational lake a few years back and paved a three-and-a-half mile loop around the lake. Two loops. Seven miles. You ready?'

He bounced from foot to foot like a boxer before a round. He winked. 'I was born ready.' We'll see about that, I thought.

He motioned forward with an outstretched palm. 'Ladies first.'

'Sure. One thing first.' I unzipped the little pocket sewn into my right arm sleeve and pulled out a stick of Juicy Fruit gum. I stuffed it into my mouth and chewed. The familiar taste made my mouth water.

'What is that? You run with gum?'

'Yep. All runners have quirks.' I pointed to my mouth. 'This is mine. I never run without it.' With that, I quickly transitioned from a casual jog to a well-paced run within a hundred feet. My muscles relaxed in the rhythm. I timed the thump-thump cadence of my strides against the song I always started my run with to be sure I didn't run too quickly. 'On Top of the World' by Imagine Dragons played softly in my ears; quiet enough that I could still hear the pounding of my feet and the strides Landon was taking behind me.

Three miles in I concentrated on keeping my stride, even down a steep hill. I shook out my arms, first the right then the left. Each one took its turn dangling at my side. The sweat that had pooled in the crease of my elbow ran down my forearm. With new blood rushing to my arms, I was readying my body for the steep incline that followed.

'Holy hell,' I heard Landon say between heavy breaths.

I smiled over my shoulder. 'You OK back there?'

'Yep. I'm fine. Just fine.' He was clearly trying to convince himself.

I chuckled and spent the next few precious strides blatantly checking out the God of a man behind me. Somewhere in the last three miles, he'd taken off his shirt and tucked it into the waistband of his shorts. His abs rippled with each stride, a full six pack that was a shade lighter than his arms, which were tanned a dark olive. His corded muscles remained flexed as his arms pumped back and forth. Good Lord, the man was the perfect combination of strength and agility. So lithe. Not muscle-bound. 'Good. Wouldn't want you to quit on me now.'

I felt the hill start under my feet, so I turned my attention forward. I heard Landon curse behind me halfway up. 'Almost there,' I managed through heavy breaths.

'Fuck me. This sucks.'

We neared the trail head where we started, so I slowed my pace and stopped at the entrance sign for a much-needed drink. 'You want to wait here? Your trainers are going to kill me if you pull something.'

'Fuck that. I'll die before I stop," he managed between gulps of water

My breath had finally recovered after the hill. 'Competitive?'

He threw his water bottle into the grass and sprinted a few strides. 'You have no idea,' he said over his shoulder. 'I'll beat you back if I have to crawl.'

I lost sight of that amazing smile when he turned to face forward. But at least I got a chance to stare at his backside. I'd let him lead for a few miles. Let him think he'd challenge me. He wouldn't. I knew it. His strides were constant on the even ground, but it was only a matter of time.

The music I had chosen for this run started to mellow out, with soft blues mixed with a little Barry Manilow, my dad's favorite. I spat out the flavorless gum as I prepared for the last two miles. I pulled out my ear bud and hung it loosely around my neck.

An ache took root under my right ribs, so I focused on exhaling puffs of air loudly like a weight-lifter attempting to bench press two-hundred pounds. Each time my right foot hit the ground, I forced myself to exhale, and the shooting pain eventually gave way to a dull ache.

The exhaling combined with the chilly morning air caused phlegm to gather in the back of my mouth. Without thought, I turned my head to the right and used my tongue to gather the extra saliva. As I took a breath to spit, my brain reminded my body that I was just a few strides behind Landon. I wasn't sure whether hocking a loogie was frowned upon on a first date. Would he be completely turned off by it? Screw it. I couldn't run two more miles with this in my throat. Decision made, I turned my head. I spat as quietly as I could, hoping I could get away with it.

Landon didn't look back, so I thought my stealth had worked.

Then he turned his chin over one shoulder, offering me the silhouette of his square jaw and high cheekbones. 'Damn. I was hoping you swallowed.'

'I do that too.'

'Promises. Promises,' he playfully chided.

'I never make a promise I can't keep. You'll see.'

'Damn. If I could get hard right now, I would.'

I pushed the ground away with the ball of my foot to lengthen my stride. Each one brought me closer behind Landon. His audible gulps of air and uneven strides told me he wasn't feeling too good. He turned his head towards me when I pulled shoulder to shoulder with him.

'I'm dying,' he managed. At least that was what I think he said.

'Only a mile left now. You can do it.'

'No. Really, I don't think so.'

I couldn't help the mischievous smile that spread across my face as I picked up the pace and pulled in front of him. Over my shoulder, I goaded him. 'Start crawling, then.'

'You better run, woman. If I catch you, you will regret it,' he warned.

With the intense need to show off, to impress him, I forced my tired legs to pump through the fatigue that tightened them.

Only a hundred yards left. You can do anything for a hundred yards. The pain is temporary. I sprinted as best I could up the hill, and when the trail head sign came into view, I stared at it like I could will it closer.

Within twenty seconds that felt more like double, I passed the sign and slowed to a walk. With my hands laced on top of my head, I turned to find Landon.

But he wasn't there.

I took a few heavy breaths as I waited. Then I started to worry. Seven miles without training was not a good idea for anyone, no matter what good of shape he was in. Panic had just started to rise in my throat when I saw him appear over the top of the hill. At first, all I could see was his head bobbing. His heaving chest with rivulets of sweat running down the cracks of his stomach muscles emerged next. The last things to be revealed were his legs that struggled to maintain his stride. He probably could have stopped and walked faster, but he wouldn't allow himself. The competitor in me recognized the one in him as he pulled up next to me.

He leaned over with his hands on his knees. Sweat dripped from his face to the concrete below until he snagged his shirt from the waistband of his shorts and wiped his face with it. It took a full minute for him to regain his breath, but he still hadn't made eye contact with me.

With his gaze towards the concrete, he panted out, 'I can't believe you do this for fun.'

I chuckled. 'I don't do this for fun. I do it for how I feel afterwards.'

For the first time, he turned his chin to make eye contact with me. One eye was closed as he was looking into the sun. 'Yeah. 'Cause feeling like I'm going to puke is certainly desirable on a first date.'

I patted his back playfully. 'I wouldn't if I were you. From personal experience, puking usually reduces the chances of wall-banging sex.'

He straightened. His flirtatious smile matched my own. 'Wall-banging sex? That's one thing where I *do* like how I feel afterwards.'

'And during.'

'Definitely during.' He tapped my ass as we started to walk slowly towards my house. He rubbed his palms together mischievously. 'And now I get to call the shots for the whole day.'

I quickened my pace from a casual walk to a slow jog.

'What are you doing?' He asked, a horrified look widening his eyes.

'Only if you can keep up.'

Landon let me take a shower first while he watched TV. Since he wouldn't tell me where we were going, other than it was going to be casual, I decided to wear a pair of tight jeans and a blue, short-sleeve T-shirt. My hair still dripping wet, I found him splayed on my living room couch, one hand tucked under his head.

I yanked the snarls out of my hair. 'Your turn.'

He didn't move. 'Everything hurts,' he moaned.

It was funny, sure, but I also felt a little guilty. 'Your coaches are going to kill you.'

He sat up slowly and stretched. He shrugged as he stood. 'I have more time between starts. I'll be fine.'

He grabbed his bag full of clothes and toiletries from the foyer. His still bare, muscled chest passed me in the narrow hallway, close enough that I could smell the musk and sweat left over from our run.

I smacked his shoulder. 'Yuck. You don't smell fine.'

I expected him to mutter an embarrassed apology. But the ever-confident, self-assured man didn't even bother to turn around as he limped through the bathroom door and clicked it shut behind him. But before he did, he made sure I heard his lighthearted jab. 'Fuck off, feisty one.'

Chapter Five

'Is this OK for lunch?' Landon asked as he pulled into a local bistro in downtown Boulder known for its locally-sourced, organic ingredients. 'I guess I don't really know what runners should have after a big run.'

'This is fine. I'm starving.'

He turned off the engine, leaned over the sleek, leather console, and pointed his finger at me. 'Stay right there. Don't move.'

I saluted. 'Yes, sir.'

'Music to my ears,' he sing-songed before he unfolded his long legs from the car, shut his door, and rounded the hood in quick strides. He opened my door with his right hand so he could offer his left.

I'd never been one to swoon over chivalry, but I couldn't fight the warm, floating feeling I got in my chest when Landon pulled me out of the low car. He guided me to the front door of the restaurant with his left hand pressing into my lower back, which didn't budge when he opened the door to the bistro with his right.

We both ordered the daily special and sat down in a worn, oak booth to wait for our food. 'So, tell me about the half marathon you're running. By the way, I didn't say it earlier when I should have, but you were really impressive today. I'm no runner, but you seemed like you still had a lot left in you at the end.'

'Thanks. I felt pretty good, but seven miles is a lot different from thirteen.' The waitress brought our food on plastic trays, so I paused while she asked us if we needed anything else. After we shook our heads and took the first few bites in silence, I answered. 'I plan to run the Georgetown to Idaho Springs half marathon. It's an iconic run in Colorado that most runners want to be able to say they've done. It's almost all downhill from one town to another, along a highway that curves through the mountains. The road follows a creek the whole way, and from what I've heard, it's a really peaceful, scenic run.'

I was taking another bite when Landon began his next question. Before he spoke, though, I noticed his eyes glued to my mouth as I licked a drop of sauce from my thumb. 'What got you into running?'

'I tried it in high school and fell in love, I guess.' The safe answer.

'What we did this morning seems like a hard thing to fall in love with. Why do you do it? What about running made you fall in love?'

My jaw stopped chewing. It was a casual-enough question, one that I got asked a lot. But, for some reason, I didn't feel like offering the patent answer I usually gave.

'What?' Landon asked at my pause. 'Did I say something wrong?'

I shook my head and swallowed the lump of food that felt like it was stuck in my throat.

'I ... keeps ... shape ... time ...' I stopped my own stammering.

Landon put down his fork and leaned back against the back of the booth. He studied me, penetrating me with those eyes that rarely missed much. 'Let me guess. One of those dark corners?'

I didn't want to answer directly with the truth. Using a hypothetical answer let me gain enough distance to come near the truth. 'Some of the best runners I know spend their entire lives running from something. If they manage to get far enough away from it, they'll have proven something.'

Landon leaned forward and placed his elbows on the

table. 'Is that something always the same for *these* runners?'

'That they're enough.' My eyes misted even though I willed them not to. 'They simply want to know they're enough.'

His eyes softened as his hand reached across the table to wrap around my wrist. His other hand reached for my mouth. His thumb tugged on my bottom lip, freeing it from my nervous bite. 'Don't we all.'

Our eyes met for a few seconds before Landon pulled his hand away, picked up his fork, scooped up some salad, and continued the lunch with casual conversation like we hadn't shone any lights into dark corners.

Fifteen minutes later, Landon's Mercedes purred to life.

'Where are we going?' I asked as I rolled on some lip gloss.

He studied me as I completed this mundane task. He swallowed heavily before turning his attention back to the road. 'Tsk. Tsk. You don't get to know. And I hope it's killing you.'

I pretended to stab myself in the chest. His chuckle made an ache settle between my thighs. I shifted my legs, trying to gain more pressure in the spot that throbbed with need. Every little detail about Landon made me want him more. The way his left wrist draped across the top of the steering wheel. The way his body leaned slightly towards mine. The way his right hand rested on the gear shift, ready to up-shift and down-shift like a racecar driver. For some reason, I felt I could watch all night the coordination of his foot pressing on the clutch and the flick of his wrist on the shifter. The car progressed through the gears smoothly, and, with each acceleration, my back was pressed into the seat, making me tingle with want. The way he pushed and pulled all the right levers and sticks at the right time made me want to leap across the console and straddle him. I desperately wanted to find out if he could master my body, my pleasure, the way he was controlling his car.

'Almost there. Have any idea yet?'

I looked out the window, recognizing that he had driven us to Longmont, a town outside of Boulder. 'I've only been here a few times. Jenn, one of my best friends, lives here. But I don't know what there is to do here.'

He smiled devilishly. 'Good.' He turned two more corners and parked in a mostly vacant parking lot. I looked for a sign, but since I couldn't find one, I unbuckled and reached for the door handle.

'Nuh. Uh.' Landon said like he was chiding a toddler. He pointed at me just like he'd done outside the restaurant.

I pursed my lips to hide my smile as my hand returned to my lap.

Landon's body leaned across the console. His lips pecked my left temple. 'That's more like it,' he said before he exited the car, rounded it, and plucked me out like it was some ritual he had to complete.

His hand guided me up the sidewalk where I was finally able to read the only sign. 'Miniature golf? You're taking me miniature golfing?'

'Yeah. So? My date. My choice. Remember?' He paid the old man at the front desk who gave us a score card and tiny pencil.

I mimed zipping my lips closed as we chose our balls and putters in the small shack of a clubhouse.

I was surprised when Landon hastily laid his putter against the wall and stalked over to me with heated eyes. I had milliseconds to register his firm hand at the nape of my neck pulling me toward him, before his lips clashed with mine. His tongue pressed, circled, and stroked as my squeak of surprise gave way to a moan of pleasure. He pulled away seconds later. He licked his bottom lip and stared into my eyes. 'I've wanted to do that all day. I couldn't wait any longer.'

I leaned forward and pecked his full bottom lip. 'I have no idea what made you think you had to wait.' I kissed his chin.

'Don't.'

Along his jaw.

'Deny.'

In front of his ear where his muscles flexed under my lips.

'Us.'

A bite to his earlobe.

'Anything.'

I pulled away to meet his feral stare with my own. His hand gripped my hip bone. 'I'm going to have a hard time putting the brakes on with you.'

I didn't know him well enough to know if that was a bad thing. 'Does that bother you?'

'Only if it bothers you.'

Nose to nose, I gave him an honest answer. 'Not at all.'

The front door chimed when a family with small children entered the lobby. Landon stepped back and plucked his putter from the wall. Silently, he took my hand and led me to the first hole.

'What are we playing for?' I asked.

He didn't pause writing our names on the score card when he answered, 'Head.'

A hearty laugh burst from my throat. That was something I'd say. 'Where have you been all my life?'

He turned his attention from the score card. 'I don't know,' he murmured distantly. Disquiet raced down my spine at the emotion I saw on his face so I turned and placed my ball on the rubber mat, and lined up for the first shot. I swung what I thought was gently, but the ball rolled too quickly past the hole by a good six feet.

I groaned when he whistled. 'Damn, muscles. You didn't have to sock it so hard. Watch the master,' he joked as he stepped in front of me and swung his club. The ball rolled slowly towards the hole where it stopped mere inches to the right.

He tapped the ball in for a score of two while I took three hits to get it in the hole. Five holes later, I was still behind by one stroke, mostly because I wasn't a very good judge of speed. It would have been more, but I got a lucky break off the blade of the spinning windmill.

As we played, our competitive banter fueled my lust that boiled under the surface like a dormant volcano. My body was aware of his slightest touch, a small caress here, a firm push there. The brush of his fingertips. The strength in his grip. It all took me back to the night at Ascent. When I closed my eyes I could feel his fingers circling between my thighs while his other hand kneaded my chest.

With my thoughts lost in that night, my skin beaded with sweat despite the cool spring air. The slight breeze blowing from the north, strong with the scent of spring tulips and daffodils that were planted along the course, blew the hair off my temples and neck. My exposed skin pebbled as I remembered how he'd nipped those sensitive places at the club.

'Nina?' Landon's voice pulled me from the memories.

My eyes snapped open to his.

His two long strides brought us chest to chest. He chucked his putter into the grass and spun me around so that his erection was pressed against my ass.

'You need some help, Nina.'

Yes. I needed some relief from this fire he had stoked.

'Your speed has been off all night. You're hitting it too hard.' With one arm on each side of mine, his firm grip circled my knuckles. He guided the putter in my hands. Back and forth. Back and forth in a lazy, rocking motion that made me whimper with want. 'It's all about the rhythm. Isn't it?' He purred, and I knew we weren't talking about a golf swing.

48

He moaned into my ear when I bent my knees slightly, dipped my hips, and pressed back against him.

'Step forward. Now we're going to hit the ball. And you're going to get a hole in one.' I followed his command, inching my right foot forward, then my left. He followed, his front glued to my back. I felt the weight of the putter as it pulled back and with the same speed accelerated forward. The ball dinged against the head of the putter. Our heads turned at the same time to watch the ball skirt around the hole and come to a stop a few inches beyond.

He exhaled the breath he'd been holding on the delicate skin below my ear. 'Damn. Story of my life. A few inches too long.' He punctuated the innuendo with a small thrust of his hips into mine.

I laughed and rested my head against his shoulder. 'Silly man. There's no such thing as a few inches too long.'

His teeth nipped my earlobe. 'You won't be saying that when you're begging for mercy.'

With that, the heat of his body left mine. He picked up his putter and hit his ball like he was unaffected by our exchange. Yet I didn't miss that before he tapped in with a score of two, he readjusted himself with a grimace.

Two holes later I placed my ball on the starting rubber and searched the course for the hole, as it wasn't immediately obvious. After inspection, I realized I had to hit my ball into the alligator's mouth, which was slowly opening and closing. The ball then traveled through a tube buried in the ground and came out in a smaller area where I could then putt it in the hole.

'I got this,' I said, confidently. 'This has to do with aim. Not speed.' I nodded to the alligator. 'First time,' I predicted.

'You're calling it?' Landon looked surprised.

'Yep.'

'Let's do a side bet, then, Babe Ruth. The player who takes the fewest hits to make it into the alligator's mouth gets to ask one question. The loser must answer truthfully.'

I wiggled my butt. 'No problem. Be ready to pay up.'

I studied the pattern of the alligator's mouth, counting the seconds it took to open and close. When I thought I had the timing down, I swung the club and watched as the ball rolled quickly into the alligator's mouth. It rattled against the metal animal before it went into the tube and came out the other end where it rested a foot from the hole.

'Nice hit.' Landon raised his arm for a high-five. The loud slap tingled my palm.

'Thanks. Now you've got to get it in on the first try.'

'I've never had that problem,' he deadpanned. Completely focused on his task, he placed his ball on the mat, studied the alligator's motion, and hit the ball.

The ding of the ball as it hit the snout of the alligator and rolled backwards was the sweetest sound I'd heard in a while.

I bit my lip to try to hide my smile.

'Damn. Damn. Damn,' he cursed as he walked up to the ball and lined up the next shot.

Which also hit the snout and rolled backwards.

Landon's nostrils flared in frustration. 'Fuck me.'

I willed the laughter to stop forcing its way out of my throat.

Obviously fuming, he stepped up to the ball and hit it too quickly without properly timing the shot. The clang of the ball as it collided again with the metal was the last straw. I bent over in breath-stealing laughter.

'Motherfucker …' was the first cuss word in a string of otherwise indecipherable expletives. He raised his club above his shoulders as he stalked towards the offending alligator, like he was going to take a full swing at the green head. He stopped himself short and one-handedly tried to tap in the short putt.

My knees gave out in laughter as he zoomed the putt past the mouth.

'Easy, muscles,' I mocked as I gulped precious air.

His head fell back as he closed his eyes. 'Cocksucker …'

His knuckles turned white on the club, and he lifted his knee like he was seconds away from snapping the club against it.

'Cool it, chuckles,' he said to me as he lined up his next shot. He took a deep breath before he tapped it into the alligator's mouth. His ball rolled through the tube and came to rest with a kiss against mine.

'That sucked hardcore,' he said to me as he led us down the pathway. My stomach ached as I tried to control my giggling.

We both tapped in, and the rest of the holes passed quickly, so much so that I was surprised when we stepped up to the eighteenth and final hole. A frog croaked in one of the ponds as the sound of a child's laughter drifted from a distance. 'What's the score?' I asked.

He didn't have to pull out the score card from his back pocket. 'You're down by one stroke. If you win this hole, we end up tied.'

'What does that mean for our bet?'

He shrugged. 'We'll have to 69, I guess. Ladies first,' he finished.

I stepped up to the final hole, which bent right then left. It was one of those holes that if you hit the angles just right the ball would bend easily around the corners. I placed my ball on the mat and started to line up the shot. In my peripheral vision, I saw Landon step up behind me.

'No way, buddy,' I warned, pushing him away with the palm of my hand. 'I can tell what you're trying to do."

His hands went up at his sides. 'Fine. I won't touch you.' His arms straightened when he laced his hands behind his back. He leaned in so closely that I could feel his breath at my ear. But he wasn't touching me.

He whispered, 'How do you like your sex? You like to be in control?'

I tried to focus on the ball. The swing. But I had to answer him. 'Some nights.'

'And the other nights?'

Straight back, straight through, I thought. Don't screw this up. 'I don't.'

'Ahh … those are the nights I'm most interested in. I bet you'd like me to tell you to go to your knees …'

'You're just trying to mess up my shot.' It was working. I listened to his every word, my body motionless.

He continued as if I hadn't spoken. 'You'd wait for me on the bed if I told you to. You'd let me tie your hands to the bedpost and fuck you any way I wanted. You'd even let me mark you with my come, wouldn't you?'

My breath came in pants as my heart beat wildly against my ribs. 'Yes. Yes I would.'

'Hit the ball, then. The sooner we're done here, the sooner we can get started.' My stiff arms swung the club much too hastily, and my ball went sailing past the hole and filtered into a low area, far away from the hole.

I turned on him, furious, and hella turned on. A dimple-laden, satisfied grin was spread across his face.

I pointed my finger at him, only mocking fury now. 'You cheated.'

He shrugged a shoulder. 'After this morning, I had to get my pride back somehow.'

And two hits later, he did, beating me by a total of two strokes. The afternoon had turned humid, and I was suddenly thirsty. We started walking back to the small clubhouse. 'I'm going to get a Coke. Do you want something? My treat.'

'Not so crazy about you paying, but if you insist –'

'I do,' I interrupted.

'Then I'll have a Coke, too.'

I took his putter from him. 'You can wait here. I'll take our putters back and get us our drinks.'

Landon sat down on a concrete bench, crossed his ankle over his knee, and stretched his arm over the backrest where he patted it twice. 'I'll save this spot for you.'

I turned towards the clubhouse with a goofy smile on my face. I'd had a great time. He was playful. Competitive. Gave compliments easily. Confident. And, above all, he radiated sexuality in wavelengths that matched mine.

When I stepped into the clubhouse, there were quite a few families waiting in line to golf, so I put the putters away and got in line to buy our Cokes.

Five minutes later, Cokes in hand, I went back outside and found an empty bench. My eyes scanned left then right, but I couldn't catch sight of his blond hair anywhere. A quick glance at his Mercedes in the parking lot told me he was still here, but I couldn't see him.

That's when I heard the faint ding of metal, followed by a deep thud.

Ding.

Thud.

Ding.

Thud.

Then I knew exactly where he was. I walked down the hill to the batting cages. Almost all miniature golf courses have batting cages attached to them, and I should have known Landon couldn't stay away. I thought I'd turn the corner to find Landon in the fast pitch cage swinging at balls shot out of the automated machine. But before I rounded the corner, I caught Landon's slightly higher voice he uses when he's teaching something. I peered around the corner so I could watch without being seen.

'Time the beginning of your swing with a quick tap of your left foot. Good,' he praised a young boy of no more than ten. The boy's eyes lit up. He wore a batting helmet two sizes too big and held a bat that looked a little too heavy for him. Spurred on, he got back in his batting stance and readied for the next pitch.

Landon watched from outside the cage. He leaned against the enclosure. One ankle was crossed over the other, and his fingers were wrapped around the chain-link squares as he offered further advice. 'Now, your hands should start the swing.' He observed a few more tries. The boy whiffed and hung his head in frustration. 'You're doing good, buddy. Keep trying.' The boy lifted the bat again and barely made contact with the next two balls. The automatic pitching machine clicked and stopped spitting out balls, so the boy started to walk away.

'No. Stay right there, big-hitter.' Landon turned the latch on the gate, stepped inside the enclosure, and latched it shut. He reached into the front pocket of his jeans and pulled out a small pile of change. He searched through it for a combination of coins, and, finding them, shoved them into the machine's slot.

'Before we start the machine again, I want to show you something.' He reached for the bat, and the boy handed it to him with stars of admiration in his eyes. Landon took a batting stance, tapped his left toe, and started his swing in slow motion. I couldn't hear everything he said because he faced away from me, but I caught some of it. 'Use your hands to start … tuck your elbows in … load your legs …'

Landon's body isolated each individual movement of the swing, demonstrating and re-demonstrating. The boy nodded when Landon handed him back the bat. Landon stepped out of the enclosure, closed the latch, and stood, his feet separated in a wide stance with his arms crossed.

He looks exactly like a coach. I know one when I see one.

He clapped his hands twice. 'We don't need home runs, Connor. Just contact.'

Connor hit the button that started the machine, and seconds later balls started racing towards him. He hit a few. He completely missed a few. He fouled a few off backwards and at odd angles. But the more he tried, the better he got. By the end of the two-minute session, Connor's good hits outnumbered the bad. And more importantly, the smile that lit his face could fuel the sun. He threw down the bat and helmet and raced out of the cage to high-five Landon, who reached down to Connor's height.

'Nice job, buddy! I'm so proud of you. I knew you could do it.' Landon offered his knuckles for a fist bump before he put his arm around Connor's shoulders. Connor strained his neck upward to look at Landon like he was Superman. The odd stirring in my chest caught me off guard as I watched them walk side by side. Having children was so far off my radar, even NASA couldn't find them. But, damn, I think my ovaries just flipped over and spit out a dozen eggs.

Someone sniffed behind me, making me jump a mile in the air.

'Sorry,' she said, wiping her eyes. 'I didn't mean to startle you. I'm Connor's mom. I was watching too. Connor needs this more than your man could ever know.'

I thought about telling her Landon wasn't my man, but she continued before I had the chance.

'Connor's dad and I divorced last year, and he doesn't see his dad much despite my best efforts. Connor craves male attention. I'm sure he'll be talking about this for a week.'

As the two walked closer, Connor's mom leaned in conspiratorially. 'Let's pretend we just met in the line to get drinks.' She held up her own two bottles of Coke. 'We'll walk around this corner talking like new friends. Then neither of us has to explain why we eavesdropped.'

'Good plan. Let's go.'

We stepped around the corner. 'So where did you say you're from?' The mom asked as if we were continuing our ten-minute conversation.

'Boulder, but we're just here visiting friends. You know, that roommate I told you about earlier.'

'Oh, yeah. I remember.' She smiled as we stopped a foot away from Landon and Connor.

'Sorry it took so long,' I said to Landon as I handed him the plastic bottle, dripping wet with sweat. 'A lot of families were in line in front of us, so we had to wait.'

He twisted off the cap and drank a few swigs. Then he brought the bottle down from his curved lips. With a furrowed brow, he looked inside the bottle then inspected the outside of it. I saw the moment when his investigation turned into a hypothesis. He looked around at the four Coke bottles, all dripping sweat, with what was most likely warm liquid inside.

He tilted his head sideways as he studied me.

Damn it. I couldn't meet his eyes.

His guess confirmed, my charade exposed, the tips of Landon's lips curled into a knowing smile. We made eye contact and he winked as he took another drink of the tepid liquid. He knew I'd snooped. And the thought amused him as I squirmed next to him.

Landon wiped away excess liquid from his lips before he spoke. 'I was just offering Connor here some tips.'

He reached his right hand out to Connor's mom to shake hers before he placed it back on Connor's shoulder. 'I'm Landon. Nice to meet you. Connor has some real promise. He says he's going to play some summer baseball.'

'I'm Alyssa. Nice to meet you, Landon. Yes, he's going to –'

Alyssa's explanation was cut off by Connor's excited scream. 'Wait. Did you say "Landon"? I knew you looked familiar. You're Landon Griesen, aren't you?' His eyes widened in an awestruck stare.

Landon ruffled his hair with a humble smile. 'I am. Do you want to come to a game sometime? Maybe I can get you some field passes while I'm still pitching in Denver.'

Connor's vocal cords wouldn't work, so Alyssa answered for him. 'That would be amazing. Thank you.'

Landon pulled an old receipt from his wallet and scrawled his cell phone number on the back. He handed it to Alyssa. 'Here. Call this number in a few days with some dates you two are free, and I'll try to set it up.'

Both thanked him as Landon took my hand. 'No problem. Have a good day.' Connor waved goodbye as we walked away. Thank you, Alyssa mouthed, clearly fighting emotions she didn't want Connor to see.

Landon nodded his acknowledgement before we turned and walked to the parking lot.

I debated on whether or not I should tell him I deliberately hid to overhear the lesson. Hell, he already knew, but maybe I should be honest. 'That was a really nice thing you did,' I said as Landon opened my door.

I stepped in when he answered, 'I love helping. Someday, I can see myself as a coach. I'm obviously no hitter, but I've seen enough Major League hitters to know the basics.' I didn't miss the wistful, longing look on his face before he closed the door, walked around the car, and opened his own door.

When he sat and started his car, he didn't say anything, so I decided to clear the air. 'Are you mad I spied on you?'

He waved my concern away with a flick of his wrist. 'No. I had a suspicion you were watching. It doesn't take *that* long to buy drinks. But when I figured it out, I really liked seeing you blush.' His finger and thumb pinched my cheek like a grandma does to a toddler. I playfully swatted his hand away. 'After all the things we've said and done, for *that* to be the cause of your first blush …'

He was interrupted when his phone dinged in his

pocket. He reached into his pocket to retrieve it. 'Sorry. I have to check this. Not very many people have this phone number, so it could be important.'

He read something on his phone while I pretended not to stare at him. He took his sunglasses off, pinched the bridge of his nose, and yawned. 'Oh man.'.

'Is something wrong?'

His face turned towards mine, regret and disappointment in his eyes. 'I'm going to have to drop you off and head back to Denver. You know the team goes on a ten-day road trip starting tomorrow morning?'

'Yeah.'

'Well, our flight was cancelled in the morning, so we have to leave tonight. All players have to be at the stadium, ready to board the bus for the airport by six.'

I checked the clock on the dashboard. 'You're barely going to make it.'

He peeled out of the parking lot and quickly merged into traffic. 'I'll make it. Don't worry. But sorry we have to cut the night short.' His warm right hand rested on my thigh. 'I was really looking forward to finishing what we started.'

I covered my hand with his and used my first finger to trace his knuckles. 'Me too.'

Despite my disappointment, I couldn't deny that the flame of lust we'd fanned all day was still burning low in my core. As he accelerated on to the highway to Boulder, I unbuckled my seat belt and leaned over the console to stroke the denim covering his inner thighs. 'But nothing says we can't take advantage of the time we do have.'

The darkness of his aviator sunglasses hid his eyes from me, but his reaction was clear when his lips opened and a moan escaped. He widened his knees as I felt his erection grow under my hand.

'Time for me to pay up,' I said as I unbuttoned his jeans and pulled down his zipper. He lifted off the seat so that I could pull down his jeans just enough to gain access.

'Fuck,' he hissed when I pulled down his boxers and rested the waistband just below his balls. He was granite hard as he rocked his hips upward, seeking friction from my hand that barely fit around him.

His width was solid but the most impressive part was his length, that reached past his belly button. The rest of his body was long and full. Why I expected this part of him not to match, I didn't know. My core clenched, begging to be filled by him. 'Wow,' I praised as I leaned forward, the leather console biting into the side of my ribs.

I felt the vibration of a low rumble in his chest. 'I wasn't joking. Here,' he added, and guided me away with his forearm.

'What?' I asked, confused.

'Let me make this more comfortable for you.' He lifted a small lever on the front of the center console and slid it back so I could lean over without it pressing into my ribs.

I grinned as I leaned forward. 'I don't even want to know what Mercedes calls that feature. Do you have to ask for it specifically?' I deepened my voice, mimicking a man's low rumble as he talked to a car salesman. 'Ya, I like that car over there, but I'm still on the fence. Can you add the fellatio assist device? Great! Then I'll take it.'

Landon snorted out laughter as he shook his head. 'No, unfortunately the truth is much less sexy. The console moves back so that the passengers in the rear seats can have closer cup holders.'

I looked to the back seat. 'I call bullshit on that. They say that to sell it to the housewives, but no one buys a Mercedes for cup holders.'

As Landon sped by cars in the fast lane, I leaned towards him once more. My breath puffed on the velvet skin of his erect penis as I asked, 'Any requests?'

His right hand pushed gently on the back of my head. 'None other than you get started now.'

I smiled at the impatience laced through his voice. My lips stretched as I sucked his head into my mouth, the girth wiping away any lingering smile. He sucked in a breath above me, and his hand pushed more insistently. I circled my tongue around the head twice before I flattened my tongue and opened wider. I squeezed with my hand at his base as he hit the back of my throat. I paused, focused on breathing, and allowed my throat and jaw to adjust to his size.

'Yes,' he whispered into the silence of the car. 'Your mouth is fucking fantastic.'

I swirled my tongue as my mouth pulled up and my hand pressed down. I sped up the pace of my descent, and each time, his hips pressed upwards, begging for more. My own need swirled through me, a heady rush of endorphins that spurred me on.

On one plunge, I paused with him lodged deeply at the back of my mouth. I moaned as desire vibrated like a tuning fork in my belly. His dick twitched in my mouth each time I moaned. I pushed my mouth down an inch more to take him all. The small patch of hair at his base brushed my nose as I held still and swallowed three times. Needing breath, I lifted my head up and off while my hand pumped vigorously. Salty pre-come slid from his slit and mixed with the shiny saliva on the rest of him.

'You're so good at this, I'm not going to last. Please. Do that again. I want to come like that. Please,' he added. His thigh shook under my hand as the engine revved with a swift acceleration.

I licked my lips and took him in my mouth again in short, heavy sucks. Then I sunk onto him again, slowly and with the most suction I could manage. He hardened even more in my mouth as he hit the back of my throat. I used my right hand to gently knead his balls. They pulled tight and contracted in my hand.

His erection pulsed in my mouth. I began swallowing

when I felt the first hot spurt. 'Yes. More. More,' he hissed in desperation. 'I can feel you swallowing me.' The rest of his curses were indecipherable as he came. Seconds later, he softened and I pulled away. I wiped my mouth with the back of my hand and turned to look at him for the first time since we'd started.

His black pupils dominated his normally light eyes. His cheeks were flushed a deep pink as he breathed through his full, parted lips. His eyes left the road for a second to stare at my lips. He lifted his hand and brushed his thumb across my lower lip. 'You're all red and swollen. That mouth will be the end of me, I swear.'

'I told you I never make promises I can't keep,' I said.

'No doubt about that. No woman has ever been able to take all of me before.' He stopped himself, horrified that he'd finished that sentence aloud. 'Sorry. That was terrible of me to say.'

I playfully punched his shoulder with a laugh. 'Oh, please. I didn't suck you off under the illusion that this was your first time. I take it as a compliment.'

He shook his head. 'You're an odd woman, Nina. I've never met anyone like you.'

'Good thing?' I asked.

'Good thing,' he concluded as he held out a half-full bottle of warm Coke. 'Coke chaser?'

I took it from him and screwed off the lid. Before I brought it to my lips, I joked, 'Such a gentleman.' He laughed under his breath as I took a drink and screwed on the cap.

'So now it's time for *you* to pay up.'

'Ah, yes. I almost forgot. Go ahead, shoot.'

A series of questions raced through my curious brain. Why I settled on the one I did, I couldn't tell you. 'I noticed earlier when you talked about coaching and helping Connor, you got this far-away look in your eyes. It made me wonder if you're unhappy, although I couldn't imagine why.' He waited through my pause as I formulated my question. 'So, I guess what I want to ask is, are you happy right now being a Major League pitcher?'

'Of all the things you could have asked, *that* is the question you chose?'

'Yep.'

He turned his head to study me then returned his eyes to the road as he answered quietly. 'That's not an easy answer. I'm not actually a Major League pitcher right now, so that's one thing that I'm not happy about. But before the injury, I remember being happy. I remember carefree nights of fast cars and faster women. I was living the life I'd always dreamt about. Most days, I was happy to pitch every fifth day, but there were times when I wished life could be different.'

'How so?'

'Growing up, I never really wanted to be a pitcher. I wanted to be the home-run king. A power-hitter who hits a walk-off homer in the bottom of the ninth inning. That was my dream. But it wasn't to be. I was good batter, but I was a *great* thrower, so my coaches made me into a pitcher despite my protests. I can't really pinpoint the moment when I gave up that dream.' Something snapped him out of his wistful, reflective stare. 'Jesus. I sound like an ungrateful whiner. I have nothing to be sad about. I have had, and will continue to have, a great pitching career, one that most players would give anything to have. So to answer your question: yes, I'm happy.'

Whether he was trying to convince himself or me, I wasn't sure. Probably both. I wanted to ask so many questions, but he cut me off with a quick change of subject. 'So we have a long road trip starting tonight, but we'll be back in Denver. Two weeks from now on Saturday night, I'm scheduled to start against the Rays. I'd love for you to come. You could sit with the rest of the families as my guest, and I could get you a field pass.'

Every part of me wanted desperately to watch him pitch again, but a seed of worry embedded in my chest and took root. It would be an epically bad idea for me to go to a game as Landon's guest. Worry turned to guilt at the secret I'd been keeping, the lie I'd perpetuated by not saying anything.

Tell him, a voice spoke in my ear.

No. He'd want nothing to do with you if he knew the truth, I argued back.

The second voice won. 'I'm not sure ... by myself ...'

'Oh. Maybe you don't want to sit with the families. That's fine. I guess I didn't think about you not wanting to sit around a lot of strangers. Do you want to bring some friends? I'm sure we can get you a suite or something.'

Going with a group of friends who might act as a buffer against exposing the truth was a good idea. 'I think I can probably get Tanner's company to let me use their suite. A group of my friends and their boyfriends sometimes come to the games, so I'll ask if they're free. If they are, all of us will definitely be there.'

His eyes lit like Connor's had after a good hit. His hand reached over and rested on my thigh. 'I'd really love for you to be there.'

Chapter Six

Everyone's coming! I texted Landon. *Tanner's firm let us use their suite. I'm excited to see you pitch tonight.*

My phone dinged seconds later. *It will be really nice 2 b home. Missed you.*

I stared at the final two words, wondering how we'd gotten to the missing part so quickly. For the last two weeks, he'd been on a road trip, and all that time, I tried to deny that I'd missed him, too. But the occasional phone call or text would make me think of him; sometimes for an hour afterwards.

It's just because you're looking forward to actually getting to have sex with him, I reasoned. Surely that was it. Once I had him in my bed, this preoccupation would go away.

Sorry. Too soon? he texted when I hadn't replied.

I mulled over my answer. Was it too soon? A part of me, the part I pushed down deep, didn't think so. Friends could miss each other. But I went with what was much more comfortable: *Nope. Missed U 2. Especially those parts of you I met on our drive home. I'm hoping we actually get to a bed this time.*

When a reply from Landon didn't come, I bit my lip in worry. I'd made light of what might have been a true expression of emotion by doing what I do best. The memory of Tanner's accusation at the baseball game made me grimace: 'I also know you well enough to know that you say the most outrageous thing that comes to your mind when you're hiding your true emotions.'

Me 2 was his vague reply minutes later. No smiley

face. No emotion. *Going into clubhouse now, so can't text anymore. C U on field after the game.*

'Quit sexting Landon and come drink with me.' Hannah walked into my room and handed me a cold bottle of beer.

I walked over to her, reaching out my hands to her like I was trying to feel for her in the dark and wasn't having any luck. 'Wait. You're actually here. You're alive!' I joked. Hannah's stuff was at our apartment we shared, but she rarely was. She spent most of her days and all her nights at Beckett's house, so, in effect, I had only one roommate – Ansley.

'Fuck off, Marcel Marceau.'

I grinned and tapped my glass bottle against hers. I pointed the end of my bottle to her. 'That was a good one. Cheers.'

We both took a long drink. 'I've missed you too. Even though you'll never say it, I knew you meant it,' Hannah said.

'I do miss you, which is why I'm looking forward to tonight. Who's coming?'

'It will be you and your might-as-well-be husband Beckett. Jenn and Declan are coming.'

'Wait? Declan? I thought …'

'Yep. I guess he came back from Hollywood. They figured it all out. Ingrid's a bitch, and life is awesome. They're in luuurve.' I batted my eyes in exaggerated infatuation.

Hannah's smile was warm. 'I'm glad. Who else?'

'Ansley's coming too.'

'Really? She doesn't join us much.'

'I know. And you're going to flip when I tell you.'

Hannah leaned in. 'What?'

'She's bringing a date.'

'I've never even *seen* her talk to a guy when we go out.'

'I know. I think his name is Zach. That's the whole group.'

Hannah finished her beer; a rare, hesitant look on her face.

'What? Just ask,' I prompted.

She answered immediately like she was getting in her question before I changed my mind. 'Does Landon *know*?'

'Fuck no, he doesn't know.' I chugged the rest of my beer.

Hannah's head cocked slightly to the left. 'When do you plan on telling him?'

'Never. He's just a fuck like the others. Wait. I need to clarify. He will soon be just a fuck.'

'Is my dear, sweet Nina losing her touch? What is this, like the third date and you haven't screwed?'

'No. We keep getting interrupted. But we won't tonight. I already told Ansley she needed to stay somewhere else so we'd have the place to ourselves. And, Lord knows, you won't be here. Nothing's going to stop us tonight.'

All the couples drove down to Denver separately since we'd all be staying in different places overnight. We agreed to meet Landon at a bar for drinks after the game before we headed back to the house, but I was sure we would all scatter after that.

I purposely left Boulder early so that maybe I could run into Landon before he went out to the bullpen to begin warm-ups. I parked my car at the front of the lot at 5.30. Given the game didn't start until 7 p.m., I was early enough that very few fans had arrived. Landon had given me and my friends field passes that allowed us into most areas of the stadium that were normally closed to the fans. I flashed the pass that was hanging on a lanyard around my neck to the security guard.

He smiled warmly and nodded for me to enter without

looking at my pass. 'Hi, Nina. Haven't seen you here in a while.'

'I know. It has been a long time.' I ducked my head as I passed, embarrassed I couldn't remember his name. 'Have a great night.'

'You too,' I heard him say as I rounded the corner and walked down the long hallway to the training rooms. Most of the players were already out taking batting practice, so I figured this would be the safest time for me to be here. I peeked my head into the first training room. It was empty save ribbons of athletic tape strewn across the floor. The second matched the first, and I was about to give up when I heard voices further down the hall.

I caught the end of a sentence. 'Feels good tonight. The time off was a good idea.' I recognized Landon's voice immediately.

I walked on the balls of my feet until I came to the doorway. The door was propped half open, but I could see Landon lying on the padded training table.

A blonde with breasts the size of cantaloupes leaned over Landon's torso as she stretched his right arm into odd angles. His long-sleeve T-shirt hid all his rippling muscles. 'Tendons feel loose. Range of motion is good. All the extra stretching has helped.'

And I knew just who had given him all that extra attention on the long road trip. The way she said that last sentence left no room for interpretation. Yet, Landon lay silent and motionless with his eyes closed. He grimaced every now and then.

'Right there,' he'd say, and the blonde would repeat the motion until his body relaxed into the stretch.

She patted his arm twice and he sat up, one foot on the ground. He took a long drink of water before he said, 'Thanks.'

She took a step closer, clearly breaking any professional barrier. 'Let's do another *personal* rub down tonight? You'll need it.'

Landon closed his eyes and dropped his chin to his chest. 'I told you, Laura.'

Ahhh … of course, this was Laura.

He continued, firmly but kindly, 'We should not have gotten together that night. I do *not* mix business and pleasure. You work for the team, and I am an employee. We cannot do that again, and if you continue to ask, I'll have to request another trainer.'

She stepped back. 'I know. I just thought maybe …'

'No maybe's.' Landon stood and began grabbing his gear, so I backpedaled as quickly as I could, hoping my shoes wouldn't squeak on the tiled floor. I slipped into one of the empty training rooms seconds before I heard Landon's cleats clink down the hallway. The dugout door banged when it closed behind him.

I exhaled the breath I'd been holding, and as the air left me, a feeling of betrayal filled the space. He'd not been entirely honest about his relationship with Laura, and while Laura certainly wasn't the ring-wrapped wife I'd thought she was, she was definitely more than he intimated. Like a hot air balloon rising, anger heated me, fueling my quick stride out of the room, down the hallway, and up to the empty suite where I seethed by myself in silence.

I told myself I shouldn't be so affected by their conversation. Why it angered me so, especially when I was keeping secrets of my own, I couldn't figure out. We had no whispered promises across wrinkly pillows – nothing that said we were anything other than a fun time. Hell, that's all I ever wanted, what I was good at. It was time to bury these silly emotions that were ruining the simplicity of our hook-up. Maybe it was a good thing I'd overheard them; it reminded me not to get emotionally involved.

Determined to drown the emotions before everyone else showed up, I poured myself two beers from the suite's keg and sat back down with my feet propped on the railing. By the time Landon jogged from the dug out across the diamond to the outfield bullpen five minutes later, I'd finished the first beer. I couldn't take my eyes off him as he ran. His legs looked longer today, his blond hair a shade lighter, his sunglasses sexier, his stride more confident. His pitching coach met him in the bullpen as he circled his arm quickly in both directions. I could see Landon nod at something the coach said before the door to the bullpen closed, and I could see nothing.

'Hey. You're here early,' Jenn said as she walked into the suite. I stood, and we shared a warm hug. 'I miss you, girl.'

'I miss you, too.'

'Thanks for inviting us,' Declan said as he reached over to give me a hug before he stepped back, hip to hip with Jenn.

With one of his arms wrapped around her waist, Jenn looked seconds away from a Scarlett O'Hara swoon as she turned her chin to peer into his eyes. They'd apparently gotten over their misunderstanding since Declan returned from Hollywood, and I was happy for them.

Hannah and Beckett arrived soon after. Hannah rushed with a noisy scream to Jenn and me for hugs while Beckett went to the keg and poured two beers. Silently, he walked to her side and handed her one. Ever the true gentleman who didn't mind taking a backseat to Hannah's energy, he sipped his drink, letting her reunite with us. We caught each other's eyes, and he lifted a hand in a small wave while Hannah twittered on.

'… And she said that because of my dissertation, I was being considered for a fellowship!' She finished with the big reveal.

'Congratulations!' Jenn raised her glass.

'Here! Here!' I yelled as the three of us toasted. Each of us took big gulps and settled into the first row of seats

70

in the suite. A voice cleared behind us.

'Hi, everyone,' Ansley said tentatively. 'This is Zach.' She introduced us all, and we shook his hand.

'I'm not sure I'll remember all the names, but it's nice to meet you,' Zach said.

I went to the keg and poured him a beer. Handing it to him, I said, 'Here. If you don't, you can at least blame it on this.'

Zach accepted the cup with a thankful smile. He took one drink and handed it to Ansley. She took a sip and handed it back to him. This, combined with his arm around her hips, spoke of an intimacy I hadn't expected from Ansley. Although this relatively new roommate and I were as different as two people could be, we shared one similarity. There was something about Ansley and the way she carried her reticence, her hesitancy, that said life had taught her lessons the hard way. If there was anyone to rival my dark corners, it was Ansley. But where we diverged was my defense mechanism was to appear like I let everyone in, hers was to let in no one. Zach had somehow broken through her barbed-wire defenses. I wanted to know the story.

The announcer called for everyone's attention to sing 'The Star-Spangled Banner,' and afterwards, I grabbed a bag of sunflower seeds and planted myself on the end of the first row of seats. Each of the couples sat side by side carrying on intimate conversations with their heads tilted towards one another. They'd occasionally share a smile that spoke of familiarity and comfort. Other times, they sat silently, contented to simply lace their fingers together. For the first time ever, I felt like the odd woman out. I didn't like the feeling, but I didn't give myself time to ponder why.

The PA announcer started, 'Welcome on this beautiful Saturday night to the sell-out crowd here to see your Denver Raptors take on the Ft. Lauderdale Rays.' He introduced the starting line-up, and near the end, my adrenaline spiked. I knew what was coming, prepared myself for it even, but I couldn't control my body's reaction to watching him emerge from the bullpen. Part nervous, part angry, I was a pool of conflicting thoughts, made even fuzzier by my third glass of beer. I sat the almost empty cup on the floor, telling myself to go easy for a while.

'And welcome back to the field, former All-Star Landon Griesen.' Landon emerged from the bullpen seconds later to loud applause. I would have thought that this time wouldn't affect me as much as the first. I'd seen this all before.

But the opposite was true. Now, I knew more about the man who filled out his uniform in all the right places. I knew he was fiercely competitive. I knew his playful side could also be extremely sexy. And I knew he took time to offer guidance and praise to kids like Connor. By the time Landon had walked up the mound and took the ball from the catcher, my heart was racing, my chest lifting with heavy breaths.

'Nina.' Declan called to me from the middle of lover's row. He pointed to the mound as he leaned forward. 'This is who you're dating?'

'We're not dating.'

He rolled his eyes. 'OK, so this is who hooked us up with field passes for after the game?'

'Yep.'

Impressed, his eyebrows lifted before he sat back in his chair.

Landon threw his first warm-up pitch. I studied his every movement, glancing away only for a second to check the radar gun. I blew out an anxious breath.

Before the first batter came to the plate, Landon stepped off the mound and completed the same ritual he had when I first saw him pitch. When he pointed to the sky, I narrowed my eyes, wishing I could decipher who he was thinking about.

The only thing different about this ritual, though, was as he walked up the mound, he turned towards our suite like he was searching out someone. Across the sea of people, our eyes met and his smile widened, lighting his face for a second until he turned away and dug his cleats in the dirt.

Something rattled in my chest. It literally bounced, ricocheted like something had come loose.

'Not dating, my ass,' Beckett said sarcastically from the far end, loud enough that everyone in our suite chuckled.

Staring ahead, I lifted my right hand to flip him off. I heard his rumbling laughter across the suite.

The umpire called the beginning of the game. The batter stepped up to the plate. Landon came set for the first pitch. A curveball. Right over the plate. Strike one.

I laughed so heartily that Jenn, who was sitting next to me, looked at me funny.

'What are you laughing at?'

'Oh, nothing. Inside joke.' I knew it was intended as such when I saw the tips of Landon's lips lift in a mischievous smirk as he prepared for the next pitch. He'd thrown that pitch on purpose. No one throws a curveball for a first pitch with no strikes on the hitter. It's a pitch that's almost always used to get a guy out when he already has two strikes.

'Inside joke? Not dating, my ass,' Jenn repeated, and the rest of my friends laughed.

The first batter grounded out, the second struck out, and the third popped out to the infield. With three outs in the inning, Landon walked to the dugout with the rest of his team. Just before he reached the steps down into the dugout, he lifted his chin and found me in the crowd.

When our eyes met, he smiled slyly at the joke he knew

I'd catch.

And then he winked.

'Not dating, my ass,' everyone in the suite said at the same time. Seconds later, they toasted their glasses in uproarious laughter.

I couldn't help but join them.

Nearly five innings into the game, I finally allowed myself to relax. He looked good, great even. Better than he had his first start. The Raptors were up comfortably, and if he completed the fifth inning, he would be the pitcher of record, meaning he would get the win even if he didn't pitch after this inning.

Zach and I met at the keg as we filled our cups. 'I don't know much about baseball, but Landon looks really good,' he said.

'He looks a lot better. I bet he won't be in the minors much longer.'

'Oh? Where will he go?'

'He's only here for a few starts to be sure his arm is fully rehabilitated.' I pointed to the field. 'With more starts like this one, he'll go back to the Major Leagues within a month.'

For some reason, I didn't want to think about that, so I changed the subject. 'What do you do?'

'I'm a dancer. Ballet, mainly.'

'Cool. So, I'm guessing that's how you met Ansley?'

'We've actually known each other a while, but, yes, we reconnected recently through ballet.'

I really wanted to open that can of worms with a blowtorch, but since Landon was trotting out for the fifth inning, I excused myself. 'You're coming to the bar for drinks afterward, right?'

He lifted his cup. 'Absolutely. Wouldn't miss it.'

This time, I didn't sit. I stood at the back of the suite along the glass wall. The flags in center field hung loosely, and with no breeze, the evening air had turned humid. My cotton T-shirt clung to my back uncomfortably. Needing air on my overheated neck, I pulled my hair into a loose bun.

I rocked nervously back and forth from foot to foot, counting every strike, every ball. He hadn't given up a run yet, and I knew the competitor in him not only wanted this win, but to pitch a five-inning shut-out. The first two batters grounded out on only a few pitches. The third one, though, fouled off a lot of pitches, making Landon throw more without any rest. It was a battle of wills, and it showed in stress lines on his face. In between pitches, he pulled off his baseball cap and wiped the sweat off his forehead with his sleeve. On the twelfth pitch of the at-bat, the hitter made strong contact and drove a ball to the outfield. I held my breath as the ball sailed in its arc in slow motion where it was caught near the wall by the center-fielder.

He'd done it. If the team held the lead through the last four innings, he'd get the win.

'Fuck. That was intense,' I whispered under my breath. 'I can't imagine what I'd be like in a game that actually meant something.'

'You can come sit down now,' Jenn said, patting the chair I'd been sitting in all night.

I plopped down in the seat, tired and wrung out.

Apparently Jenn could read the frazzled state of my nerves. 'You seemed pretty nervous there,' she said, pointing to the field. 'Not dating, my –'

'Oh, shove it,' I interrupted good-naturedly.

She leaned over so her shoulder bumped mine. 'I bet you guys don't stay at the bar more than a half hour.'

I spent the next four innings catching up with Hannah, Jenn, and Ansley. The guys formed their own little group, allowing us to reconnect. The game ended with the

Raptors winning by five runs. The stadium had emptied after the fifth inning, which meant the seven of us were able to get down to the field rather quickly. The teams were still shaking hands when the security guard let us on to the field. I didn't spot Landon right away. Stupidly, I walked towards the dugout and away from my friends. On the top step, Landon was talking with someone. His eyes turned to find mine like he could sense me looking at him. He waved me over with a smile while he nodded at something the other person said. It wasn't until I got closer that I realized he was talking to Coach Craig.

My stomach fell to my feet as the coach's eyes followed Landon's gaze to me. Craig's eyes widened in surprise before he waved me over enthusiastically. I couldn't find a reason to make my feet move, but I had to. I felt like a prisoner walking to my own death, and there would be no last-minute pardon.

When I got to the dugout, Landon's forehead rippled with confusion as the head coach's arm went around my shoulders. He pulled me in for a hug as he pecked my temple. 'You didn't tell me you'd be here.'

I looked up into his proud eyes. 'Hi, Daddy.'

Chapter Seven

'Griesen, I'd like you to meet my daughter, Nina.'

Landon's look of shock and confusion gave way to a split second of what looked like pain. He schooled it quickly before he raised his right hand for a handshake. 'Please. Call me Landon.'

His grip on mine was feather soft, not the strong squeeze he gave me when we met at Ascent. The eyes I was normally able to read gave away nothing, like he'd pulled on a mask, which made my stomach churn. I would have preferred anger, I think.

'Nice to meet you, Landon. You had a good outing tonight. Your stuff is looking better.'

No graceful, humble smile crossed his face. No dimple peeked out. 'Thanks. Coach and I were just talking about that.'

'I probably won't have you for more than one or two more starts, I'd bet,' my father said. 'Too bad. My other pitchers have already learned so much from you.'

'Glad to hear that, Coach. Excuse me, please. I'll let you two catch up while I get some ice on my elbow.'

'By all means. This was your longest outing in a while. Be sure to take care of it,' my father said.

'Will do,' Landon said over his shoulder as he looked away. I willed him to finish with 'Nice to meet you, Nina,' or 'See you around, Nina,' but nothing came.

My father turned me by my shoulders to face him. 'Sweetheart, I didn't know you were coming to the game.'

'It was kind of a last minute thing.' Not really the truth.

The only man I'd ever loved pulled me into a tight hug.

The only arms I'd found comfort in circled my shoulders. When he pulled back, his eyes, those light blue orbs that had lightened as he aged, misted. 'I've missed you, baby girl. Missed sharing this with you.' He gestured around the field.

My eyes stung as tears formed. I swallowed twice before I answered. 'I've missed you too, Daddy. Seeing a game without you just isn't the same. I thought about that tonight, actually.'

'I've always told you that you could come with the team on the road for a year. I'd pay your way. We could see the sights in each city in between games.'

Man, did I ever want to spend that precious time with my father, made more precious when I didn't know how much time he had left. Years of travel and poor eating had taken a toll on his heart. But while part of me loved the idea, I knew it wasn't practical. I'd built a life of my own. My dissertation writing. My friends. My apartment. My church. The list went on.

He must have seen my scowl even though I tried to hide it. This conversation never turned out well for us. His fingers lifted my chin so that I could see the truth in his eyes. 'I know you have your life, Nina, and hanging out with your old man isn't probably on your to-do list. I can tell myself all I want that you've made a life of your own with your school work –'

I laughed. School work. He made it sound like I was still working on my ABC's. 'You mean my dissertation? That pesky little thing,' I added sarcastically.

He continued like I hadn't interrupted. 'But no matter what I tell myself, I miss my little girl playing with her Barbies in the clubhouse as I got ready for a game.'

'I remember that.' The ache in my chest twanged with the memory. Since it was just Dad and I when I was growing up, he would take me everywhere with him. Thankfully, the majority of the baseball games were played during the summer months, so I rarely missed school. I'd been to more cities across the US by the time I was ten than most adults. I'd been in hundreds of 'closed-door' team meetings, although I never paid attention to what was being said. He'd tell the guys to watch their language around me, and I'd pretend not to hear when they slipped. In one summer, I went from having very little family to a team-full of dads looking out for me, stopping to play Barbies or have tea parties in my dad's office after practice. Those were the best of days that got me through the worst time of my life.

'Me too. We'll always have those memories,' he said, as he patted my shoulder. He took a deep breath. 'Sorry I brought it up again. You have to do what makes you happy. I'm proud of you no matter what.'

A single tear escaped my eye, and I quickly brushed it aside. 'Thank you. I love you.'

'Hey, Nina!' Hannah yelled as she walked over to us. 'We couldn't figure out where you went for the longest time.'

'Sorry. I saw my dad, and I thought I'd come say hi.'

Hannah's eyes widened in a stare that said 'I hope Landon doesn't see you talking to him.' Hannah knew who my father was, and that I hadn't told Landon that he was trying to bang the coach's daughter.

She schooled her worry quickly as the rest of our friends joined us. I introduced my dad to each one, some of whom he'd met before.

'I better go, Dad. We're going to a bar for drinks.'

He didn't raise a questioning fatherly eyebrow. He also had post-game drinks. And his was plural, too. 'Have fun!' He said. I watched him walk away with a slight limp from the knee replacement he had when he'd retired, a melancholy feeling taking root in my heart.

'Let's go.' Jenn tugged on my arm. 'Landon's meeting us there, right?'

'Yep. Let's go,' I said wearily, my heart heavy for so many reasons. Missing my dad. Worrying about his health. And the glimpse of hurt I saw cross Landon's eyes when he realized what I'd been hiding. And I had to face him tonight in the bar. What would he say? Even worse, would he say nothing?

Hannah eyed me suspiciously, given I'd never been one to drag my feet to the bar, but she didn't say anything. She linked her arm around mine, and as we walked slowly behind the others with our elbows entwined, I fought the urge to rest my head on her shoulder.

I had been nursing my beer for over an hour when I concluded he wasn't coming. I'd texted him: *U coming?*

Then, ten minutes later, I wrote again: *Please. Let's talk.*

When I didn't get any responses, I wrote one more time: *I'm sorry.*

I nearly jumped out of my chair when my phone dinged seconds later: *Not in a bar.*

He was right. The conversation we needed to have couldn't happen with six sets of ears overhearing our dirty laundry.

'I gotta go.' I grabbed my purse and left the rest of my drink on the table. 'Sorry, guys.'

Beckett stood up, worried. 'Are you feeling OK? Do you need a ride home?'

'No, I've had half a beer in the last two hours. I'm fine.'

'Why are you leaving?' Jenn asked.

Hannah nudged her with her elbow. When Jenn looked at her, Hannah gestured to the empty chair. I saw the moment Jenn realized what Hannah was saying. She's leaving to go find him.

Jenn's mouth curved into an O before she smiled, wishing me luck in the genuine, compassionate way that made Jenn who she was.

I waved goodbye to the rest of the group. 'Let's all get together again soon,' I said, meaning it.

They murmured their agreement as I walked past the bouncer at the front door. Two steps into the chilly May air, I pulled my phone from my pocket. *Give me your address. I'm coming to see you.*

You good to drive?

His concern for my welfare, despite his justified anger, made me feel even sorrier I'd ever been untruthful. *Yes. For sure. Address?*

He texted me seconds later. It was a street I knew well. Many players and coaches through the years lived in those high-rises not only because of their proximity to the stadium but because of their prestige. The hip, young crowd with money to burn bought a condo there. It was perfect for the ball player who was on the road in the summer and had no time to mow a lawn. Most likely, though, the condo he was staying in was owned and furnished by the team for players like Landon who needed a short-term place to stay.

The building was exactly how I remembered it when I pulled into the guest parking spaces in the underground garage. I took the elevator to the posh main lobby where a uniformed guard stood watch. 'Nina. Here to see Landon Griesen.'

'He called and said you'd be coming. Take the elevator on the right to the tenth floor.'

'Thank you.' My shoes clacked on the travertine floor as I crossed the lobby, pushed the button, and waited for the elevator. Its doors opened with a ding thirty seconds later, and I stepped in and pushed the button. The car glided upwards so smoothly that I couldn't tell how fast it went.

The first thing I saw when the doors opened was Landon. He was standing in the hallway with his left shoulder pressed against the wall. His right elbow was still wrapped in ice. His left ankle was crossed over his right, and his hands were wedged in the front pockets of his jeans. His eyes were down, focused on the carpet. Deep in thought, his mouth dipped into a frown.

He looked up when he saw me standing just outside the elevator. He didn't say anything – just stared at me like he expected us to have this conversation in the hallway.

I broke the heavy silence. 'Let's talk in your condo. I'll leave as soon as you want me to.'

He nodded, turned, and started walking down the well-lit corridor. I followed, acutely aware of the fact we weren't walking side by side. He stopped at an unmarked door, turned the handle, and stepped inside first.

He closed and locked the door behind me as I stood in his wide entryway. The building had been converted into high-end housing years earlier as part of the downtown revitalization projects. Before it was housing, it was a commercial building, which was still evident in the open, high ceiling with visible ductwork, and the exposed brick walls.

He walked to a black, leather couch and sat down. I followed him and sat on the other end of the couch, my knees facing him.

He broke the silence with a quiet announcement. 'I'm angry you kept that secret from me.'

'I don't blame you. I'm sorry.'

'I can understand why you hid that you are the *coach's daughter*.' He said the last two words like he was still in disbelief. 'You had to know I wouldn't be with you if I knew who you were.'

'Yes. That was the only reason I didn't tell you.'

'So, what was the plan? When were you going to tell me?'

I winced.

'Never, right? It was just going to be a fun, one-night

fling with a famous baseball player. And I'd be none the wiser.'

Yuck. I didn't like the rolling in my stomach. 'That was the plan.'

'But when the plan changed and you went on *dates* with me, shouldn't you have told me then?'

'Yes. But ...' I couldn't finish, and I couldn't meet his eyes.

His voice rose. 'But what?'

'I knew that you wouldn't want to see me anymore.' And that would have really bothered me.

He leaned forward with his elbows on his knees. He held his head in his hands as he blew out a deep breath. 'I understand why you didn't tell me. I really do. But it doesn't make me feel better.'

'I understand. I would feel betrayed if I were you. You deserved to know the entire story to know what you were getting into.'

He stood quickly. Angry, he paced in front of the couch. 'Jesus. I even told you I thought your *dad* should be replaced.' He stopped pacing and turned towards me. 'Does he know?'

'Of course not. I wouldn't tattle to him like middle-school gossip, and I certainly don't tell him who I'm involved with.'

'Involved with,' he repeated. He scowled like he'd tasted something sour. He didn't say anything for a long while, mulling over the phrase like it had bothered him. 'And it would continue to be something you didn't tell your dad?'

'Of course it would. But you and I both know you're not going to be here another month, if that. You'll probably be 700 miles away back in Dallas.'

He scoffed like he didn't believe me and continued pacing again, this time more slowly.

Desperate to break the silence, I repeated, 'I'm sorry. I

wanted a chance to get to know you, and I knew that you never mix business with pleasure, and –'

'I've never told you that. While it is certainly true for good reasons, I've never used that phrase with y –' His stare held mine. I'd cut myself off a second too late. Embarrassed I'd admitted to eavesdropping, I lowered my eyes to the ground. I felt the red rush of shame heat my throat, then my cheeks in the silence that followed.

I sensed that he'd stopped pacing, so I looked up. He cocked his head while he studied me. His voice was gentler when he spoke again. 'You heard me say that to Laura, didn't you?'

I resigned myself to the truth I wasn't proud of. 'Yes. I came early to see you, and I caught the end of your discussion.'

He flopped onto the couch and rested his head on the back of the couch. His eyes staring at the ceiling, he started, 'I guess this is where I apologize too, isn't it? We both kept very different secrets for very similar reasons. I suspected that if I told you I'd been with my trainer, that you would assume that all of our late-night sessions turned into sex.'

'Well, that doesn't seem so far-fetched, even now.' Over my initial embarrassment, I couldn't help the jealous sneer that tinted my words.

He lifted his head so that I could read his eyes. 'It was a one-night mistake weeks before I met you. One I've never repeated.'

'Even over this long road trip?' Damn my heart for beating so hard.

'Especially not over this long road trip. How 'bout you?'

I sucked in a breath. 'No one,' I whispered.

He moved down the couch so that our knees touched. 'What about Tanner?'

This time, I was able to meet his eyes with the full

truth. 'He is in the past for me; like Laura is for you. He was fun, but he's found someone he loves, and I'm happy for him.'

His hands, one cold and one warm, reached for mine and held them in my lap. 'We have enough dark corners to fill a house, don't we?' He tried to use humor to cut the tension in the room, but I didn't feel like laughing. He exhaled and rubbed his forehead. 'And we have more of them, don't we?'

A wave of panic mixed with nausea rolled into my throat. I can't tell him tonight. 'Yes. But …'

He interrupted. 'I know it would be ideal for us to start over with no secrets, but we both know it would be impossible.'

My eyes misted with tears caused by something I couldn't understand. I looked down at my lap. 'Yes, it would.'

'So let's call a halt to this truth marathon. Sound good? When and if you want to tell me more, you can.'

I met his tentative smile with one of my own. 'Same goes for you.'

His fist nudged my shoulder. 'So when do we get to have this wall-banging sex you keep talking about? You sure know how to keep a guy on edge.'

The full, hearty laugh I allowed myself melted away some of the night's tension. 'Sorry. Not tonight.' For most of the day, hell, for the last two weeks, I'd looked forward to all-night sex-a-thons with this God of a man. But something inside me, inside both of us, was currently too raw. I felt like my insides had been rubbed bare with a wire brush. Whatever had been exposed was too sensitive. I had to have time to scab over.

But of course, I didn't say that, so I went for the easy answer instead, which was still truthful. 'It's already late, and I have to get up early for a run before I go to church tomorrow morning.'

'You go to church?'

'Yes.' Our conversation nearly over, I yawned from the exhaustion weighing down on my shoulders and giving me a headache.

'First time I've heard that excuse,' he said skeptically, like he didn't believe me.

I shrugged and walked towards his door. 'It's the most honest excuse you've probably ever heard, although I doubt you've heard many at all. You can come with me if you want to.'

'Thank you for the invitation, but I think I'll head in early for some extra therapy since tonight was a long outing.' He must have seen the frown on my face when he mentioned 'extra therapy' because he soothed, 'Don't worry. I'm scheduled with Derek tomorrow. And every day after that if you like.'

'Your call.' I shrugged like I didn't care, but I really did. 'I'm not some insecure girlfriend you have to answer to.'

'What are you then?'

'A friend with a lot fewer secrets.'

Landon bit his lip as he smiled. 'I like that.' His genuine smile turned playful, naughty. 'Do we still get to fuck?'

I laughed at his boldness and the hopeful, puppy-dog plead in his eyes. A man with a good sense of humor had always been my kryptonite, and I found myself laughing more around Landon than anyone else. I schooled a look of mock horror on my face. 'Absolutely. I better have rug burns on at least three parts of my body before next weekend.'

He stepped closer to me. 'Is that a challenge? You know I love challenges.'

I lifted my chin so our lips met in a soft kiss. 'That's what I'm counting on.'

'You won't be disappointed.'

'Promises. Promises,' I mocked.

'And there goes that smart mouth again,' he joked, then sobered. 'Good night, Nina. I'm glad we could work it out,' he said as he unlocked and opened the door.

'Good night,' I echoed as I took a few steps down the hallway, but remembering something, I turned around. Landon was leaning against the door jam.

'What?' He asked.

'Nice curveball.'

Chapter Eight

The scabs had already started to form the next day. Feeling less raw and more myself, I called Landon after church to ask him a favor. 'You guys are off on Tuesday, right?'

'Yep. But don't think I'm spending my day off running. That was hell on Earth.'

'No running. I have a favor to ask of you.'

'OK,' he said tentatively. 'What's up?'

I could hear male voices in the background, echoing off what sounded like the concrete walls of the training room. 'Is this a bad time? I can call back −'

'Fuck off, dude,' he said to someone in the room. His attention returned back to the phone. 'Sorry, Cal was giving me shit. I went to another room, so you have my attention now. What's up?'

'Well, I'm on this church co-ed baseball league, and one of our guys is out. His wife just had a baby. We're ahead in the league standings, and we're playing our rivals from Manchester. Man, I hate those guys. They beat us last year in the finals, and −'

Landon's burst of laughter made me pause.

'What?' I imagined his pursed lips as he tried to contain his amusement.

'Nothing,' he managed.

It clearly wasn't nothing. 'What?' I asked again, more forcefully.

'You're playing in a *church* co-ed baseball league, and you just said you *hated* them. That's …' he searched for a word, '… rich.'

Even though he was on the other end of the phone, I

narrowed my eyes in mock anger. He did have a point, though, so I decided to move on. 'Well, we can't find anyone else to fill in, and I would ask one of my girlfriends, but it has to be a guy to maintain the required balance of guys versus girls. I was hoping that …'

He laughed again, this time more heartily. 'You're calling in a ringer? To your co-ed church league?'

I let his laughter roll through the line for a few seconds before it ebbed into silence. I couldn't deny the smile plastered across my face. 'The Lord helps those who help themselves,' I offered, only half-serious.

The burst of laughter on the line was so compelling I couldn't help but chuckle. Finally, he pocketed his amusement, his tone turning more deliberate. 'I'll do it. But on one condition.'

'Don't worry. I'll feed you first. We'll have lunch at noon and then we'll go to the game at two. Then we can go back to my house.' My voice lowered to emphasize my insinuation.

He growled. 'I'm not worried about food, Nina. But I will take you up on staying at your place. My one condition, though, is that I don't pitch.'

'Wasn't expecting that one, but fine by me. You mind me asking why?'

'I spend my *entire* life pitching. I want to do something else. I want to hit and play outfield.'

'Hell, if you come, you can play every position you want to. Twice.'

'Wait? What? You're breaking up.' He was coming in loud and clear, so I knew he was playing with me. 'I didn't quite catch that. I can take you in every position I want to, twice? Great! Sounds awesome!'

Funny, funny man. 'Good one,' I started.

Without a single crackle in the cellular connection, he continued. 'Can't quite hear you. Gotta go to practice. See you on Tuesday.'

He hung up, and I sat on my bed, imagining his perfect body covering mine, taking me in every position. Twice.

Barely after noon on Tuesday, we shared a pepperoni pizza on the patio of a local restaurant. The spring sun burned hot today, making me thankful for the shade of the white and red umbrella over the table. Mid-week, the restaurant was vacant save for a few businessmen who decided to eat in the air conditioning instead. 'This is good,' Landon said after he took a bite of pizza. 'Never been here before.'

I took another bite of greasy goodness. A thin string of cheese stretched from the slice to my mouth and, stubbornly, wouldn't break. When it finally did, I thought I'd caught all of it, but Landon smiled and reached over. His thumb wiped a thin string of cheese off my chin.

'I must admit, I'm a little worried you shouldn't be playing today.'

'Why?'

'Well, what if you get hurt? I know some guys in the majors have clauses in their contracts that say they can't play recreational sports: ride a motorcycle, go skydiving, or ride a four-wheeler. Things like that.'

'My contract doesn't mention anything about co-ed, church baseball leagues, so I think we're good. Plus, how am I going to get hurt playing the outfield? Can anyone actually hit it in the outfield?'

'Sometimes. I don't know. You could pull a muscle or something. I don't want to be responsible for delaying your return.'

He rolled his eyes. 'Well, if I get a pulled muscle, I'll go in and get extra treatment. Feel better?'

'My dad would *kill* me.'

He took another bite and grinned while he chewed. 'Nina, I thought we covered this already. What your dad doesn't know won't hurt him.'

The legs of the metal chair scraped on the concrete

when I stood and leaned over the table to slap his shoulder. He pulled back, balancing on the back two legs of the chair, just out of my reach. 'Easy, kitten, easy,' he joked.

I curved my fingers to look like claws and hissed. He simply laughed. It felt good to be back to our normal banter. I sat back down with a wide smile and took another bite. When I did, he shifted the conversation.

'So, you know what I do for a living, but I realized as I was driving here that I didn't know anything about you. Are you off work today? On a Tuesday?'

'I'm a doctoral student at the University of Colorado. I usually teach two classes of freshman English each quarter, but school is out for the summer, so I don't have any scheduled classes. This summer, I plan to finish my dissertation so I can revise it, defend it, and hopefully graduate at the end of the year. Every waking minute is spent working on that behemoth.'

He sipped the last of his Coke, the straw noisily straining to suck up the last of the liquid. The waitress came over, quickly replacing the empty glass with a full one. 'Cool. So, what can you do with a doctoral degree in English? Do you want to be a professor? That's hot, by the way. I'd totally love to do a professor.'

I smiled, trying to mask the unease I felt every time I was asked these questions. 'Something like that.'

'Is that regret I hear? Disappointment? Did you change your mind?'

I took one more bite and chewed. He waited through my silence, so, sighing, I began, 'At one point, all I wanted to do was be a professor at a university. I imagined spending my days researching all my favorite authors in between teaching classes. For so long, I wanted to be part of academia, to go to conferences, to get my papers published.'

He leaned forward. 'But?'

'But ... some of the luster has worn off. Academia is

cut-throat. I don't want to spend the rest of my life reading terribly written freshman composition papers on global warming. And I don't know the actual statistic, but it's something like for every twenty doctoral graduates, there is one job opening. And even if you are lucky enough to get a job offer, you have to be willing to move at a moment's notice.'

'And you don't want to?'

'Maybe for the right job, but I love Boulder. I couldn't imagine living anywhere else. Especially for a job I'm not even sure I want anyway. I went into this because I loved writing and reading. I loved studying language, but somewhere along the line, the joy in it was sucked dry.'

'Even in your dissertation? You don't like that either? Are you going to finish it?'

'Oh, it will get finished even if I'm on my deathbed. But it might actually be the cause of my death.'

'So I assume it's not going well. What's it about?'

'That's a long story.'

He looked at his watch. 'I've got ninety minutes. You done?' He gestured towards the two slices of pizza left.

When I nodded, he signaled for the waitress. He handed her his credit card without looking at the bill. 'Let's walk on Pearl Street while you tell me about it. I gotta walk off that pizza before the game.'

He signed the credit card slip and handed me one of the two peppermint candies the waitress left with the bill. He led us to the exit where we turned right on to Pearl Street, a sidewalk full of small boutiques, food carts, and eccentric artists. The plastic crinkled as I opened the candy and my tongue tingled as I sucked the mint. When I talked, it clanked against my teeth. 'Have you heard of Jane Austen?'

'Sure. I think one of my girlfriends in high school made me sit through a movie based on her book. Some romance like 'Pride and …'' He paused, unable to remember the rest.

'*Pride and Prejudice*. It's one of her most famous novels, along with *Sense and Sensibility*.'

'I recognize that title too.'

'Most people do. She wrote six full novels and many shorter works. My dissertation focuses on *Sanditon*. My favorite part about it, and the part that also frustrates me to no end, is that it is a fragment. She died before she could finish it. Every time I think of it, I imagine Austen learning of the sickness that would take her life as her mind is generating this idea for a novel, a novel she knows is so different from everything else she has written. She knows it could be her masterpiece, so every day she sits at a desk, madly scribbling this amazing idea, knowing that she's racing death to get it on paper.'

Landon stopped walking. Hands in his front pockets, he turned towards me. With a somber tone, he concluded, 'And she didn't make it. That's so sad.'

'Especially when she was just getting to the good part. Two pages before the end, the heroine finally gets to see the hero, but we don't get to see them interact.'

'Hmm. OK now I'm interested. Since I'm not familiar with the story, tell me a little about it.' He walked up to a cart selling hand-made straw hats. He picked up a few, turned them over to inspect them, and put them back. Then he chose a wide-brimmed, floppy sun hat. It must have passed inspection because he put it on my head. I had to admit it kept the sun out of my eyes, and it was the most stylish. He circled me, inspecting the hat from each side. He pulled out his money clip and handed the hat maker a twenty dollar bill. 'Keep the change,' he said with a nod to the artist, who stared at him like he was high. He probably was.

Landon walked away, guiding me with a hand on my lower back towards another cart full of jewelry. I pointed to the hat. 'Thank you, by the way.'

'You're welcome,' he said, a bit distracted as he looked at the jewelry.

'You really want to know the story of *Sanditon*?'

When he nodded, I continued. 'OK. The story follows the heroine, Charlotte Heywood, who is invited by the Parker family to leave her family's home in the country to visit a summer vacation spot, Sanditon. Sanditon is a small tourist village on the coast where people go to bathe and breathe in the sea air, believing that it cures various illnesses. While she is in Sanditon, Charlotte meets a variety of people, most of whom Austen uses to satirize vices like self-importance and hypocrisy.'

Apparently not finding anything he liked, he walked towards another booth, this one manned by an artist selling charcoal sketches of horses. 'Very good,' he praised the artist, before he walked on. 'Keep going. I'm listening. Austen satirizes vices of self-importance and hypocrisy.'

'Yes. For example, Charlotte meets Sir Edward, whose chief vice is to be "seductive". He basically thinks he's God's gift to women, and in order to woo them, he memorizes lines of poetry he clearly doesn't understand. Then there are the two Parker sisters, who are convinced they are suffering from life-long illnesses the doctors simply don't understand. But Charlotte soon correctly concludes that the sisters pretend illness out of boredom or want of attention. The last vice is the self-important way some of the residents participate in charity. One of my favorite lines in the novel is that Charlotte abhors those do-gooders who give to others simply for "the glory of doing more than anybody else".'

'That's still true today. I've met all three of those types of people.'

'Absolutely. Nearly two centuries after she wrote the novel, it's still relatable. That's the beauty of literature.'

'OK, so Charlotte goes on this vacation, meets all these people, and observes all these characters with obvious flaws. Then what?'

He walked into a building I knew well. The door dinged as we opened it. A cool blast of air conditioning welcomed us into the empty store, so I took off my new hat and sunglasses. The clerk behind the counter asked if we needed help, and when we declined, she told us she would be in the back room doing inventory if we needed assistance. I took a breath to start telling him about the introduction of the hero. 'Charlotte hears …'

He held up a single finger. 'Hold that thought a second. You ever been here before?'

'Yes. It *is* quite famous in Boulder. This lady makes all her own perfumes. I wear one of hers, actually. It's –'

He held up his hand to interrupt me. 'Wait. Don't tell me. I want to guess.'

'There's over fifty scents! OK, have at it,' I gestured towards the wall where the bottles were lined up on the wooden shelves. They were sorted by type, including flowers, spices, and nature. He stood in a wide stance in front of the wall and crossed his arms over his chest. His shirt stretched across his broad, muscled back, and his jeans hung off his hips without looking sloppy.

He scrunched his forehead, deep in thought. 'Go on. Go on. You were saying. Charlotte hears … what?'

'You want me to talk about my dissertation while you guess which scent I wear?'

He nodded as he stepped forward to smell a scent. He popped open the top of the container, sniffed it, and shook his head before he replaced the cap and put it back on the shelf.

'That's definitely not it. You're not a girl who wears flower scents, so I think I can eliminate all of those.'

He was so right, and his ability to understand the type of perfume I'd chosen reminded me how observant he really was. Last year, for Valentine's Day, a guy had given me some rose-scented perfume, which showed just how little he understood me at all. It had landed in the donate to goodwill pile as the door clicked shut behind him.

'You're right. You've narrowed it down to thirty-five.'

He smelled a few more, eliminating categories as he went. He stopped in front of a sign that read "Nature" and nodded. He smelled a half dozen before he grabbed my arm and tugged so I was standing in front of him. His arms wrapped around my waist as he leaned forward and ran his nose along the side of my throat. I tilted my head, lengthening that side of my neck. I closed my eyes and listened to him breathe against the goosebumps pebbling on my neck.

He took two deep breaths, then groaned. 'I thought I asked you to talk about your dissertation.'

'I heard you, but I didn't think you were serious.'

His right hand snuck under my shirt and wedged under the top of my jeans. 'I'm serious. You're fucking sexy when you go all professor on me. Makes we want to dress you up in heels and glasses so I can fuck you while you lecture me about some nineteenth-century shit. Now, fucking tell me what Charlotte hears.'

His hand ventured lower as I began; my voice low and raspy. 'Charlotte hears through the Parkers about their eldest brother, Sidney, who I think is intended to be the hero. They often talk about him in passing; some of it good, and some of it bad. They say he is very "clever", that he has a good sense of humor, and throughout the first chapters, Charlotte is repeatedly told that Sidney can make everyone laugh. That's a quality that usually makes for a great hero. Austen loved her witty, funny men.'

Landon smiled. 'And you?'

'Insufferable. I hate it,' I said, sarcastically.

I felt Landon's smile against my neck.

'But he also has a vice: he is a man who "lives too much in the World to be settled". Charlotte is told "he is here and there and everywhere". For an Austen hero, that is usually the kiss of death. All of the previous Austen heroes are of a place. Mr Darcy has Pemberley in *Pride and Prejudice,* and Mr Knightley has Donwell Abbey in *Emma*. All these heroes are as stable and settled as their estates. So, in Sidney, Austen had a new hero, and that is one way that this novel was going to be different from her others.'

I sucked in my stomach when his hand dipped under my panties and cupped my sensitive flesh. One finger started to swirl. 'One way? What are the others?'

I licked my lips, trying to concentrate on the conversation. 'Usually, Austen ...' I stuttered when my breath hitched. What was I saying? 'Usually heroes are intimately connected to their families, but we get the sense that Sidney has purposefully chosen to distance himself from the vices of his family.'

At this, Landon's finger stopped moving, and he removed his hand before he stepped back, taking his heat with him. His eyes clouded over, darkening to a slate grey before he turned his head away, probably to hide the scowl that crossed his face. I'd hit some nerve I didn't know was exposed.

I tried to smooth out the ripples in his stormy ocean eyes. 'I don't blame Sidney, by the way. Who would want to be around self-important hypochondriacs who compete with each other over how much charity they can participate in? Yuck. That sounds awful.'

Landon still didn't look at me, so I continued, hoping to move past whatever had soured his mood. 'So that's the story. She sees Sidney pull up in his carriage, he gets out, she likes how he looks, and that's the end.'

Landon's thoughts were still distant, so I said, 'You figured out which one yet?'

He walked over to the shelves, took two jars off the shelf, and smelled each one. 'This one,' he said, holding up Stormy Night. It smells like expectation, like the energy in the humid air right before a thunderstorm. It makes me feel like I'm sitting on my grandpa's front porch watching the horizon light with shutters of lightning.'

'You're right.'

He put the jar back on the shelf and looked at his watch. 'We should go if we want to make it to the game on time.' He opened the door for me to exit. The humidity made my glasses fog over in seconds.

We walked in silence, a heavy cloud hanging over what was otherwise an enjoyable afternoon.

He grabbed my hand as we walked across a street to his Mercedes parked at a street meter. He let me in first, then himself. When he sat down, I heard him sigh and force lightness into his voice. 'So, do you spend your dissertation talking about how *Sanditon* is different from her other novels?'

If this was where he wanted to go, I didn't mind it. Hell, I could talk about this for days. He started the car and reached his right hand behind my headrest to check traffic as he backed up.

'There are two parts to my dissertation. The first one was easy. It is a literary analysis that fleshes out all of the themes I told you about. The second part has proven the most difficult. I'm attempting to use my analysis to help me write the last two-thirds of the novel.'

'Whoa. So, you're finishing Austen's story?'

'Yep. It's not an entirely new idea. Many other people have tried it as well. What is making it difficult for me is that I'm not entirely convinced that Sidney and Charlotte end up together. I can easily imagine their best of times. I've written scenes where they sit across from each other at the banquet table or in a crowded parlor and their eyes meet in this amazing moment. They share a knowing smile, both of them laughing at the folly they're surrounded by. They share the love of satire and humor. They both can't stand the hypocrisy of their society, and they see in each other a rare being that rises above it.'

'So there must be worst of times if you aren't convinced they end up together.'

'I can't figure out how to resolve the conflict I see them facing, so my writing muse has left me. I haven't been able to write more than a page in the last week. You see, they both meet in a place that neither of them calls home. It was a spot to visit, to vacation, but not a place either of them will ultimately end up. Each of them has separate lives; we've been told Sidney is a man of the world who can't be pinned down.

'Similarly, we're told that Charlotte is close to her tight-knit, country family, who is happy in their humble surroundings. They both have their separate lives in separate places, and each is either unwilling to or unable to sacrifice that life. While they may have great chemistry in *Sanditon*, I can't figure out how to make it into a happily ever after. And because Austen seems to be doing so many things differently in *Sanditon* than in her other novels, I worry that I'm imposing a happily-ever-after ending on something that wasn't going to get one.'

'Then maybe it won't get one.' He shrugged like it was no big deal.

Landon pulled into the gravel parking lot next to the softball fields. He turned off the engine and started to get out of the car.

That's why he didn't hear me say, 'That's what I'm afraid of.'

Chapter Nine

The humidity had spiked in the two hours between lunch and the start of the softball game. White clouds with shadowed bases billowed in the blue sky. A strong wind from the south blew my hair into my mouth before I had a chance to tie it back. I met Landon at the back of the car to grab our gear from his trunk.

'I heard we're supposed to get storms tonight,' Landon said, pointing to the sky. 'I believe it. In Texas, those are the types of clouds we get hours before severe weather.'

'You think we'll get the game in?' I asked.

He turned his head to scan the horizon. 'Sure. We won't play a full game anyway. There's a mercy rule, right?' He leaned in conspiratorially and winked. 'They might not last five innings.'

He walked away with his gear, and seeing that his good mood had returned, so I grabbed his elbow, wanting an answer to a question I'd been formulating for a while. 'So, slugger," I started playfully. "Tell me something. Why are you so adamant to play outfield?'

'For the first time in my life, I want to be the guy who gets to stand out in left field and doesn't do shit. Then, when my one and only chance to be a hero comes, I run down a ball, smash into the outfield fence, and rob the guy of the homerun. I get to be the guy who saves the pitcher from the consequences he deserved from what was probably a really crappy pitch.'

I laughed. 'Guess what position I play.'

He narrowed his eyes in deep thought. 'I bet you can catch well. First base.'

I shook my head.

'You're pretty fast. Shortstop?'

'No.'

'Are you going to be in the outfield with me?'

'I wish. Nope.'

Exasperated, he huffed. 'Just tell me.'

'I love third base.'

He stopped walking and snaked his hand around my back to pull us so close that our noses touched. 'I love third base too, and I can't wait to make it there tonight.' He licked his lips before he sauntered away towards the bench where the rest of our team sat.

I ran after him so that we arrived at the team's bench at the same time. 'Hi, everyone. I told you I found someone to replace Will, and here he is.' I held out my hands in a Vanna White-like reveal. 'This is Landon.'

Utter silence.

Landon broke it, casual as can be, like twelve sets of eyes weren't staring him down. 'Thanks for letting me join you guys.'

'Letting you? Ha, that's a funny one,' Libby joked. 'Manchester is going to crap their pants when they see *him* warming up.'

'Is he pitching?' Another teammate asked hopefully.

'Nope. We wouldn't deprive you of your start, Greg. Landon's going to play left field instead.

The team, of course, agreed, all of them watching him out of the corners of their eyes as he changed into his cleats and stretched. No one knew what to say or do around this world-class athlete. The normal, good-natured ribbing between teammates gave way to a silence that stretched to the first inning.

From across the diamond, I could see the Manchester players getting ready, unprepared for who they would face. Jackson, one of the players I'd partied with a few times, walked over to me. 'See you got a new player, Nina.

Who'd you find to take Paul's place?'

I played it casual. 'His name is Landon.'

'Cool.' Jackson's voice dipped as he stepped closer. 'We getting together tonight?'

Landon looked up to me from the grass where he had been stretching his hamstrings.

'No. Not tonight, Jackson.'

The burly man with ebony hair shaved in a military-style cut shrugged. 'No problem. Another time maybe,' he said as he walked away.

I heard Landon's growl as he stood up. His chest purposefully bumped my shoulder as he rumbled in my ear, 'Church league, huh? He wants you.'

'Well, he won't have me. I'm all yours tonight, slugger.'

'Damn right,' he grunted as he stepped away and grabbed his glove. He jogged to left field, shoved his hand in the leather, and punched his right hand into the center of it, a gesture that said 'bring it on.' He leaned forward with his hands resting on his bent knees, readying like he was taking this very seriously.

I took my position at third base, fifty feet in front of him.

When I leaned forward, mimicking his fielding position, I heard his exaggerated moan behind me. 'Ah, hell. Now how am I going to concentrate?'

I turned my head over my shoulder and winked as I wiggled my hips back and forth. He shook his head and laughed.

The breeze blowing in from the outfield brought with it the sound of Landon's favorite exclamation. 'Damn, woman,' he'd say when I leaned over.

Greg, our pitcher, got two Manchester batters to pop up lazy fly balls and one to roll a gounder to third, so we all headed back to the bench since it was our turn to hit.

I heard Landon's breath as he jogged behind me. 'You

are *so* going to get it tonight, you tease.' When he passed me, Landon turned his attention quickly to Greg. He held up his hand for a high five and praised, 'Nice pitching, man. You looked great.'

Greg's eyes widened to the size of silver dollars. 'Thanks.'

'Here. Let me show you something.' He pulled Greg aside, who followed like a puppy. Landon grabbed a ball and wrapped two fingers around it. He flicked his wrist a few times and pretended to throw the ball in slow motion. I sat on the bench as I watched Greg hang on his every word. The two were so engrossed and our first two batters got out so quickly that we didn't have anyone up to bat when we should have.

'Landon. You're up, man,' a guy yelled. Landon put down the ball, shook Greg's outstretched hand, and grabbed his batting gloves and a bat he'd brought. He winked at me as he jogged to the plate. He tapped it twice, circled the bat, and took his batting stance. His chiseled profile rested over his left shoulder while I stared at his ass. A few women teammates chuckled next to me when one made a comment about his backside.

All mine, I growled to myself. At least for tonight. And hopefully for as long as he's in Denver. Landon watched Jackson throw the first pitch, timing the step of his left foot with the pitcher's movements. He did the same to the second, and when he timed it well, I knew Jackson was dead meat on the third pitch.

He had the nerve to throw a third fastball in a row. Landon's foot tapped, perfectly timed. His hands started his swing as he extended through the ball, which dinged loudly as it made contact with the metal bat. The ball soared over the infielders' heads and landed between the outfielders, twenty feet in front of the wall. Landon rounded first and ran to second base. With one foot on the base, he pulled each finger out of his batting gloves and tucked them into his back pocket.

I think I might have moaned when he leaned over, his elbows near his knees as he readied to run. 'Next batter,' someone yelled. 'It has to be a girl.' We didn't have a set batting order.

'Nina. How 'bout you?'

'Me?'

'Sure. Hit him in,' Greg said, pointing to Landon at second base.

I grabbed a bat and walked to the plate. When Landon saw me, he clapped his hands together twice and yelled, 'Hit me home, babe!'

At the endearment, Jackson turned to second to study Landon more closely. He looked back to me, quizzically. I pretended not to notice him staring as I practiced my swing a few times.

In the spirit of good-natured ribbing, Landon yelled, 'This guy's got nothing.'

Jackson's eyebrows lifted. He came set for his first pitch, one that was way too high and way too close as it snapped into the catcher's mitt near my chin. I squeaked as I stepped back. It might not have hit me if I hadn't moved, but it was difficult for me to tell. Regardless, Jackson's intent was clear, especially when a sneer crossed his face.

The second after the ball hit the mitt, I saw Landon stand ram-rod straight from his running position. His shoulders squared to the pitcher's mound as his chest puffed out, readying for a fight. Blood pumped through the veins in his arms as his fingers curled into fists. He took two steps towards Jackson like he was ready to storm the mound.

His footsteps stilled when I held up my flat, open palm. I wanted to take care of this myself. That asshole had taken it too far. Please, let me handle this, I pleaded silently with Landon as I watched him battle with himself. He wanted to give the guy a piece of his mind, but he also wanted to follow my request. He paused to think and then took two steps backward to second base. He leaned over again, ready to run, an intensity in each of his movements. This man was competitive to the core. And protective. And that made me molten hot.

Jackson threw another pitch, this time much lower. I didn't swing at that pitch or the next, waiting for the one I wanted. The next pitch was closer to the strike zone, but low, so I dropped the head of the bat and made contact, trying to steer it past the first baseman and into the outfield.

The ball was hit sharply but not high. It skirted along the ground and escaped the outstretched glove of the first baseman. It trickled into the outfield slowly enough that I was able to round first and head to second. With two outs, Landon had started running on any contact, and he easily rounded third base and touched home plate.

He immediately looked back to me and pointed. 'Great hit, slugger!' he yelled before he high-fived the line of teammates waiting for him at the bench.

Five innings later, we were winning by two runs, but Manchester had guys on second and third base with two outs in the inning. I didn't know the batter, but he looked strong. 'Back up two steps,' Landon yelled from the outfield. 'I bet this guy pulls the ball to our side.'

I took two large steps back and readied. He swung and missed on the first two balls, but on the third pitch, he swung hard and popped it up to left field. I pointed in the sky to show the outfielders where the ball was in the bright sunlight straining through the clouds.

Landon immediately started running forward, his eyes trained on the falling ball. Each stride was long and measured as his run turned into a sprint. Everything seemed in slow motion except for the ball speeding towards the ground, made even worse by the wind blowing in from the outfield. I saw his last stride push off the ground. I saw the moment both feet kicked behind him as he laid out, fully splayed. He reached out with his glove at the last minute so close to the ground I couldn't tell if he'd caught the ball or not. I also saw the way his arms caught his fall, his elbows hitting the ground so hard that his head snapped forward. He rolled onto his right side, his back towards me, before he rolled completely onto his back.

My breath left me in a stifled 'oh no.' Full of worry and fear, I tried to make my legs run to the outfield, but they wouldn't move. I could see the headlines now: **"Star Pitcher Out for Season"**. All the work he'd done to get back might be for naught. He wasn't moving other than the rise and fall of his chest, signaling his quick breaths.

'Landon. Oh my God,' I managed to yell, my feet finally starting to move. Then his left, gloved hand raised off the grass and showed everyone the ball safely nestled in the webbing. The center-fielder reached him first. They laughed about something as the center-fielder offered Landon his hand and pulled him off the grass. Smiling, they chatted as they jogged towards me. Landon tossed the ball to the mound for the next inning, and as he trotted by me, he clicked his tongue and winked. 'All day, baby. All day.'

Minutes later, I found him sitting on the ground, searching for something in his bag. 'I knew I put it in here,' he said as he pulled out a red apple, rubbed it against his dirty shirt, and took a large bite. Juice glistened on his lower lip as he chewed with the most serene smile stretched across his face.

Chapter Ten

After the game, we stopped at a sandwich shop and drove back to my vacant house. A line of dark clouds that extended across the horizon raced us home. Small, white wisps hung ominously down from the dark bases. The flashes of lightning lit the sky as the sun snuck away. Landon parked his car in Hannah's parking space in the garage; Lord knows, she wouldn't be using it. The minute the garage door closed with a groan, a bolt of lightning streaked across the sky, cutting open the clouds that happily poured out the heavy rain.

'Just in time,' I said, as I flipped on the light in the living room and pulled open the blinds that covered the large, glass door that led to the deck. I cracked the glass door open a few inches to let in the breeze and double-checked that the screen door was not letting in too much rain. 'I love a good storm. I could stand here just watching it, smelling it.'

Landon walked over to my living room couch and grabbed a large blanket off the back. He flapped it twice to unfold it and laid it down on the carpet in front of the glass door. 'Let's have a picnic here,' he proposed as he sat cross-legged and started opening the paper wrapped around his sandwich.

I grabbed a beer for me and water for him and joined him on the floor. The continual strobe of lightning flashes was even more dramatic when I turned off the overhead lights. The small lamp in the corner provided enough light for us to eat. I leaned against the couch, stretching my legs out. I took a bite and laid the sandwich on my lap.

'So you're a man who likes his condiments,' I said when Landon took the first bite of his sandwich that was literally dripping with added ingredients.

He wiped some sauce off his lips with a napkin. Grinning, he pointed to my sandwich. 'I can see you aren't.'

'Definitely not. No mayo. No mustard. Nothin'.'

'I keep learning something about you every day.'

My jaw stopped chewing as I pondered his comment. He meant it playfully, but there was an intimacy to his comment that pitter-pattered through my chest. There was so much more to learn about me, about him for that matter, and for the first time in a long while it didn't bother me that he was unearthing me; daily discovery after daily discovery. Most of the tough stuff was buried much deeper, anyway. Even the small revelations, the ones I hid from virtually everyone, had proven surprisingly painless.

Maybe it was because I knew our friendship had an expiration date that was fast approaching. It was easier to open up to a man who'd likely be gone in a month.

Regardless of the reason, there was no doubt that Landon had at some point uprooted my carefully laid plans of a one-night stand. Now he was the first man other than my dad who made me feel like telling half-truths was a full lie. He was the man who I was going to break my no sleepover policy with; the first man I wanted to see in the morning with creases on his face from my pillows. I could see him now, looking unbelievably hot in the morning with his tousled hair arranged around his face. His morning stubble would scrape against my cheek …

'Earth to Nina.' Landon waved his hand in front of my face. 'Where'd you go?'

The valleys and ridges of his playful smile were lit by a flash of lightning. With each strobe, I catalogued every little detail about his face that made lust pulse low in my core.

110

His cocked eyebrow.

His tight-fitting T-shirt.

The way his collarbones met in a perfect valley at the base of his throat.

His dilated pupils that turned his ocean blue eyes a dark navy.

The way his playful smile faded into a look of pure lust – a look that had to have mirrored my own.

I put down my sandwich on the paper it had been wrapped in. When I slowly crawled over to him, he swallowed. The paper from his sandwich crinkled when he pushed it away. When our faces were inches apart, I stopped and sat back on my knees. 'Let's learn some more. I don't want to wait anymore.'

A gust of wind blew heavy rain on to the glass door where it clung as it fell in sheets. Thunder banged a second after a bright flash with the type of percussion I could feel in my chest. The force made the glass flex and vibrate.

He leaned forward so our lips brushed. 'I want to learn how you taste.'

I tried to press against him harder, but he denied me, his lips moving down my chin to my throat. His hand pressed against my chest so that I fell backward, my arms braced behind me. I stretched my legs out when he kissed around the collar of my T-shirt. His hand tugged the corner of my shirt so one of my shoulders was exposed. He kissed where my bra strap dug into my skin.

'Why did we wait so long?' I whispered when his teeth grazed my sensitive skin as he bit the strap and drew it off my shoulder.

He smiled. 'You taste good right here.'

I felt the whisper of his tongue as he kissed along my collarbone. 'And here.'

Up my neck to my ear. 'And here.'

Across my cheekbone and down to my jaw, where he took a deep breath. 'Stormy Night,' he repeated. 'Lift up your arms,' he instructed, and I followed. He slid my shirt up and off and unhooked my bra with a hand behind my back in one smooth motion.

'Looks like you've had some practice,' I teased when my bra fell away. He threw it onto the couch and stared at my chest, not bothering to acknowledge my joke. Both his hands circled my wrists where they held my weight behind me. He pulled my hands forward and eased me back so my elbows landed softly on the plush carpet.

More reclined now, I watched as his mouth took over the worship his eyes had started. He sucked one nub into his mouth, gently first then with more force. I moaned when his hand kneaded my other breast in the same rhythm. He pinched one nipple as he lightly bit the other, making my hips shoot off the blanket as I moaned.

His lips descended slowly to my belly button, where he kissed as his fingers unhooked my jeans, slid down the zip, and pulled them down and off my legs. Save for a pair of lacy panties, I was exposed to his gaze that ran up and down as he memorized each curve.

His fingers tickled along the top of my panties before he pulled them off. He opened my legs with firm hands on the inside of my thighs. 'Stay on your elbows,' he commanded. 'I want you to watch me.'

His lips brushed against my core, close enough so I could feel the heat of his breath when he said, 'Can you see my tongue?'

I started to say 'no,' but then his tongue darted out, and with a long lick took his first taste. 'I can,' I said after the first few licks gave way to sucking and a hint of teeth. My head dropped backward when a hard gust blew small droplets of rain racing through the screen door. The cool mist coated my overheated skin, sending goosebumps down my legs.

'No. Eyes on me. They never move. I want to see them when you come.'

I lifted my head, my eyes meeting his as his tongue darted out again. Two fingers nudged at my opening. He entered so slowly I felt each of his knuckles as my sensitive skin parted for him. As I looked down, my stomach lifted and lowered in heavy breaths. His fingers circled inside me as his tongue laved my clit with quick movements, back and forth and around.

The tell-tale tightening made my breath hitch. 'I'm close.'

His mouth left me as he sat up. His thumb quickly took over where his mouth had left. He pressed and circled as he leaned forward, his lips next to mine when he said, 'I learned you flush right before you come. It starts at your chest.' The fingertips on his other hand brushed a line between my breasts.

'Then your throat reddens. Your cheeks get rosy and your eyes go glassy. Your breathing changes too, doesn't it? Every part of your body is readying for what it knows is coming. See. There go your eyes.'

His thumb pressed one last time as his fingers scissored inside me. Waves of electricity bolted through me and I expanded and collapsed like air after a lightning strike. I tried to keep my eyes open like he'd asked as crests gave way a flood of endorphins that tingled my skin.

'And the rest of you follows,' he whispered. I shivered as he pulled away a minute later. He stood over me, his feet planted outside my knees. My elbows were raw from supporting my weight. I collapsed onto my back as Landon towered over me. The blanket had been bunched and pushed aside when I came, so the soft fibers of the carpet caressed my back.

Flashes of lightning illuminated him every few seconds as he reached behind his neck with both hands and tugged his shirt over his head. My senses hyper alert, I could smell the rain. Its earthy, salty scent spawned a warm feeling in my chest like hot caramel running over ice cream, melting it with its heat. He unbuckled his belt and pulled it through the loops with one hand. He dropped it to the floor where it clanked and settled. He pulled down his jeans quickly, although it seemed to take forever. His muscles flexed as he stepped out, one foot then the other. His stomach was concave it was so tight. So lean. So strong. So perfectly sculpted.

'Hurry. I need you,' I begged as he pulled a condom from his jeans, ripped open the packet, and rolled it on. He knelt on his right knee first and spread his weight over me. From toe to chin, there were thousands of little, tiny points our skin rubbed and brushed, and I was aware of each and every one.

I felt him nudge my opening, so I wrapped my legs around his back. His lips took mine, languid at first as he inched forward, penetrating so slowly I could feel me part and give way.

'Now I'm going to have a different memory every time I'm in a thunderstorm,' he said, as his girth widened me. The possession took so long I swore a half dozen times he was fully seated, but he kept going until with a fierce growl into my mouth his hips bucked forward the last inch. His balls slapped against me as my lower back arched off the carpet.

'Oh, fuck!' I screamed when Landon hissed and held his body against mine as I writhed and twisted my hips against the sensation. I'd never felt so full.

Mercifully, he pulled out halfway before he plunged in quickly this time. With each penetration, he tried a new angle, first shallow, then deep. He watched my face and my chest as he tested. A small smile would lift his lips when I let out a moan. He grinded against me, pressing on the sensitive nerves both inside and out. His right hand went under my hips and lifted me onto him so forcefully I yelped and grabbed the back of his neck. 'Again. Do that again,' I managed.

Lightning struck again, lighting the dark corners.

'This is the one place where you're not a challenge. You're so responsive. I can play your body like a sonata.'

It was true. He was playing every string of my nerves with harmonies and cadences that quickened to a crescendo. I tightened my legs around his waist. 'Play on, maestro.'

He grunted. 'Do you know how that makes me feel right now? To be able to do this to a woman like you?' His voice was so reverent.

I shook my head, unable to put voice to it even if I knew.

'Like a fucking king.'

His abs tightened when he shoved into me, filling me as he lifted my hips in the rhythm he chose. That angle rubbed my upper back on the carpet fibers, burning this moment on to each vertebrae. I whimpered when he twisted a nipple between two fingers.

'And she tips over again.' I grabbed his hard biceps, my nailbeds turning white with the force. The second hovered, timeless and weightless, like the moment at the top of the rollercoaster. The next second, I zoomed forward, unable to control the momentum. Along for the ride, I let him buck into me, prolonging the force of my orgasm as it twisted, turned, and settled.

When my body stilled, he pulled out and tugged at my hips. 'On your hands and knees. Face the window.'

I did as he said. He knelt behind me with one knee raised and a foot braced on the ground for extra leverage. The rain pelted the window along with occasional dings of hail. He thrust forward so quickly in this position that I cried out. My arms gave way, so I collapsed onto my elbows. The small light in the lamp flickered and gave way to darkness as we lost power.

'I told you that you had this comin' after all that ass waving and winking you pulled at third base today.'

He plunged forward repeatedly, the sound of our flesh pounding together audible even through the rumbles of thunder. His hands encircled my hips and pulled me backwards onto him. One hand left me a second later. I knew what was coming, but I couldn't prepare myself for the intensity. Would it be soft? Would it sting?

His palm connected with my backside twice in quick succession, the slap loud and sharp against the rumbles of thunder. My back arched as the sting gave way to a heat that spread, radiated, diffused, as it sunk into each pore.

'Fuck. We learned that too, didn't we? You love getting spanked. I felt you tighten around me.'

His other hand smacked even harder twice more. I pushed backwards into him, begging with my hips for more. 'It'll make me come. Please.'

He grunted. 'You got one more?'

'I'm not sure the second one ever stopped. So sensitive. Feel everything.'

'Fuck. I know.'

Using his leg for leverage, he lifted his pelvis and drove downward for an even deeper penetration. I gave up trying to hold up my head and rested my cheek against the carpet where I welcomed the friction rubbing my cheek raw. Out of the corner of my eye, flares of lightning outlined his torso with all its edges and valleys. I closed my eyes, memorizing the moment's perfection. The smell of the rain. The chill on my feverish skin. The echo of rumbling thunder. The flicker of lightning that seeped through my eyelids.

He grew impossibly harder, nudging a new place in me, making me crest one last time. A final slap of his hand tipped me over.

'Yes. I feel you. I feel you,' he chanted as he pumped into me, his grip on my hips sure to leave marks. 'You're making me go over too,' he said before he growled and held himself deep inside.

116

How much time passed I couldn't say, but soon he softened, pulled out, and rolled us so I lay next to him. He pulled off the condom and wrapped it in a napkin. With my cheek on his shoulder, I got a good look at his eyes for the first time. Black with desire and satisfaction, they searched my face first.

'You good?' He asked.

My eyelids were suddenly so heavy. 'Better than good.'

He chuckled and with light fingertips traced circles on tender parts of my body. I flinched when he found the raw skin on my upper back, elbows, and knees.

Through my half-lidded eyes, I saw his smirk. 'What?'

'I won the challenge.'

'Challenge?'

He pressed on those sensitive areas one more time. 'Rug burns in three different places.'

My hand circled one of his fingers and brought it up to my cheek where the sweat made it sting. 'Make that four.'

Chapter Eleven

Hours before the sun rose, I woke from a dream. Landon's warm body, half covered by a thin blanket, was splayed across the bed. His arms stretched sideways, claiming his space as his chest lifted in even, shallow breaths. I snuck out of bed, tied my robe around myself, closed the bedroom door, and raced to my laptop on the kitchen table. It wouldn't power on fast enough as words, phrases, paragraphs that I thought might never come back flitted through my head. My heart beat furiously as I prayed I wouldn't lose those precious descriptions, that fleeting dialogue. My muse had returned, and my fingers flew over the keys, trying to reach out and seize every word, racing a feeling that soon the ideas would disappear. At times, the images in my head refused to be captured by the blinking cursor, language such an inadequate way to describe what I saw so clearly in my imagination.

Simon's hair curled and fell over his eyes as he leaned forward. His graceful bow fit the formality of the drawing room and the company of Lady Denham ... something didn't match though ... something was off. He did all the motions right. Nodded at the right time. Clapped when Clara finished playing the piano forte. Yet, he distanced himself. It was his eyes. They were dark, but not black. Occasional flashes of light bespoke his disquiet like this drawing room was the last place he wanted to be ... Every time Charlotte looked over, those eyes were trained on her, searching, exploring, trying to find a truth she schooled behind the temperament bred into her as a young lady. Her back was straight, her hands in her lap, her expression warm and affectionate to meet all the expectations ... must be lovely company ... must be respectable and pleasant ... the epitome of civil, well-bred manner ... must please ... be obliging.

Exhausted by the charade of it all.

Her dress ruffled as she shifted her legs ... tired of sitting ... tired of pretending. The fatigue threatened to consume her and burned her from within ...

'Excuse me, please,' Charlotte said with a small curtsy and a promise to return. She let the drawing room door click shut before she picked up the cursed skirt and ran faster than her shoes allowed. They fell off in the corridor ... she didn't care. Escape from it all. Freedom beckoned from the back parlor door a few steps away. She lunged, pushing open the heavy wooden doors. They banged behind her as the thunder rumbled and rain soaked her proper attire. She ran to the middle of the garden, the bottom of her dress coated in mud in only a few steps. She'd have to hide it later, but as she stood in the middle of the dying azaleas, her arms outstretched and head tilted to the sky that cracked and opened with sheets of rain, she allowed herself a blissful moment of not caring. Her hair stuck to her face as drops fell into her eyes and her mouth. Lightning flashed above her, its crooked fingers crossing and stretching wherever it pleased. She envied that flash its freedom, its ability to decide.

She thought no one saw her stretch her arms to the dark sky. But he did. He'd followed her despite his every attempt to stay away. He knew what would happen when he followed her into the rain. And it did happen when his lips tasted the drop of rain on hers.

Two hours later, pages of disconnected thoughts and incomplete sentences filled the screen, but I was satisfied. Utterly exhausted, but satisfied.

Somewhere in there, Charlotte and Simon allowed themselves to be alone for the first time. They had sat in the stuffy drawing room long enough, saying everything with their eyes. Their lips did the talking then, a feverish rush fueled by their mutual distaste for fitting in.

I saved the document and closed my laptop. I grabbed the glass half-full of water, took a sip, and turned towards the hallway, looking forward to snuggling back into Landon's warm chest.

'Holy shit! What are you doing here?' I screamed when I realized I wasn't alone. The glass fell from my hands and shattered on the kitchen floor.

'Don't move,' Landon said as he walked towards me. He'd been leaning against the doorframe joining the hallway and the kitchen with his arms and ankles crossed. He'd watched me write for God knows how long. His boxers, his only clothing, hung low on his hipbones.

His hands wrung through his hair in worry. 'Jesus. Don't. Step. Anywhere. There are shards of glass everywhere.'

'You scared the hell out of me.'

'Ditto. It wasn't fun waking in the bed alone.'

'You thought I bolted from my own house? Not my style. I've been known to leave beds in the middle of the night, but never my own.'

He gestured to my laptop. 'You usually write at 3 a.m.?'

'No. My muse came back. I *had* to write.'

A smug look crossed his face as his chest puffed out like a muscle-bound Neanderthal. 'Ahh. So it was the amazing sex I gave you that woke that little lady up,' he

121

joked.

I laughed. 'Something like that.'

Landon's smug smile sobered as he looked at the field of glass at my feet. He held up his open palms. 'Just stay there, but take off your robe and throw it to me.'

'The fuck you say? Not in the mood, dude.'

He rolled his eyes. 'Difficult woman.'

He got down on his hands and knees and lifted his eyes to mine. 'I could have used it to push away the pieces of glass into piles, giving you a little walkway to get to the bedroom. Then we could have cleaned it up tomorrow morning.' His flattened hand hovered over the broken glass. 'But if you would rather me use my hand …'

'No!' I screamed. 'You'll get cut. What about pitching?' He smiled and lifted his hand. He knew what my reaction was going to be, and he was probably never planning on using his hands anyway. Damn him. I unknotted the belt of the robe and slid my arms from the sleeves. I threw it at his back as he knelt on all fours. I stood naked and cold, my feet rooted to the chilled kitchen tile.

He tugged the robe off his back, wadded it into a ball, and used it like a plow to create a small path for me to walk. He set it aside carefully, and I lifted my foot to step forward.

'Wait,' he said, crawling forward. 'I don't know if I got it all.'

He reached out his hand and this time touched the ground, brushing it softly to be sure it was safe.

My pulse skyrocketed. 'Stop, Landon. Stop!' I yelled louder when he kept moving. 'Your hand!'

'I'm using my left,' he whispered. 'Don't worry about it.'

He finished brushing his hand along the floor, stood up, and blew off a few flecks of glass from his hand before he held it out to me. I walked three tentative steps on the balls of my feet before my hand took his.

I followed him down the hallway and crawled into bed beside him. His arm curled around me as he snuggled into my back and rested his chin on the top of my head. 'Tell your fickle bitch of a muse to wait 'til morning next time. I'm freezing,' he joked.

'I'll relay the message.' My voice sobered. 'Thanks for helping with the glass.' The way he'd looked, so careful, so meticulous, as he crawled on the floor to ensure my safety, was burned into my memory – like when you stare at the sun, you can still see its outline when you close your eyes minutes later.

'You're welcome.' He kissed the top of my head and added, 'If I had to, I'd have used my right.'

At 8 a.m., my muse didn't wake me. It was the slanting rays of light peeking through the venetian blinds, and the heat of the man snuggled so close to my back that I was sweating. He stirred when I turned towards him, but he didn't wake up. Damn him, but he was beautiful in the morning light. No trace of drool. No snorting, stinky breaths. Just tousled hair that hung over his forehead and over his closed eyes. My hand itched with the need to brush it back. I gave in and reached my hand up. I arranged the silky strands, lighter on the edges than at the root, along his temple as I catalogued each detail of his face. His thin nose, his full lips, his light eyebrows, and his thick eyelashes that fluttered open. I saw the moment his eyes focused on me.

He smiled. 'Good morning.'

'Good morning,' I echoed with a devious smile as I pulled up the sheets over my head and pushed myself down his body. He rolled onto his back.

'Good morning to me,' he hummed as I tugged off his boxers. I kissed a line along the inside of his leg from his knee to the base of his impressive morning wood. I wrapped my hand around the tip and pulled upwards, exposing the underside of his balls to my tongue. My tongue flattened as I licked and sucked. His hips flexed and rolled, begging for more, so I licked up the length of his shaft and took the tip in my mouth with a hard suck.

'Now *this* is how I like to wake up,' he whispered. My hand gripped his base tightly as he filled my mouth. His hands snuck under the blanket, and, by touch alone, he pulled all my hair away from my face. He held it between his thumb and finger at the base of my neck. I sucked harder and increased the speed.

'Yes,' he hissed. 'So close, but I want to be in you instead.' His hand holding my hair tugged, pulling me off him. I crawled up his body and straddled his length. I reached into the drawer of the bedside table, ripped open the condom, and rolled it over his erection. I tilted him upwards and notched him at my entrance.

'Now this is how *I* like to wake up,' I mimicked, and he chuckled. That died away quickly as I slowly slid down his shaft. Tight from last night's lovemaking, my walls first protested then gave way.

His eyebrows furled, and he closed his eyes. 'Fuck. You're so tight.'

I whimpered, which made him open his eyes. He folded a pillow under his head so he could see where we were joined.

'Almost there,' he said as his hands went to my hips, guiding and pushing.

He hissed a 'yes' when I was finally able to take him all. I couldn't move in this position at first. I was so full. So stretched. I waited some seconds before my hips started making small circles. Back and forth at this depth, he rubbed the end of me while my clit was pressed against his pubic bone.

'Fuck. Get yourself off like this,' he encouraged. He reached up to cup the underside of my breasts. He pushed them together with his strong hands. 'I love how your tits sway every time you move.'

'Hold them while I bounce on you,' I said, my hips lifting and slamming down on him in rapid succession. I ground my clit against him before I repeated the rhythm, my thighs burning from the strain.

His eyes turned feral. 'I'm not going to last long like this.'

'Then don't,' I panted.

His chin tilted upwards as his eyes closed as if he was in pain. 'Not without you.' 'I'm with you. Just a little … so close …' The knot of nerves tingled and swelled.

His fingers and thumbs pinched my nipples, making me scream as the first flash sparked and ignited all the nerves through my legs to the arches of my feet where they curled and pointed.

So struck by the intensity, I lost the pounding rhythm.

'No. Keep going. Make it longer,' Landon said through gritted teeth. His hands gripped my hip bones and lifted me off and shoved me back down. His abs flexed, pushing his pelvis upwards every time his hands brought me down. I was on top, but he was fucking me.

The muscles in his face flexed as he tried to maintain control. 'Give it up, Landon. Come in me. Fill me.'

His jaw relaxed when he shouted, 'Fuck yes. Yes. Yes. Yes,' with each throb as he emptied into me.

His glassy eyes opened seconds later as his breath recovered. His hands gave up their grip on my hips as he flung his arms above his head. He stretched, all-sated male.

That was when I saw it. I don't know how I'd missed it before. He'd always worn a shirt around me, I guess, or at least an ice pack. And the living room had been so dim last night I must have missed it. A large scar lined the inside of his right elbow. The gentle curve of it contrasted with its angry pink color. I knew he'd had surgery, so why the scars took my breath away, I didn't really know. Maybe it was the realization that this man was human, something other than the casual jokester, that he was able to suffer pain and injury like the rest of us.

Or maybe the scars in me recognized his.

'Oh, Landon,' I gasped.

His eyes shot open. 'Nina? What's wrong?'

Wordlessly, I leaned forward and brushed my lips against the smooth, slightly shinier skin.

And he let me. I heard him exhale shakily as my fingertips traced the scar forward and back, forward and back.

When I sat up, he offered a gentle smile. I returned it and laid my ear on his chest. My head lifted slightly with each of his breaths, and I closed my eyes to the metronome of his thumping heart.

His fingertips brushed up and down my spine for a long while. His voice was raspy when he asked, 'Where do I kiss?'

'Hmmm?' I asked.

'You have them too. We just can't see them.'

Minutes later, he swatted my ass. 'Let's get that glass cleaned up so you can make some pancakes, woman.'

And with that, I knew we were back to the playful camaraderie that allowed us to pretend our scars were well healed. I rolled over and stretched like a lazy cat. 'I'll be right here while you clean it up. Let me know when it's done.'

The swat on my ass was much harder this time. 'Ouch!' I yelled as I rolled over and tried to swat him back. But he was much quicker and he anticipated my move, so he easily dodged out of the way, grabbed his boxers, and retreated behind the locked bathroom door.

'That fucking hurt,' I yelled to him as I rubbed the

126

reddened spot.

I heard the water running in the sink. 'You loved it,' he said.

He had me there. I did. I really did.

As I pulled on my lounge pants and a T-shirt, my cell phone rang on the nightstand. I picked up the phone, scowled at the caller ID, and answered on the last ring. Why was he calling this early on a Wednesday morning? My chest tightened.

'Pastor Tom? What's wrong?'

'Hi, Nina.' His warm, soft voice was edgier this morning, causing a spike of adrenalin to race through me. 'Sorry to bother you so early, but you are head of the outreach committee, so I needed to contact you as soon as possible this morning.'

'Tom. You're scaring me. What's wrong?' I repeated.

Tom sighed, then began. 'I'm sure you heard the storm last night. Well, we got a lot of rain and lightning, but our sister church in Bethel didn't fare so well.' He paused. 'The church and a lot of the town is gone, Nina. A tornado hit there last night. Three people died, and many are missing.'

'Oh, no. Anyone from the church?' Bethel Presbyterian was our sister church, meaning that we combined a lot of our efforts on big projects and often celebrated religious holidays together. We often played in leagues against each other and had eaten countless potlucks at their local park.

'Thankfully, none yet, but it's really early. The church is a total loss, which is why I'm calling you. We need to organize a group of volunteers to start clearing the rubble after the emergency management team gives us access to the city, which will be probably another two or three days. I really need you to head that, Nina. I'll get Preston to collect donations for rebuilding, but with all the insurance claims that need to be filed, I'm sure construction won't start for a while. Our main focus right now should be on helping them salvage what they can and get rid of everything else. Let's get a group together for Friday, OK?'

'I'll do it. No problem.'

'I knew I could count on you. I'll be in touch a lot in the next few days when I know more.'

'OK. Thank you.' I ended the call and stared at the phone in my lap. I'd been to that beautiful, old church many times. Its mahogany woodwork and stained-glass windows were priceless. Churches weren't made like that anymore. And that was true of a lot of the congregation, too. Mary. Carter. Will. Names and faces floated through my head as my eyes misted. I prayed that none of them were among the unaccounted for.

My mind immediately made a list of everything I needed to do. Coordinate volunteers. Find dumpsters and gloves. Organize food and water for the volunteers. The list went on.

The bathroom door clicked and opened. I heard Landon's footsteps down the hall, into the empty kitchen, and back down the hall. 'Nina. Where are you and why are you not making me ...' His question halted when he saw me sitting on the bed. He strode over and knelt in front of me.

'What's wrong?' His hands gripped mine around the phone. 'Someone call?'

'Yeah.' I related to him what happened last night and how much it troubled me.

'Friday, huh?' Three lines of worry crossed his forehead.

'Yeah. That doesn't give me much time.' I thought that was why he was worried, so I couldn't have been more surprised when he stood and, as he paced, said, 'We have a game that night, but I'm not scheduled to start, so maybe the team will let me go for a leave of absence for that day.'

'What?'

He stopped pacing and his eyes met mine. 'I want to go there with you and help.'

Sweet, sweet man. This reaction to help gave me a peek into his gracious soul. 'Really? I don't want to get you in trouble.'

He waved off my concern with a flick of his wrist like it was a bothersome fly. He pulled on his pants and tugged his shirt over his head. He stuffed his money clip into his back pocket and grabbed his keys. 'There won't be a problem. I'll talk to Coach Craig today –' he smiled at the name, '– and I'm sure he'll understand. In fact, I'm going to be late for my therapy, so I'm going to take a rain check on those pancakes.'

'You probably don't want one. I'm a terrible cook.'

'That makes two of us.' He leaned down to kiss my lips. 'Thanks for a great night. And a great morning.'

'You're welcome, and thanks for offering to help on Friday.' He leaned in for another kiss, which I granted. Then I slapped his ass with a pop against his jeans. Damn, my hand stung. 'Now get your ass out of here before I tie you down and force you to eat my pancakes.' Then I added, 'Tell Laura and her double-d twins "hi" for me.'

He chuckled as the door shut behind him.

Chapter Twelve

When news came out about the tragedy, it wasn't difficult to find volunteers. My phone spent the next two days attached to my ear with people pledging their time and resources. Pastor Tom often called with updates on logistics, and, thankfully, good news that all other residents were accounted for.

On Friday morning, I woke before my 5 a.m. alarm, dressed in old, ripped jeans and a long-sleeve T-shirt, and drove to Bethel. I parked in the pre-arranged volunteer parking lot just outside the city limits. Red Cross vans and semi-trucks full of supplies surrounded the area. I boarded the shuttle, which was no more than a tractor pulling a large hay trailer, and told the driver where I was volunteering. Three women and two men joined me. We introduced ourselves, but our casual conversation died away within a few minutes when we pulled on to Main Street. The tornado couldn't have made a more direct hit had it used GPS. Two blocks away, green trees still stood, although with fewer green leaves. The ornate flowering trees that lined Main Street's sidewalks had been shredded. What looked like foot-long sticks stuck out from the ground, the remnants of tree trunks. The trees had just begun to flower, so the ground was littered with what looked like snow. Piles of petals clung to half-collapsed doorframes. All the roofs were caved in, each building marked for demolition with a red X on what was left of the front façade. Each X told a story of people's hopes and dreams and the death of their livelihood: a tailor here, a lawyer there, a barbershop down the street. The eerie silence made it feel like we were riding through a ghost town. Maybe we were. Many small towns never came back from something like this.

'Dear God,' the woman next to me muttered between the fingers covering her parted lips. 'They lost everything.'

'First stop for anyone volunteering at Bethel Presbyterian,' the driver called. I gasped, unable to recognize the area I'd been to countless times.

I gathered my supplies and made my way down the trailer's steps and onto the ground below where my heavy footsteps made a path in the petals. Through the tears pooling on my eyelids, I could see the towering, majestic oak in the front lawn had toppled, littering the ground with millions of three-inch long twigs that crunched under my feet.

The all-brick building was unrecognizable. In my optimistic dreams, I thought maybe the dire descriptions had been dramatized, that I'd be able to spot a few missing pieces from the stained-glass window over the front door. But the reality was that not only were the pieces of glass nowhere to be seen, but the heavy, mahogany front door wasn't either. There was no roof, no walls except for half of the northern-most wall. From the sidewalk, I saw the pews in their still-perfect rows like hell hadn't visited all around them.

'Nina,' Pastor Tom's voice came from around the corner. 'You're early. Thanks for coming.'

I couldn't make my mouth work. The shock of it all, the loss, was too much.

Pastor Tom stepped closer and circled his arms around me. 'It's a lot to take in. I've been here for twenty-four hours, so I've gotten somewhat used to it.'

'Will they even come back? The town … it's gone. Everyone will just cut their losses and move to a bigger city.'

'That's why this is so important.' Pastor Tom gestured

132

to the ruins behind him. 'If people see their church rebuilt, it might help the town survive.' He stepped away, a look of fierce determination on his face. 'Time to get to work.'

I dried my eyes and stood straighter. 'Let's do this.'

'Hey, Preston,' Pastor Tom called. 'Nina's here. Let's have you two organize everyone when they get here.'

Preston, a young, up-and-coming lawyer in Boulder and a happily married father of two, walked quickly to our side. 'Good morning, Nina,' Preston welcomed as Pastor Tom stepped aside to direct other volunteers.

'Good morning,' I said as we walked around the building and put on our gloves. 'Where do we start?'

He directed me to a pile of splintered wood near a dumpster. We started picking up the pieces we could on our own, but others were so large we had to work together. Each piece of wood we tossed into the dumpster cracked and settled, causing a cloud of dust and dirt to rise into the air.

'How's the fundraising going?' I asked, since Preston had been put in charge of raising donations for the initial rebuilding costs before the insurance settlements were received.

'Amazing. The response has been phenomenal. Our congregation has already pledged nearly ten thousand dollars. And last night at the Denver Raptor's game, the Red Cross collected another four thousand from the crowd.'

'That's great. It's only been a few days, too.'

He nodded. 'But that's not even the best part. On Wednesday night, Pastor Tom received a check for fifty thousand dollars.'

'What? From who?'

He lifted his eyebrows when he leaned in. 'It was anonymous.'

'Oh, God,' I said, backing away. I couldn't catch my breath. It might be anonymous to everyone else, but it wasn't to me. My heart knew immediately who had written that check and wanted no glory or recognition for it.

I then whispered to Preston, 'I'm going to check on something in the front. I'll be right back.' I walked around the east side that was thankfully vacant to collect my thoughts. My heart beat wildly, and I swallowed against my dry throat. His donation wasn't done in order to be seen. It was done out of compassion for people he'd never met, for a church he'd never been to.

'Oh God,' I repeated, overwhelmed by emotions. 'Oh God.'

'I think you were saying that Tuesday night,' Landon said in a voice full of exaggerated manly bravado as he rounded the corner. His chest was puffed up as he sauntered towards me. 'Thinking about me when I'm not here, huh?'

I had been, but not in the way he thought. I decided in that moment not to tell him I knew of his donation. The shock over his anonymous generosity must have been painted across my face, so I smiled, attempting to cover my shock with a come-hither look from under my eyebrows. 'More than you know,' I said, as he wrapped his hands around my lower back. I tugged on the hair at the nape of his neck to bring him closer for a chaste kiss.

'Thanks for coming.'

The bright morning sun backlit his smile. 'I wouldn't miss it. Where do you want me to start?' He asked as he pulled a pair of work gloves from his back pocket and slid them on. I showed him to the pile I'd been working on and introduced him to Preston. The guys shook hands and began work in silence.

I picked up a few bricks and starting carrying them to the dumpster. 'Sorry I couldn't be at your start last night. I was busy coordinating volunteers. How did it go?'

He threw two large pieces of wood into the dumpster

like they were matches. He turned away quickly to shield his eyes from the dust that flew up. 'No problem, I understand. It went really well. Best one yet, in fact.' He grunted as he threw in a large piece of concrete. 'I got another win, but more importantly, the movement of the pitches is coming back. The best part is that I feel really good this morning,' he added.

'And the curveball?' I joked.

'Never better,' he said as he bit his bottom lip and stared at my chest. 'Must be all that practice.'

I slapped his shoulder. 'Cool it. Don't get me all riled up.'

He laughed and went to help Preston carry a particularly heavy load. I left the men to work together so I could walk around front and help organize the volunteers that were due this hour. I made sure the water bottles were being passed out and that the lunch service we'd ordered was delivered.

An hour later, I gathered everyone to eat. Landon and Preston were some of the last to quit working. They shook hands and went in different directions, Preston to find his wife, and Landon to sit next to me. We sat quietly side by side on makeshift benches and ate sandwiches and chips. The afternoon sun had burned off any cloud cover, and with spring quickly giving way to June, the temperatures climbed into the upper eighties. Sweat wetted the hair along my forehead and temples as I handed out extra bottles of water, some Band-Aids, and a few pairs of safety glasses.

The rest of the day went quickly, but because I was in charge of organizing the effort, I didn't see Landon much. For two hours, I joined some of the Bethel church members as they walked through the remains of their church for the first time. Some picked up Bibles strewn on the floor. Many were missing covers, others had pages falling out of them, but the parishioners clung to those rare discoveries like they'd found hidden treasures.

'What will we do?' Mary asked no one in particular as she picked up a broken candle.

'We'll rebuild,' her husband Will vowed, although he sounded like he was trying to convince himself.

My heart ached for their loss. I told them so, but the words didn't seem adequate enough. Nothing was going to help this situation but time.

Depressed and needing some time alone, I walked around the north side and sat below one of the only trees left standing. Many of the branches were bare, so it didn't provide much shade. But the rough bark that scratched my back as I leaned against it reminded me how tough something needed to be to survive. From my secluded spot under the tree, I saw Landon pushing a wheelbarrow full of debris to the dumpster on the sun-drenched west side. The afternoon sun baked the skin on his shoulders and back. His damp shirt hung from where he had taken it off and tucked it into the waistband of his jeans. A sheet of sweat made his abs shine in the bright light. His baseball hat was turned backwards, and his sunglasses were wrapped around his eyes, accentuating his high cheek bones.

'Landon,' I called as I stood up and walked towards him. He put down the wheelbarrow and smiled. I walked to him, wrapped my arms around his sweaty lower back, and lowered my forehead into his chest. I felt him pull away.

'I'm sweaty,' he objected, but I pressed my forehead against his collarbone, stopping his retreat, and closed my eyes. Sensing my mood, he wound his damp arms around my waist. He dipped his chin and rested it on the top of my head.

Then he sighed, 'You want to talk?'

I shook my head back and forth. We stood like that for a while, entwined in something new and different. The birds chirped around us as they looked for the remnants of their nests, their song a reminder that life went on. A strong gust of wind blew so much dust around us that some specks stuck to the perspiration on Landon's shoulders and arms. I tilted my head to the side and ran a single finger through the flecks. They parted, leaving a line of skin underneath. I'd made three parallel lines when I felt his breath hitch under my cheek. I started to ask him about it when someone spoke behind us.

'It's 4 p.m.,' someone said.

'Thanks,' I called. I pulled back, and Landon allowed me to. 'We're scheduled to leave in fifteen minutes. I'll meet you at the front so we can ride the shuttle back together.'

He frowned and looked around him. 'But there's so much to do.'

Such a gentle, kind man. 'You've done all you could with the time we have. Another shift is coming this evening and more this weekend.'

He picked up the wheelbarrow. 'Are you coming back this weekend?'

'Yes. I'm in charge of volunteers, so I'll be here Saturday and Sunday at least. I have a Monday meeting scheduled at the university, so I can't then. But then I'll probably spend some time here next week.'

He stopped next to the dumpster and began throwing in rubble from the wheelbarrow. He blew out a breath before he said, 'I wish I could be here, but we have games both days. I got one day off, but not the rest.'

My hand encircling his elbow made him pause his work. 'You've been very gracious with your time.' And your money, I wanted to add, but I didn't want him to know I knew yet. 'Here, let me help,' I added and grabbed the smaller pieces from the wheelbarrow. We emptied it quickly and loaded it twice more before Landon pushed the empty wheelbarrow to the front for the next wave of volunteers to use.

He put back on his wrinkled T-shirt. He took off his hat and sunglasses and rubbed the sweat off his forehead with the sleeve. The skin was whiter around his eyes and on his upper forehead where it had been protected from the sun.

'Oh, no. You got a sunburn. Did you use sunscreen?'

He rolled his eyes and put back on his hat and glasses. 'No, Mom,' he ribbed as we stepped onto the waiting shuttle. The diesel engine puffed a small black cloud as it took us away from what was left of the church. Each rut in the dirt road jostled us side to side. His arm wound around my back and pulled me to his side.

'What's for dinner? You're feeding me, right?' He joked.

'Sure. What do you want?'

He leaned in. 'You,' he whispered.

It was my turn to roll my eyes. 'That's a given, but after I get a hot shower.'

He looked forward before he spoke under his breath. 'I'll take you any way I can get you.' His thumb rubbed an inch of skin on my shoulder, up and down and in circles, as we road back in silence.

My hair was still dripping wet from my shower when I answered the door to pay the delivery guy. I put the box down on the coffee table in front of the couch and walked to the bathroom. I cracked the door open slightly, and a puff of steam hit me in the face. 'Pizza's here!' I shouted to Landon, whose shape I could barely make out through the frosted glass door of the shower. The water immediately turned off.

'Thanks. I'll be right out,' he called as he pulled down a towel that was hung over the shower door.

I shut the door with a click and went to get plates and drinks. I flipped through the channels, landing on a baseball game between the Dallas Stars and New York

Yankees. He joined me on the couch, chose a slice of pizza, and bit into it without bothering to use a plate. He watched the game as he ate three slices, and I watched him, although I pretended not to.

He'd brought a change of clothes, but he'd put back on his old, ripped hat. The edges of it were darker since it absorbed water from his hair. The longer pieces of hair at the back were just starting to curl into loose waves as they dried. He watched the game like a scout. I could see him memorizing small details, details I most surely missed, cataloguing them for later when he'd be playing against these very same players. He'd huff at what he thought was a bad call or nod in praise when a pitcher got a hitter to strikeout. The thought that in the near future he'd be on that screen rather than watching it from my living room couch spurred me to take advantage of the time he was here.

I wrapped my lips around the cool glass as I finished off the rest of my beer. I took his bottle of water from where he held it in his lap and placed it on the table where he'd propped up his feet.

I threw one leg over his lap to straddle him. His attention went immediately from the game to my chest. He didn't even bother to ask what I was doing. My voice lowered seductively. 'It's time for me to thank you for all your help today.'

He reached for the remote and clicked off the television. The muted glow of dusk filled the room so there were more shadows than light. 'But with one stipulation.'

His beautiful lips pursed together in amusement. 'OK. I'll bite. What is it?'

'You let me thank you for the donation you made to Bethel Presbyterian.'

His eyes flashed with shock only for a millisecond before he covered it, and that's when I knew he wasn't going to tell me the truth. 'What donation?'

'The one you gave to Pastor Tom on Wednesday night before the destruction was reported in the press. The *anonymous* donor earmarked it for Bethel Presbyterian and knew to contact Pastor Tom. There's only a handful of people who could have known to do that. And who has *that* much money just sitting around?'

'Fifty thousand dollars is not a lot of money.'

He realized his mistake as soon as he said it. 'Busted,' I said as I playfully pointed one finger into his chest. Then I turned more serious. 'Did you not want me to know?'

His eyes wouldn't meet mine. Instead, they stared at his hands that gripped my hips tighter by the second. 'I didn't want anyone to know. I donate anonymously to many charities.'

'Why?'

'Why do I donate or why did I not want you to know?'

'Both.'

His chest lifted with a large breath. When he exhaled, he laid his head back on the top of the couch so that he spoke to the ceiling. 'I donate because … of personal reasons.'

'One of those dark corners we're granting each other?'

'Yes,' he whispered. His Adam's apple bobbed when he swallowed and as he spoke. 'I never want anyone to know because I don't do it for the recognition. Those people who go on television and talk about how much they've given to others throughout their lives make me wonder if they do it for the right reasons.'

'"When you give to the needy, do not let your left hand know what your right hand is doing, so that your giving may be in secret". Matthew 6,' I whispered. 'Beware of practicing your righteousness before other people in order to be seen by them …'

To my utter surprise, Landon finished, '… for then you will have no reward from your Father who is in heaven.'

When his head tilted up, his eyes finally met mine. His mouth didn't move, but he said more than I could process. 'I … didn't know you were religious.'

'I'm not. I grew up in a household that *pretended* to be religious. I guess maybe as an adult I'm trying to live out what they professed to believe.'

Every time I learned something new about him, it made we like him more. 'I like that …'

'Leave it, Nina. Please,' he growled, the deep baritone of his voice a clear warning. Then his eyes blinked heavily before he repeated more softly, 'Please, just leave it.'

'OK.'

'So now we've discussed this *stipulation* of yours …' His arms finished the sentence for him as they circled around my ass and pulled me inches forward so his erection pressed against my center.

I rubbed up and down his shaft through our jeans as I unbuttoned his. I leaned forward so our lips met in a kiss that ignited the need I'd stored up since our last night together. I'd felt like a match all day, ready to light with the slightest strike. My tongue sliding against his, like a match against its matchbox, created a reaction in me that burst and flared in me. I lifted off to pull down the zip with a rasp. When my hand reached into his boxers, he caught it.

Against my lips, he said, 'Let's go to bed.' His right knee was bouncing under me in anticipation.

'OK, but whatever you do, don't stop kissing me.'

He growled, 'Like I ever could,' as he stood and carried me into the bedroom. His hands under my ass kneaded as he walked. His foot kicked open the door where it banged loudly into the wall. Seconds later, he threw me onto the mattress.

'Strip,' he commanded as he pulled off his own jeans and shirt. 'I don't have a lot of patience tonight.'

He grabbed a condom from his wallet and placed it on

the bedside table as I stripped, my shirt and jeans followed by my bra and my lacy underwear.

His gaze followed the last to the floor. 'As much as I hate to see those go ...' Landon crawled across the mattress and lay down so his body covered mine. It practically vibrated with an energy I hadn't felt from him before. '... I like this a lot more.'

'Me too.' I wrapped my legs around his waist and scraped my nails down his back.

I felt him wince in the near darkness. I placed my open palm against the skin on his neck and back. It was warm to my touch like it had been kissed by the sun's heat. 'Sorry, I forgot about your sunburn.'

'You're going to make me forget about it in just a second.' He leaned over to grab the condom from the table, his weight pressing against my chest. I bit my bottom lip as I watched him roll it on.

His thumb pulled my lip free a second before his tongue licked across my lip, the beginning of a fervent kiss. He sucked in a breath as he notched himself at my entrance. He pulled away from the deep kiss to say, 'Fuck. I've got no patience tonight.'

He shoved in with one strong thrust, so hard that my back arched and I screamed, 'Landon! Oh God.' The rest was indecipherable as he pounded into me. His hands grabbed mine and stretched them above our heads.

'Wrap them around the headboard,' he said as he let them go. 'Push back against me. This isn't going to be tender.'

My knuckles must have turned white with my strong grip. 'Fucking do it. I need it,' I panted. I screamed when he crushed against me, stretching me and filling me.

He bent one of my knees to my chest and hooked his elbow underneath it so he could pound into me at this new, vulnerable angle.

My body braced, tensing for his penetration. 'Relax for

me. Don't want to hurt you.'

I felt the shake in his muscles as he tried to hold himself back.

I willed my muscles to release, and when I did, he plunged so deeply the headboard banged into the wall with a thump. He continued the rhythm. All I could do was hold on. I rode his wave of passion, of want, until my fervor matched his. I bucked up into him as he drove down into me, the skin on our bodies sliding easily with a thin layer of sweat.

His eyes clenched shut when he moaned. 'Damn. I can't hold it. This one's for me. The next will be for you.' He pounded again, beyond control, beyond restraint, until his back bowed. He held himself still inside me, planted deep, as his member throbbed inside me with his release. One of his hands gripped the sheet next to my shoulder so hard that his knuckles were colorless. The other covered mine around the headboard. The blunt edges of the wooden slats cut into my knuckles as his grip encircled mine.

As he came back down, I felt parts of his body begin to relax. First went his arms, then his shoulders and hips. He rolled to the side, wrapped the condom in a tissue, and turned back to me. With his head propped up on his bent elbow, he finally looked at me. 'You didn't come, did you?'

'Nope.' I hadn't even considered lying. Not my style. Sex was one of the only things I was truly honest about. I turned on my side to face him and propped my head on my arm, mimicking his pose. 'The sex was great, don't get me wrong. But I don't really come with that kind of sex.'

'Who knew?' He mocked surprise. 'That works in all the porn I've seen.'

I smiled at his joke, glad we could laugh about it.

He rolled onto his back and pulled me in so my cheek rested on his shoulder. 'Give me an hour and I'll be ready again.'

I yawned. 'I'll take an hour of sleep after today. Wake me up when you're ready to rock my world,' I said against his chest, the last thing I remember until his kisses woke me hours later.

Those kisses tickled my toes under the covers before they brushed up the back of my knee and stroked my clit. His breath puffed against me. 'Wake up, sleepyhead.'

'Mmm ... I'm awake,' I hummed as he kissed up my stomach to my breasts. He sucked one nub into his hot mouth. His tongue massaged the distended flesh until I whimpered.

His mouth popped off. 'I'm going to do to you what I had no patience to do earlier. I was so on edge. I needed you. I had to have you. Now I get to take my time.' The full weight of his body pressed against my chest and hips as he feathered kisses in all my favorite places. 'You won't be able to get away. Your body belongs to me.'

I tried to wiggle out from under him to prove I could, but if I was honest, I didn't really want to. And if I was brutally honest, it felt good to fight. 'Landon ...' was all I could say since I couldn't make sense of my contradictory emotions. If I allowed myself to simply feel, I would say that it felt good for him to claim my body. Yet we both knew this fling had an expiration date. Why would he stake a claim to something he was sure to leave? Why did it feel so good when he did?

'I see I've hit a raw nerve,' he said against my other breast. 'There's a part of you that doesn't want to belong to anyone, especially to a man you know won't be around much longer.'

I nodded.

'I know that, and that's what attracts me to you. You're this fascinating combination of being utterly available for anything, yet you're untouchable, unreachable. You're like a wild horse, up for the biggest adventures yet you refuse any reigns.'

I wiggled again, more forcefully this time, but his weight on top easily held me down. It was strange how much he enjoyed watching my struggle. Even more strange was my reaction to it. I loved that I couldn't get away despite my feverish attempts. He was too strong. I stopped fighting. My chest sawed up and down from my exertion as we stared at each other, unblinking.

'You want to tame me. Is that it?' I asked.

'No. I'd never want that. But I don't want anyone else to try, either.' He let that sink in before he continued, 'What if I have to go soon? It kills me to think someone else will ...' He paused curiously and looked over his shoulder. 'Wait here for one second. I have to grab something.'

He rolled off my body and walked across the room. He watched over his shoulder to see if I would move.

For a fleeting second, I considered it. Hell, all I wanted seconds ago was to be out from under him and his claiming gaze. Now, without his weight covering me, I didn't feel the need. The appeal to flee, to fight, was gone.

He found his overnight bag near the bedroom door. He rummaged in one pocket then another before he found what he was looking for. In the near dark, I couldn't see what it was. He returned to the bed, laid next to me with his leg slung over my hips, and held up the object to my face. Even inches away, I couldn't tell what it was. It looked like a tube of black lipstick with a plastic lid.

'What is that?'

'Eye black. You know the ...'

'I know what eye black is, moron,' I snapped playfully. It was the stuff athletes rolled on under their eyes to absorb bright sunlight. 'I've just never seen it not on someone before. Why the hell do you have some in that bag?'

'That's the bag I took with me to your baseball game,

remember?'

'OK,' I said, tentatively, still not understanding why he had it. Pitchers rarely wore it. They could see the ball just fine from the mound.

Then it hit me at the same time he said, 'I was playing outfield, remember?' He was right. Outfielders use it all the time so that they can track down fly balls better against the sun's glare.

He uncapped the tube and twisted the base. Like a tube of lipstick, the black stick inched upwards. 'So I was saying … It kills me to think someone else will be touching this arm …' He brushed the eye black down my arm so a dark line marked me from shoulder to wrist. The light touch raised goosebumps all over my body. I could see the hairs on my arm stand as he moved to my collarbone.

'… And this spot right here that makes you whimper when I kiss it. I know it's not mine, but I don't want it to be anyone else's.' He drew a line along my cleavage down to my hips. The black trail felt slightly wet before it dried in seconds. I shuddered when he continued down my leg. 'And these legs …' he hummed.

'But you're leaving. You expect me to be with no one else while you go flying around the country doing God knows what? That's insane.'

I struggled anew, this time even more forcefully, so much so that he lay on top of me and pinned my arms to my sides. I protested, 'Why are you marking me? I don't belong to you, especially when you surely won't ever belong to me.'

He stopped and rolled off and then he laid the uncapped eye black on my stomach. It rose and fell with my labored breaths. It felt like it weighed as much as a brick. 'That's interesting you say that. How do you know that? Maybe that's something I want.'

'Are you crazy?'

146

'You make me crazy. In fact, you gave me this idea today. Don't you remember marking me? You drew lines in my skin as we stood behind the church.'

'I wasn't marking you.'

'Oh? Then why did you do it?'

My heart skipped and thudded as I held my breath. I couldn't move a muscle, not even to lift a finger. I had completely forgotten I'd done that. 'I don't know. Lost in thought, I guess.'

'I'm not sure about that. But regardless of the reason, I can tell you that I liked it. In fact, I fucking *loved* it.' His fingers followed every line on my body, down one arm, up the other. Down one leg, up the other. 'I wanted you to trace lines on me, on all your favorite spots.'

He picked up the eye black again and turned my cheek to expose one side of my neck. 'Like this one. This is my favorite. Right under your ear. You love me whispering here. You like feeling my breath. You like me licking you, biting you.' His teeth tugged on my earlobe when he finished marking the spot. He threw the eye black onto the bedside table where it clanked and fell to the carpet as he climbed on top of me.

His stare was intense when he said, 'You know as well as I that this can't last forever, so can't we just pretend for one night that your body is mine?' One hand traced the line from my chest to my stomach and continued further until he circled my clit. My hips bucked at the contact. 'You'll belong to me. You'll hold nothing back until we're completely exhausted.'

'And you're mine? For tonight?' I added.

He stared so long I thought maybe he hadn't heard it. His hand urged my legs further apart and started working tight circles around my nub. Then he whispered, 'Don't you already know?'

I closed my eyes. It was easier to meet his sincerity with what felt like armor. Instead, I focused on the sensations he was wringing from my body. I writhed against his hand, begging for more pressure.

'For God's sake, Nina, for one night be an open book. Don't hold back on me. Don't hide.' His thumb pressed against my swollen nub as he speared two fingers into me. He sucked my nipple into his mouth where his teeth grazed and his tongue soothed. I circled my hips in short, quick bursts, chasing the orgasm that was waiting for the right moment to explode.

That moment was when his mouth popped off my breast. He claimed my mouth with a kiss so heated he pressed my head into the mattress. I turned my head the moment the first wave hit. 'Yes. Fuck, yes!' I screamed as each pulse vibrated higher. He removed his fingers and rubbed quickly side to side on my clit to sustain the intensity.

When I came back down, God knows how long later, nerves all over my body were pulsating, throbbing for more of the feeling they'd become addicted to. 'I gotta be in you,' he said as he rolled over, grabbed a condom, and put it on with one hand. Seconds later, he was on top of me.

His arms wound under my shoulders so one hand cupped the back of my neck, the other the back of my head. He used that leverage to pull me onto him. I slowly slid down onto him as he kissed all the places he'd marked along my neck and shoulders. My arms rubbed against his skin, blurring the lines he'd drawn so that both of us were covered in smears and smudges. The lines were wavy. The once clear edges that delineated light and dark were now anything but definite.

The rhythm he set was calm, tranquil, like those rivers at waterparks where you lay on a raft and drift down a lazy stream. I closed my eyes as he pulled his arms out from under me. I felt every kiss along the undulating black lines on my arms and across my chest.

'These arms. You always talk with them when you're angry.'

Sometimes his tongue would dart out. Other times, it was just his soft, pink lips that caressed the spot as long as he pleased before he moved on.

His hips continued their worshipful rhythm. Unhurried, all his motions were deliberate and careful. Sometimes he held himself still inside me so I could grind my hips up to meet him at the spot I really needed. He'd whisper, 'Give me more. I want more of you.'

He sucked a spot on my neck until it was tender. 'I love feeling your pulse here.'

My nipples pebbled and I sucked in a breath. 'And these tits. So beautiful,' he rasped.

I grabbed his biceps that bulged around me. 'I'm there. Please. I'm there.'

'I know. Give me more, Nina,' He didn't speed up his hips, lose any rhythm. He kept rocking me, grinding me, until my body decided it was time.

I started to tip over, so I scrunched my eyes shut again.

'Fucking look at me. Hide nothing.'

I opened my eyes to see him staring at me. Our faces didn't touch, but aligned nose to nose, mouth to mouth, he saw everything as I flew apart, shattered into millions of tiny pieces. Overwhelmed by the emotions of the day and even more so by the revelations of the night, I felt the prickle behind my eyes. I willed it away as he stared, seeing everything.

That's why I know there's no way I was able to hide the tear that slipped from the corner of my eye to my ear, smearing the remaining eye black as it landed.

Chapter Thirteen

On Saturday night, despite working for hours in Bethel, my brain wouldn't turn off. Simon and Charlotte had something they wanted to say, so I grabbed a Red Bull and planted myself in front of the laptop even though it was nearing midnight. I'd made it to where they'd finally allowed themselves to meet alone in the gardens under the pouring rain. But in the light of day, they had to remain casual acquaintances, their politeness a mask for their attraction. Charlotte often escaped to the Sanditon library, which was usually vacant as most of the women her age were busy buying new dresses and hair ribbons. Simon knew to look for her there.

Charlotte was so focused on the world Chaucer created, she didn't hear the booted footsteps scrape across the wood floor where they stopped behind her chair.

'I knew I'd find you here, Ms. Heywood.'

She gasped as the book slammed shut. 'Mr Parker. Good day. Sir,' she added respectfully. It was the first words she'd said to him alone.

He sat on the chair across from her, pulling his coattails out from underneath. 'There's no need to call me sir.'

'Sir?' She asked, pretending not to understand why he didn't require the formality that polite society usually did. The heated kiss they had allowed themselves in the garden went far past polite society.

He huffed in frustration, but continued the charade. 'Fine, if you wish, Madam,' he added with a sarcastic bow of his head. After a pause, he continued, 'Tell me. How do you like Sanditon? Please, speak freely. My brother might have a stake in its success, but I assure you I do not.'

Charlotte's eyes softened like she was looking out over the waves. 'It is a lovely getaway. A beautiful retreat. But I am anxious to return home to my family.'

'And that is all the young lady thinks? What about the company?'

'All have been welcoming and gracious. I couldn't have asked for more.'

His next question came quickly. 'And the shopping? Why do you sit in this room when there are lovely ribbons and lace to be bought at the finest of stores? Don't you covet that new blue lace? Ms. Robbins just got in that light pink brocade that my sisters can't find enough uses for.'

Charlotte's heart did yearn for that pink brocade as she imagined whirling around in it at the upcoming Sanditon ball. It would sway as she waltzed. Simon's hand would cover hers. He'd squeeze ... But reality soon intruded. Her parents had too many mouths to feed to spend money on such frivolity. Charlotte cleared her throat and prepared the best answer she could. 'The pink brocade is lovely. Perhaps someday I will have a reason to buy it.'

'Always so proper.' His eyebrows knit in frustration as he saw through her careful answers. He stood and walked to her side where he knelt a foot from her. 'Why do you provide courteous, polite answers with me? Why do you hide what you truly believe?'

'Why would I not?'

Simon's dark brown eyes looked away for a moment, then returned to hers, steadfast and determined. 'Because I understand you. I recognize in you the mutual distaste for all of this.' His arms waved in semicircles.

'What is "this" sir?'

He glowered at her obstinacy. 'The pretension. The hypocrisy. The affectation disguised as sincerity. It's

152

exhausting to keep up. And I don't want to keep it up with you.'

'What are you suggesting?' Her voice was breathy, her tight bodice cutting into her ribs with each breath.

'Take a walk with me tomorrow evening. We'll stroll along the beach after tea.'

A voice nearing them made Simon stand quickly and take a step away.

When Charlotte accepted his invitation, her voice was schooled into the formal lilt required of a young lady of good breeding. 'I would love to meet you for a stroll, sir.'

I spent all weekend in Bethel, coordinating volunteers and sorting through rubble while managing to write some hours each night. Landon had games both nights, and while he didn't pitch, he had to be there. We talked on the phone both nights. The fatigue in his voice mirrored my own. We talked about things we did that day, how the clean-up was going, and how the team had done. We said nothing about the night he'd used eye black or the dreaded tear I cursed every time I thought about it. We ended the call with the promise to talk in the coming days. On Sunday night, I wished him well with his therapy appointment, and he wished me the same for the meeting I had with the university Monday morning.

My fingers drummed a rhythm on my chest as I lay on my couch Monday afternoon, confused and conflicted. The meeting earlier in the day had been terrible and phenomenal at the same time, which explained a large part of my exhaustion as I lay on the couch, pulled a blanket over my body, and stared at the ceiling.

At 10 a.m. on Monday morning, I'd had a scheduled meeting with the head of the English Department, Dr Karen Moore. She'd called me last week to set up the meeting, and had I been less busy over the weekend, I might have worried myself sick wondering what she wanted. It was not common to be called into her office. And it usually wasn't good news.

This rare time, it was good, or at least it would have been to anyone else. 'Good morning, Nina,' she welcomed me into her corner office that overlooked the university gardens. 'Have a seat.'

'Thank you.' I sat in the modern, leather chair and crossed my legs; waiting for her to deliver what I'd convinced myself was awful news. My legs sweated under the restricting pantyhose. I hated those things, and I never wore them, but I thought they were appropriate.

'You're probably wondering why I called you here, so I'll get right to it. Dr Clark, one of our undergraduate professors, has recently been diagnosed with cancer. The doctors think it is curable, which is good news. But the bad news is that he will be undergoing rounds of chemotherapy, requiring him to take a leave of absence for at least one full semester, probably two.'

'I'm sorry to hear that. Is there something I can do?'

She smiled a warm smile, one that calmed me. Her teeth were yellowed from years of drinking coffee. 'I'm glad you asked. We will need someone to step in and teach his classes for the next two semesters. Both focus on nineteenth-century literature, and since that is your specialty and your class evaluations have been marvelous, we have decided to ask you to fill in for Dr Clark.'

I stuttered, so surprised I couldn't speak. 'But, you could get a million people ... I mean ... you could put out a job posting and have ten interviews lined up tomorrow with scholars all over the country.'

'Not as many as you might think. It is a temporary position, remember. It will not be tenure track, and it is not guaranteed to lead to future employment. Many people will not want to move their families for such a position, and not to mention, everyone in the department knows you and respects your work. We'd love for you to join us.'

My mouth knew what it was supposed to say, so it moved before I could think. 'It would be an honor to join you. Thank you for the opportunity.'

Her nervous smile turned to a grin. She quickly came round her desk and enveloped me in a hug. Then she stepped back and offered her hand, which I shook. 'We're glad to have you on board. I'll send you some information about the classes, the old syllabi for you to review, although you can choose the texts you would like to use, and other forms for you to fill out now you will be paid a professor's salary rather than the graduate student stipend.'

I hadn't even thought about the money. Heck, I didn't even know what a professor's salary was.

'You look overwhelmed. Don't be. You have the whole summer to prepare,' she encouraged as she led me to the door. 'I'll be in touch,' she said as she opened the door.

I thanked her again before I walked out of the office. My heels clacked on the tile floors, slow at first, most likely out of shock, then faster, as my thoughts started whirling.

I threw open the doors and ran to the nearest bench, gasping for air. What was wrong with me? Why wasn't I calling everyone I knew to tell them about this amazing opportunity? It was a fantastic opportunity – of that I had no doubt. Not only would I get paid much more; I would also get exposure to teaching classes that only full-time, tenured professors usually got. This would look so good when I applied for jobs. I'd always wanted to teach, to be part of academia. No matter what Dr Moore said, I knew this was a coveted position. Hell, I could name ten graduate students in our department alone who would take the position in a heartbeat. I ought to be screaming with joy.

But as I sat on the bench overlooking the gardens full of dark purple irises, I couldn't help the bile rising in my throat. This would definitely delay work on my dissertation. My priorities would have to change, all for a position I'd dreamed about forever and now wasn't sure I really wanted. Was life in cut-throat academia really for me? Did I want to spend the rest of my life worrying about tenure and whether or not my latest article would be published in a well-respected journal? Did I want to spend weeks writing grant proposals and grading papers? The answers to those questions were less clear than they ever had been.

That was why I was laying on the couch mentally exhausted when Ansley opened the front door. I heard her take off her shoes and hang up her ballet bag in the hall closet. When she rounded the corner, she gasped. 'Oh, Nina. You scared me. I haven't seen you around in a while.' She checked her watch. 'Definitely not at this time of day.'

Lines of worry deepened on her face as she walked over to the couch and knelt down. 'Are you sick? Do you need something?'

'Not sick.'

'Do you want to talk?' She asked tentatively. We were two peas in a pod when it came to keeping emotions to ourselves.

That was why her face registered shock when I said, 'Sure.' Shock gave way to happiness when I continued, 'I got a job offer today. I'm a full professor for the next year.'

'That's great! I'm so proud of you!' Her enthusiasm died a quick death when she studied my dour mood. 'Isn't that what you want?'

'It was, but now I don't know. The life of academia I'd envisioned years ago is far different from the reality I now know exists.'

Her hand patted the blanket covering my leg. 'Maybe you're just burnt out with your dissertation. Once that's

156

over, you'll …'

'You ever ask for a pogo stick for your birthday?' I interrupted.

'Maybe …' she answered, not sure where I was going.

'Me too. I remember my seventh birthday; I begged for a pogo stick because the girls down the street had one. My parents bought me one, of course. I got it out of the package, sure that it was my new favorite toy. I tried it once the first day. I fell and hit my chin on the handles. I bit my tongue so hard it bled. The day after that, I had convinced myself it was just a first try and I would love it. I tried it again, day after day, assured that *this* was the day I'd love it. Countless scraped knees and bruised elbows later, I finally gave up, realizing it was the worst idea I ever had.'

She smiled tenderly. 'I think we've all been there.'

'Yeah. Well, I worry that working as a professor is the same thing. I'll be unhappy for years while I try to make myself fall in love with the illusion I'd dreamed up. Maybe I should just cut my losses now and ask for a scooter instead. I'd be much happier with the scooter, right?'

'I don't know. What is the scooter?'

I'd never given thought to option B. If I wasn't a professor, what did I want to do? 'I don't know,' I answered honestly.

'Well, this is just a year job, right? This will give you a chance to test drive that pogo stick and then decide if you want the scooter. I can't think of a better option, really.'

I'd never thought of it that way. 'Especially since I don't even know what I would do otherwise.' My spirit felt lighter after talking with Ansley. This wasn't a life-long commitment. It was at most a year-long commitment that would help me figure out my future, all while getting paid handsomely for it.

'Thank you for talking. I feel better now.'

She rocked back on her heels and stood gracefully. She began to walk away. 'Nuh. Uh,' I chided. 'Get your skinny ass back here and tell me the truth about Zach. You've been holding out on me.'

Her steps stopped, but she didn't turn around. She stood as still as a ghost for long seconds before she turned around, her face white. 'We're friends and we dance together. That's …'

'That's not the end of the story. You and I both know it. In fact, I'd bet my new salary that the story started much longer ago.'

'You'd win the bet,' she whispered. 'But that's a story I never tell.' Her eyes begged me not to ask anything more.

'That's fine. Do we get to meet him again?'

She swallowed. 'Opening night of our new season is in ten days. We have a cast party afterwards for donors and friends. If you'd like to come, I could get you, Hannah, and Jenn tickets. You can come to the show and then meet up with Zach and I at the after party.'

'I'd love that. I'm sure Hannah and Jenn would love to get away for a while. Let's plan on it.'

'Great. I'll set it up.' She grabbed a bottle of water from the fridge and pulled pins out of her hair. Her long brown hair fell from the bun at the nape of her neck into loose curls. She ran her fingers through the hair-sprayed strands. 'I need a shower, though, unless you were planning on getting in.'

'Go ahead. I'll use it after you're done, and then I'm supposed to head to Landon's tonight.'

She smiled over her shoulder and raised an eyebrow. 'You're seeing him a lot lately.'

'Yep,' I said simply. Both of us had stories we weren't telling.

Landon's sculpted, naked torso was the first thing I saw when he opened his condo door. Then I noticed his jeans were unbuttoned, the zipper the only thing tentatively holding up his jeans on his narrow waist.

Behind him, the blue flickering light of the television lent an ominous glow to the otherwise dark room.

His nostrils flared as I stepped into the foyer. When I tried to take a few steps towards the couch, he tugged on my ponytail, halting me. His grip on my hair made me squeak and back up so my rear slammed into his front. He bit my ear before he rumbled, 'Fucking missed this.' He took a big breath along my neck. 'You always smell so good.'

His body vibrated with energy behind me. His muscles were tight. The veins in his neck and arms looked like ropes woven under the surface of his skin. I could tell in an instant he was on edge.

On the edge of what, I didn't know.

He pushed me forward a few steps and guided me next to him on the couch. His left arm slung around my shoulders and pulled me tight to his side. His chest lifted in deep breaths like he'd just run a mile. And normally in this position his fingertips traced circles on my shoulder. This time, he gripped my shoulder so tightly his nailbeds were white.

I still hadn't said anything to him, troubled with this side of him I'd never seen. He was always so jovial, so happy-go-lucky, that I didn't know what to do with this new, brooding attitude. 'Hello to you too,' I attempted a joke, but he stared straight ahead at the baseball game muted on the television as if I hadn't said anything. His mind was miles away.

I decided maybe it was an important part of the game and he didn't want to miss it. I sat next to him in silence as we watched the Stars' pitcher strike out the first Marlins' batter before giving up a home run to the second.

'They've got him timed,' Landon said as the Marlins' batter ran the bases and touched home plate. His right hand held a baseball. His fingers continually rolled it around as he toyed with various grips. The tendons on the inside of his wrist flexed and released dozens of times. He was nervous or troubled about something, unable to sit still. His heel bounced on the carpet, his knee trembling up and down with constant movement.

I attempted to start a conversation. 'I met with Dr Moore today …'

He didn't nod or ask a follow-up question. Instead, he sat up, pulled his arm out from behind me, and cracked the knuckles on both hands.

I stood and started walking towards the door. 'I can tell you have something on your mind tonight. I'll just …'

I didn't hear his bare footfalls as he stalked up behind me. I jumped, startled when he wrapped an arm around me so forcefully I instantly changed directions. 'You'll just what? I need you here tonight.'

He walked us backwards so quickly that my feet could barely keep up with his long strides. 'Landon? What the fuck is going on?' I ripped myself from his grip.

He didn't answer me as he turned off the television. The only things fighting the darkness in the room were the lights on the horizon that shone through his floor-to-ceiling windows. I backed up against the glass that was cool through my thin shirt.

"This," he whispered simply, as if the one word explained everything. He kicked off his pants, and they landed on the floor, followed by his boxers. I allowed him to lift my arms so he could tug off my shirt and unclasp my bra. He threw it across the room and pulled down my yoga pants. He left on the lacy black thong as he spun me around so that my bare back landed on the exposed brick wall.

My breath whooshed out of me as his hips grinded against me. He lifted one of my legs off the floor, stretching the back of my leg. He kicked the other one out from under me and grabbed under that knee so I was splayed open against him, each of his elbows notched under my knees.

His hips shoved against me, making the sharp edges of the bricks dig into my skin.

He grunted as he rolled on the condom. 'You like it rough, right?'

The answer that swirled around in my brain was an unequivocal yes, but I hesitated, more worried about what was troubling Landon so much. What was he not sharing? 'Answer me,' he commanded impatiently.

'Yes …'

'Don't worry. You'll come so hard you'll beg me to stop. You're ready for me, aren't you? You wet?'

'Yes.' My thong was drenched with my attraction to this man, fed by the edge he'd been balanced on all night.

His right hand pulled the wet string from my center, the only warning I had before he pulled so hard on the string that it snapped. He wadded up the lace and threw it behind his back. A second later, he shoved into me.

'Fuck!' We yelled together as he continued pumping, slamming our hips together so that my back was quickly rubbed raw on the brick.

His eyes were glassy as if they were focused on something far away. 'Kiss me,' I whispered. He hadn't kissed me at all tonight, and I yearned for some sort of intimacy, a weird thought as I was getting banged against the wall. Normally, I was fine with this, but now … something felt wrong.

His mouth descended on mine so my head thudded against the brick. His tongue slid across mine, velvety smooth yet demanding. That was when I tasted it. I don't know how I didn't smell it on his breath before. I tore my mouth away.

'You've been drinking.'

His rhythm didn't falter. 'So what?' He grunted. 'I'm a

161

grown adult who can have a few drinks.'

'Of course. You just never do.' My voice shook with his rhythm like I was riding in a car on a gravel road.

'Yeah, well. This night I do.' His head lowered, and his teeth nipped my shoulder. His chest flush to mine, his erection seated deep inside me, he circled his hips so that his wide base rubbed my clit.

I felt the familiar tightening at my core as the rest of me went numb. 'More,' I begged. 'You're going to make me come like that.'

'Hell yes, I am.' He pulled out and on his next plunge, I cringed, my back burning with abrasions on each vertebrae.

He blinked, then frowned as he pulled out. He let down my right leg, then my left, and spun me around. His fingers caressed the scraped skin as he inspected it. The breath he exhaled cooled my skin and blew strands of hair around my face.

'Fuck. I'm so sorry. Look at your back. I wasn't thinking. I'd understand if you …'

'Just finish this.' *Whatever this was.*

His gaze studied me for a long, breathless second before his shaking hand reached for my forearm and he turned me to face the windows. 'Bend over the arm of the couch. I don't want you on your back anymore.' He guided my hips forward. The cool leather chilled the skin on the tops of my thighs and stomach as I laid forward and braced myself on the cushions.

I tucked my chin so my forehead could rest on the leather. Both his hands squeezed my ass as he grunted, 'Ready?'

I nodded against the couch, sure I was ready for whatever he felt he needed to do.

I couldn't have been more wrong.

He surged into me so forcefully that my toes lifted off the plush carpet. My legs kicked, tried to find footing, and failed. The hot pants of my breath against the black leather created a thin layer of moisture on the slick surface.

He used his grip on my hips to drive me back onto him with punishing strikes.

'Had enough yet?' he asked. It was a challenge, but it also sounded like he was begging me to put a stop to all of this.

"No. Not enough," I managed. "Keep going."

"Never enough," he added. "I can never get enough of you."

I pushed up on to my hands. The arch of my back allowed me to find my footing on the carpet with the balls of my feet. I thrust back onto him, meeting his fire with my own.

'There she is. I knew you'd love this.' He wrapped his fist in my hair and pulled back so that the tiny hairs on the edges of my scalp ached with the strain. My chin lifted and my back arched more severely as we raced to the cliff's edge.

He stopped when I didn't think I could bend an inch further. 'Just like that,' he said as his hips stilled. He held himself deep in me. I wiggled my hips, begging for the small circles that would put me over the edge.

He let go of my hair and wrapped his hand around my exposed, lengthened neck. His sweat-soaked chest covered my back, making the scratched skin burn. 'You ready for this to be done?' He hissed into my ear.

I thought at first he was talking about this raw, aggressive sex. But then I heard it in his voice, something vulnerable, something unguarded.

I shook my head. 'Not yet.'

I heard the clench of his teeth. 'I swear, Nina. You're going to be the end of me.' His hips pounded again, and his other hand wound under my hips and pressed against my clit. He circled the nub twice before I detonated, convulsing with each powerful wave that made me buck

163

and writhe against him.

'Take me with you,' he begged as he pumped one, two, three more times. I collapsed onto the couch, unable to hold my weight any longer. He shoved into me and let go. Out of the corner of my eye, I saw the moment his brow unfurled, his eyes unclenched, and his lips softened as he silently chanted, 'Yes, yes, yes.'

His limp body fell on top of mine like he'd imploded, destroying whatever was keeping him upright. I shivered from the overload of sensations. He grabbed the blanket from the back of the couch and wrapped it around us. He held it tight like it was vital to keep us warm. He arms shook as he held onto me like he was afraid I was going to bolt.

His weight was too much and he needed to get rid of the condom, so I wiggled, trying to free myself, which only made him hold on tighter.

'We need to talk,' I said, wiggling under his weight again.

'I know.' This time, he did roll off, but like he was reluctant to do it. He walked to the bathroom where I heard him flush the condom. I wrapped myself in the blanket and stared out the window, trying to process what had just happened. The outline of the front range of the Rockies loomed in the distance. The rising moon made the few stubborn peaks that were still white with snow glow iridescent.

He pulled on his jeans but didn't bother to button them as he sat next to me on the edge of the couch. He leaned forward so his elbows rested on his knees. His knuckles turned white as he gripped fistfuls of his hair. He stared at the ground and said nothing.

I recognized a troubled soul when I saw one. He didn't need me beating him up for what just happened because he looked like he was taking care of that all on his own. His hands stilled when my gentle voice broke the silence.

'What *was* that? It sure felt like you were trying to fuck me out of your system. It's like you were daring me to leave the whole time.'

He rocked back and forth and spoke to the carpet. 'I got called up.'

Understanding ricocheted through my chest. This was a goodbye fuck.

'When do you have to move?' I whispered.

His answer was just as quiet. 'I have to be there on Friday. I move Wednesday.'

Two days.

The first reaction I allowed him to see was shock. 'Wow. That was sooner than I think we expected.'

He hummed his agreement.

My second reaction was happiness.

For him?

Surely.

For me?

Well, I'd grown accustomed to people leaving.

'Congratulations. That's great news. You deserve it. You've worked hard.'

'Thanks. Don't get me wrong. I'm thrilled to be going back to the majors, but ...'

I recognized the conflict in his eyes; it was similar to what I'd felt earlier today. Both of us had just been handed something we always wanted, but we didn't feel the absolute elation we thought we would at the news. Reality was so much more complicated than our dreams.

He finally lifted his head from his hands and turned towards me. His eyes were bloodshot. The bags under his eyes made him look exhausted, weary.

'... but I thought we had more time,' he whispered.

His eyes searched my face for a reaction. I wondered what he wanted. Did he want me to be sad? To miss him? Did he want me to tell him to call me when he was in town so we could hook up? Did he want me to thank him for the sex, get dressed, and get the hell out? I didn't know, so I schooled my face into a blank stare.

I knew what my initial reaction was, though. Surprise mixed with melancholy at the loss of a friend. I'd never met a kinder, funnier, more generous guy; that was what I'd miss the most. But I'd known all along our paths were crossing for an indefinite time, so while the timing was a surprise, the leaving wasn't.

The leaving never was.

His lips curved into a frown as he closed his eyes and pinched the bridge of his nose. 'They want me back before the All-Star break. They're second in their division, and they need starting pitching to make it deep into the playoffs.'

I patted his knee as I stood, the blanket wrapped around me as I began collecting my clothes. 'I'm sure they need you.'

I barely caught his softly spoken reply. 'And you? Do you need me?'

I whirled around. 'Come again?'

He didn't repeat what he knew I'd heard. Instead, he said, 'Come with me.'

My eyes blinked twice as my jaw fell open. 'What on earth would –?'

'Hear me out,' he interrupted. 'You could come with me. Travel with the team. Stay with me at my condo in Dallas. You could sit with the wives and girlfriends in the stands on game nights and write your dissertation whenever you wanted. It would only be until October, November at the latest if we go deep in the postseason. I'd pay for your meals. Anything you needed, you could have.'

I held up my open palm as my heart raced. The picture he painted was so rosy, so inviting that I almost let myself believe it could be that easy. Who wouldn't be attracted to that life on some level? The baseball-lover in me begged me to agree. 'Stop right there. You make a generous offer, but I can't agree to go with you.'

'Why not? I see women do it all the time.'

'My life is here in Boulder. My dad is here. My friends are here. My church is here. All the resources I need to finish my dissertation are here. The university library. My advisor. I have to meet with her every week. But that's all beside the point.'

I felt his frustration growing when he huffed, 'Which is?'

'I'm not some cleat-chasing girlfriend who is willing to pick up her life for a friend she likes but barely knows. I wouldn't know anyone other than you. I'd be isolated, dependent upon you. We might have fun playing house for two weeks, but it would get old fast. That's not a life I want to live, and I guarantee you wouldn't want it either.' I pulled on my clothes, uncomfortable being naked for this conversation. 'I won't upend my life so I can sit in the stands and watch yours. And with this new job I accepted –'

'New job? When were you planning on telling me?'

'I tried to tell you about it earlier, but you were … distracted.'

'What is it?' He asked, impatient.

'I was asked to fill in for a tenured professor for one semester, maybe two. It will look amazing on my resume, and I'll still be able to write my dissertation. And I'll be making a lot more money. Most importantly, it's what I've always wanted.'

'Had you not –'

'I still wouldn't have gone with you.'

Now fully clothed, I stepped up to him. I tried to wrap my arms around his waist for a hug, but he bristled and pulled away. 'What?' I asked.

He shoved his hands in his pockets as he glared at me. 'Silly me. I thought I meant something to you.'

Ouch. That one stung a little. He was lashing out at me, angry over my rejection, but he seemed genuinely surprised, sincerely hurt I hadn't taken him up on his offer. 'You do. I consider you a close friend.'

'Close friend,' he spat. He sat down on the couch and clicked on the television. The blue glow filled the room as he stared at it, dismissing me.

I moved towards the door, and when my hand grabbed the cool metal, I heard him say, 'If you choose to go out that door, don't bother tracking me down.'

Seconds later, the door clicked shut behind me.

As I walked down the hallway, my heart ached at the loss of a good friend. I'd miss him, of that I had no doubt, and I couldn't deny the attraction to the picture he'd painted. I imagined it as the elevator took me to the ground floor. When it dinged and the doors opened, I walked to my car, part numb, part mournful, and a part angry at his childish ultimatum. Each step I chose to take away from him felt like I was walking in sand. I couldn't deny a part of me wanted to run back up to his condo and agree to his proposal. But if training for a half marathon had taught me anything, it was that the hardest steps are always against the wind.

Chapter Fourteen

The electric yellow glare of afternoon gave way to the muted oranges of early evening as Charlotte and Simon strolled along the promenade. The ocean banged its familiar rhythm of swells and crashes over their right shoulders. Wet sand stuck to the bottom of their shoes, making both wish they could take them off.

'You are the eldest of twelve brothers and sisters?' Simon repeated. 'That is a significant household.'

'Yes. We live humbly, but we're happy in Willingden. Our family is quite close.'

Charlotte's smart gaze didn't miss his attentiveness, the attraction that was spoken in his eyes. She understood it well, although this was the first time she'd ever returned such interest. 'And you, Mr Parker? Are you close with your family?'

Simon's chin lowered as he looked at her over his spectacles. 'Let's not pretend, shall we? I can stomach my family in small doses. There are only so many stories of ailments one can listen to without losing one's patience. I prefer traveling the world, seeing what it has to offer outside of this small country. Thankfully, my business allows me to do so.'

'That sounds lovely. We were never able to go on holiday often, but when we did, it was someplace close, usually to visit my mother's family in Wessex.'

The pair rounded an outcropping. Simon gestured towards a dry, elevated log. Charlotte was thankful for the moment to stop and breathe in the humid, salty sea air. He sat beside her, a respectable distance away. The retreating

tide sucked bits of sand from under their feet as it left.
'When do you plan on returning to Willingden?'

Charlotte's gloved hands rested in her lap. 'Within the week, I would guess. I'm sure father and mother are in need of my help at home.'

Simon's knees swiveled towards her. 'I will be leaving tomorrow morning to attend to business in London.'

'So soon?' The disappointment in her voice could not have been missed. He was leaving before the ball. Charlotte cleared her throat and spoke more formally. 'Your presence will be missed by all, I am sure.'

'And you?' His eyebrows dipped, imploring her for an honest answer.

'Of course I will miss you. I've become accustomed to our afternoon walks that let me escape the stuffy drawing room.'

He moved closer so his trousers brushed her dress. His hands reached for hers. 'I desire to see you again. Will your family be in London anytime soon?'

She allowed a small laugh. 'Mr Parker, I think you misunderstand me when I say we do not often go on holidays.' She sobered. 'We will not be in London in the near future.'

The look that crossed his features could only be described as confusion. 'But I do not have business to attend to near Willingden. Do you not have an aunt or uncle to visit in London? Surely –'

'No, sir. I do not. Nor do I think my family could spare me being away much more than I already have.'

Simon frowned and stood, his shadow long, as he offered her his hand. She pressed her hand into his, the warmth of him heating her through her glove. He pulled her upright, allowing their eyes to meet in a moment of shared understanding.

'So, this is good-bye,' he said, dropping their hands as they retraced their footsteps in the sand. The sun's long

rays glistened off the top of the small waves.

'Yes, sir. I believe it is,' she whispered, the only thing they said to one another during the ten-minute walk back to Lady Denham's estate.

The next morning, Charlotte watched out the window as his stylish chaise pulled away from the inn. The following day, she requested to return home, and she left Sanditon, the place patrons visited to cure illnesses, with a new sickness of her own.

I closed the laptop and walked to my bedroom, satisfied with the morning's progress. I changed into a pair of shorts and a sports bra, ready to take on the long training run. I cringed as the elastic band of the bra brushed against the row of scabs forming on my back. For the first few days, the wounds stung in the shower, a potent reminder of that night. Now, as the days passed, the raw wounds healed so the sting became a soreness that only hurt when something rubbed against it.

I'd run with more fervor over the past two weeks since I left Landon's condo. Each run lasted a little longer as I welcomed the burn in my legs and lungs. As I ran, I had time to think about that night. I had no regrets over my decision. I knew it was the right one, but I couldn't help the sadness that our friendship had ended the way it had.

I felt very little anger towards him, actually, which surprised me since that had always been an easy emotion for me to feel. How could I be angry when I was the one who chose to step away? I wasn't used to allowing myself to feel sadness, that heavy weight in my chest that got worse at night when I lay in bed.

The lack of anger paired with fond memories of our friendship was what allowed me to sit alone on a blanket in front of the television with a large pizza to watch Landon's first start back in the majors. It was surreal to watch him on television, weirder than I thought it would

171

be. It was odd to think that the image on the screen was an actual, real-life person, a man who had held my hand. A man who liked miniature golf and helping young boys in impromptu batting practices. A man who had sat on this floor to watch a baseball game. A man who had on this blanket rocked into me with gentle slides and pounding thrusts. Even though I only saw his image on television, my mind remembered the smell of his cologne after a shower, the way his baby-soft hair curled as it dried, the strength of his grip on my breast.

I watched every pitch of his five-inning start, not allowing myself a bathroom break or a trip to the kitchen for another beer. I gritted my teeth with each ball and cheered every strike. I watched for winces of pain, although the camera often, to my endless frustration, didn't show him at all after he released the pitch.

His pitches looked good with strong movement. He gave up some hits and two runs, but by the fifth inning, his team had a comfortable lead. When a relief pitcher came in for the sixth inning, I allowed myself to sit back against the couch and blow out a relieved breath.

I clicked off the television minutes later and went for a rare night run. I usually ran in the mornings, but I had energy to burn, so I drove to the campus rec center and sprinted on the treadmill until I couldn't pick up my legs again. Tired and sore, I hobbled into bed that night to dream of thunderstorms and eye black.

I still hadn't heard from Landon weeks later. My sores had healed. My friends had stopped asking about him. It was almost like he'd never existed in Colorado at all. I'd follow his starts religiously when they were on television, but beyond that, my life continued. Write. Run. Plan for the semester. Throughout my life, I'd gotten good at moving on.

'You about ready, Nina?' Jenn yelled from the living

room where she and Hannah waited so that we could all drive to Ansley's performance together.

'Five minutes, drill sergeant,' I yelled back. I slid the black knee-length dress over my head and fastened the buttons on the bodice. I slipped on my favorite red high heels and matching necklace to add some color.

I walked down the hallway and stopped in front of Jenn. With a mock salute, I said, 'Reporting for duty, ma'am.'

Hannah chuckled. 'Let's go, private. We're going to be late. Show starts at seven.'

'I'll drive,' Jenn said as we grabbed our purses.

'Yeah, you will,' I said when Jenn pushed the key fob and the lights blinked on a brand new car. 'Looks like professor life is treating you well.'

Jenn smiled as she started the Lexus and pulled out of the driveway. 'My first purchase with professor money. Not gonna lie, ladies. It doesn't suck.'

'I'll be joining you soon, I guess,' I said from the back seat.

Hannah's hair flipped in her face as she spun around in the passenger's seat. 'What? You got a job and you didn't tell me?'

I told them about the job offer I accepted, trying to hide any trepidation.

Hannah never missed a thing. 'Why don't you sound happy?'

'I'm just not sure that's the life I want anymore.'

'What changed?' Jenn asked as our eyes met in her rear-view mirror.

'I'm not sure it even has. Maybe I'm just burnt out.'

Hannah and Jenn both nodded. Jenn added, 'Finishing the dissertation sucks. Then life gets better.'

'Maybe you just need some time away,' Hannah said.

'Maybe,' I agreed, looking out the window wistfully.

Jenn practically bounced in her seat. 'Well, put miss

doom and gloom out of her misery and tell her already.'

'Tell her what?'

Hannah pivoted in her seat, a bright smile illuminating her face. 'Beckett's rented a house in the hills on Copper Mountain for the Fourth of July. He wanted all of us to come, spend the weekend, swim, and watch the fireworks.'

'Sounds just like what the doctor ordered,' Jenn sing-songed. 'What do you think? You in?'

'Of course I am. Who's coming?' I knew Tanner was a good friend of Beckett's, and while we left everything on good terms, I didn't want to open that can of worms again. Spending the weekend tip-toeing around Tanner and his new girlfriend would be more than awkward.

'So far, Beckett, me, Jenn, and Declan,' Hannah answered. 'Ansley has a performance that weekend and Tanner's in New York finishing up his project. Then you and your date, whoever that is. Which lucky man are you choosing from your harem to join you?' She joked.

I tapped my manicured fingernail to my lips like I was trying to choose; but really, only one face came to mind. Too bad he was 700 miles and a month's-full of silence away. 'I'll have to see who's available,' I deflected, apparently successfully since the conversation steered from me to Hannah's description of the rental house.

I caught only snippets of it, my thoughts elsewhere. '... infinity pool overlooks West Lake ... fireworks from the balcony ...'

Twenty minutes later, we pulled into the parking garage and walked through a glass tunnel that connected the garage to the theatre. Plush burgundy carpeting silenced our clicking heels as ushers handed us programs and showed us to our seats in orchestra center.

'Wow, I didn't know she was lead,' Hannah said as she pointed at Ansley's picture in the program.

'Me neither,' I said, feeling bad I didn't know that about my roommate. 'But most importantly, I didn't know he was the *male* lead.' I pointed to Zach's picture. I read both of the bios included in the program, realizing their paths had crossed many times. Hell, they studied at the same studio as kids.

Jenn's lips tipped into a soft smile.

'What do you know?' I asked, knowing she had connected with Ansley from day one.

'Not my story to tell,' she said, 'but I can't wait to see how they interact on stage.'

I smiled when I saw the name of the ballet, *The Taming of the Shrew*, an adaptation of Shakespeare's play – an interesting story given their history I was starting to piece together.

The lights dimmed five minutes later, and the audience clapped as the conductor took to the pit, a spotlight highlighting his entrance.

The orchestra lifted their instruments when he raised his hands, and the music started, filling the theatre with light, airy notes. As the curtains parted, my eyes searched the stage for Ansley and her bright blonde hair. The setting was a town square, so it was filled with various dancers covered in long dresses and fancy hats. I found her in the back as she walked arm in arm with her sister, Bianca.

My eyes followed her around the stage as she picked up a teacup and pretended to drink. A gentleman came over to her, bowed, and walked on when she dismissed him. Then Zach, playing Petruchio, entered from stage left, and the entire way she carried herself changed.

My heart raced with hers during Act Two. I felt her struggle, and I rejoiced with her. I felt her passion when the two of them danced alone on stage, their legs and arms entwined in a series of lifts and spins.

When the last note played and the harmony rung through the building, I joined the rest of the standing crowd in an ovation that lasted minutes. Ansley's and Zach's bows were last. She curtsied deeply and gestured to him as he bowed first to the crowd then to her. They walked formally, in long, pointed ballet strides, hand in hand to the center of the line of cast members. Their lights dimmed as the curtain closed.

Our lights came on seconds later, their brightness making me squint.

'That was beautiful,' Jenn said, wiping a tear from under her eye. 'They were really great together.'

Hannah agreed, pointing to the now vacant stage. 'There's a story behind those two. There are some things you just can't act.'

'Let's go to the after party and get the scoop,' I said, shooing them out of the row.

Jenn led the way to the party held downstairs in a parlor decorated with fresh flowers and posters advertising the ballet. We gave our names to the doorman, and he checked them off the list.

The minute we stepped inside, the waiters dressed in tuxedos handed us glasses of champagne. We had started our second glass as the cast members finally made their first appearances. Zach and Ansley were last. He ushered her into the room with a hand at her back. Her left ankle was wrapped, and she limped slightly as both of them greeted us.

'Ansley, are you OK?' Jenn asked, gesturing towards her foot.

Neither Ansley nor Zach even looked down. She smiled, 'Don't worry. It happens all the time. An old injury. I'll just stretch it out tomorrow.'

Our worries easily cast aside by their lack of concern, Hannah was able to say what all of us felt. 'You two were spectacular together. Really. That was amazing to watch.'

Zach's hand left her back and grabbed her hand hanging loosely at her side. I saw him give it a little squeeze before he said, 'Thank you. A lot of hard work.'

Hannah's eyes narrowed. 'Have you ever danced

together before? You seem to have such chemistry.'

Zach's eyes looked down to Ansley's as hers turned upwards. Their soft smiles mirrored each other. 'No, but some things are worth waiting for.'

My phone dinged in my clutch, and needing to go the restroom anyway, I excused myself and walked down the carpeted hallway. I pulled out my phone, expecting a text from my dad or an update from Pastor Tom. My breath caught at the unexpected text. From Landon.

I want to talk. I'm sorry.

A month had passed, so I never thought I'd hear from him, much less receive an apology. I'd figured his silence was a sign of his ability to move on. But the text said otherwise.

I didn't know what to type in response as I stood in the hallway, staring at my phone as people veered around me.

'Sorry,' I said as I realized I stood in the middle of the walkway. I stepped aside and sat on a red velvet settee, my heart pounding in my throat. I typed, deleted, typed, and deleted so many times, unable to decide on my response. Finally, I settled on:

Yes. Let's do. At a party now. Call you tonight. 2 hours, OK?

His reply was swift and succinct:

Yes.

'There you are,' Hannah said, sitting next to me on the couch. Her hand rested on my leg. 'Thought we lost you.' Her eyes bounced back and forth between my face and my phone still clutched in my hand. 'Everything OK?'

'Yes, but I'm not sure how much longer I want to stay.'

'No problem,' she said, tentatively, starting at me like

she was trying to decode me. 'Let's go say goodbye to Ansley and Zach. They have to mingle with donors anyway. We'll find Jenn and go.'

I nodded. Her elbow wrapped around mine as we walked back to the party. We found Jenn, congratulated Ansley and Zach on their performance again, and twenty minutes later, pulled out of the parking garage.

Hannah spent the drive home concocting scenarios that explained Ansley and Zach's history. 'Oh. Oh. Oh. How 'bout this? Let's say they were supposed to dance together, but she got hurt and he had to dance with her understudy, her best friend. What if *they* started dating?' Her stories kept getting wilder and more creative as we drove, so much so that Jenn was crying through her laughter.

'Stop! Stop!' she begged. 'I'm trying to drive here.'

I must admit that Hannah's stories were able to make me, even in my anxious, reflective mood, crack a smile. But mostly I laid the side of my head against the cool glass and closed my eyes. The gentle vibrations of the car calmed my racing mind. What did he want? Where did he want us to go from here? Was there anywhere to go with hundreds of miles and his on-the-road lifestyle between us? Did I want there to be anything between us? What exactly was he sorry for?

We pulled up to my house thirty minutes later. Hannah and I thanked Jenn for driving, and we went our separate ways: Jenn to Longmont, Hannah to Beckett's house, and me to my own. I flipped on the living room light, walked to my bedroom, and undressed. Unhurried, I hung up my dress and changed into my cotton pajamas. Before I slipped under the covers, I opened the window, allowing a breeze that smelled like evergreen trees to float through the room. The summer cicadas sang their continual, raspy song. I lit a lilac candle on my bedside table. The breaths of air billowed the lightweight curtains every now and then as I lay on my side and pulled the sheets up to my shoulders.

When my finger brushed over the 'call' button minutes later, my heart leapt, begging my finger to take it back. But I couldn't, because he answered on the first ring.

'How've you been, Nina?' He asked.

I debated what to say. That I missed him? It was true, but I hadn't been pining for him every day. That I was fine? It was mostly true, but I might sound like a cold-hearted bitch. I decided not to answer his question at all. 'Your starts have been great.'

'You've watched them?' He sounded genuinely surprised.

'Of course, all the ones on television. Why wouldn't I?'

He stuttered before he exhaled. 'I ... I don't know. I thought maybe ... we ... you didn't want anything to do with me.'

Uncomfortable, I attempted a joke to lighten the mood. 'I'll always be your biggest cheerleader. Rah. Rah. Rah.'

The silence on the other end of the line told me my attempt at levity didn't work. I heard him exhale again along with what sounded like him crawling into bed. What I thought sounded like covers rustled for a few seconds before he settled into silence. 'I'm sorry for what happened the last night in my condo. Every time I think about how your back looked, I hate myself for it.'

'It's healed. No worries.'

'I'd been drinking, you know I never do that. I shouldn't have even had you over when I was that upset. I didn't treat you well in many ways.'

'You're forgiven, Landon. We all have bad days. Lord knows, we all have regrets, me more than others.'

He hummed into the phone. I heard him mumble under his breath 'God, this is the hard part' before he continued, 'I ... want to still be friends with you. I've missed you.'

My heart twisted. It was so much easier to say it second. 'I've missed you too.'

I heard his intake of breath as he whispered, 'Thank you.' He continued, caution coating every word. 'Nina. I have no right to ask, but have you been with anyone else since …?'

'No.' The rustle on his end of the line made it sound like he dropped his phone. 'You there, Landon?'

He still didn't answer, so I checked my phone to be sure we still had connection. I decided to go with my old stand-by: humor. 'You fucking ruined me for every other man I've laid eyes on, you jerk.'

His chuckle that rumbled over the line was so familiar, so comforting, I hadn't realized how much I'd missed it. 'That was the plan,' he said, then added somberly, 'I want you to know I haven't been with anyone else either.'

Half of me felt like jumping out of bed to do a happy dance while the other half cursed the leap of my heart for caring. This was uneven ground. I had to tread carefully.

When I started to speak, he began, 'When you said you were at a party tonight, I couldn't do anything but think about some other dude wrapping his arm around your shoulders.'

'No other dude,' I reassured. 'Just me in a lonely, cold bed.'

He growled. 'Not fair. When do I get to see you next?'

'When's your next break?'

'Let's see.' His tongue clicked as I heard him flip pages of what I assumed was a calendar. 'We have a big road trip to Boston, New York, and Atlanta before we're home for a three-day break.'

I tried to do the math in my head to determine how long the road trip would be. 'So … are you free on Fourth of July?'

'Yeah, I guess I am. Man, I've been so busy I haven't had time to think about what I'm doing for the holiday.'

'Some of us are getting together at a house in Copper Mountain. Beckett and Hannah will be there and so will

Jenn and Declan. We'll do some swimming, drinking, and watch the fireworks show from the back deck. You want to come with me? Be my plus one?'

'I'd love that. I'll fly into Denver the Friday before, and we'll spend Friday night and all of Saturday there. I'll have to fly out early Sunday morning, though.'

'Sounds good. I'll pick you up at the airport and we can drive up together. Just text me when your flight arrives.'

'Will do.' His voice deepened. 'What are you wearing right now?'

I laughed, 'Don't push your luck, buddy.'

He groaned. 'A man can try.'

We said goodnight, and as I set my phone on the bedside table, I blew out the flame on the lilac candle. Ribbons of smoke diffused into the air while I tucked myself under the covers and fell asleep with a tender smile.

It felt good to forgive.

Chapter Fifteen

The figure that walked through the gate was so much more tanned and leaner than I remembered. He was an athlete before, but his short return to the majors had sculpted every line, chiseled every edge, so that the figure stood before me looked like something Michelangelo would be jealous of.

'Fuck, you look amazing,' spurted out of my mouth before I had the chance to check it.

He leaned forward so quickly he practically caught the words as they escaped. I heard him drop his bag on the tile floor as both hands tugged my lips to his in a kiss that both demanded and forgave. He pulled away when we needed a breath. He smiled and closed his eyes, his cheek rubbing against mine. 'And you taste amazing too, and ...' he took a breath and finished, '... have I ever told you how good you smell?'

I belly-laughed, 'I think you've mentioned that a time or two.'

The veins in his arm were visible when he bent down to retrieve his bag. I thought he was lean and carved with muscle a month ago but now, thinking about what the rest of him would look like made me bite my bottom lip.

When his eyes landed on my mouth, they darkened. He slung his other arm around my shoulders and pulled me closer as we walked. Our hips brushed against each other as he leaned in to kiss my temple. He whispered, 'Keep looking at me like that and we won't make it to Copper Mountain.'

I pulled my sunglasses off the top of my head and over

my eyes when we walked out of the concourse to the parking garage. 'Oh, we'd make it there eventually.'

He growled his frustration as he readjusted himself in his jeans. We had picked up like we hadn't skipped an entire month. The jokes, the ribbing, the sarcasm had returned, and I couldn't deny the relief I felt.

'You mind if I drive?' He asked when we got to my car. He threw his bag next to mine in the back seat.

I tossed him the keys. No problem. Watching him drive was foreplay for me.

He paid the parking fee and rolled down his window. His right wrist laid over the steering wheel as his left hung out the window. He took off his baseball cap and flung it in the backseat. With his hair blowing in the wind from the open window, he looked as happy as a dog hanging out a moonroof. A serene smile covered his face as he rolled up the window and turned on to the interstate.

The seventy-five mile drive on Interstate-70 that took us west of Denver into the front range let us catch up on each other's lives over the past month. He asked how Bethel was doing, I asked how reuniting with his teammates was going, and our conversation flowed easily.

'How's your dissertation?' He asked.

I leaned against the headrest. 'I got some writing done this past month, but I'm still at a crossroads. He's left Sanditon for business, and she's returned home to be with her family. I've played with multiple plotlines, trying to maintain in real life the spark they had in Sanditon. Trouble is, I can't figure out how they come back together. I'm worried maybe they just don't. His business lifestyle is far from her settled life in Willingden. In that time, a working man without an established estate was considered less respectable and a less than advantageous marriage. What would Charlotte's parents say about his lifestyle? Would Charlotte want that for herself? Would she be willing to sacrifice the close family life she knows to be with him? I find myself trying to make this into a love story and I wonder if I'm trying to do the literary equivalent of fitting a square peg in a round hole.'

'You're worried it isn't a love story.'

'Sure. And even if it is, can I do it justice? Writing about love is like trying to grasp of fistful of wind.'

He lowered the window again, but since we were driving over seventy miles per hour, the wind blasted through the car, blowing wrappers from the front seat to the back. He reached out his open hand and quickly closed it.

'Hold out your hands,' he shouted over the gusts. He brought his hand back into the car and unfurled his empty fist on top of mine.

There was nothing visible on my hands, of course, but I stared at them like there was.

'Difficult,' he said, 'but not impossible.'

We used GPS to find the remote address in the hills above the Copper Mountain Resort. After turning right onto a gravel road, we followed the manicured pathway around an outcropping and down a steep incline. One turn later, a mammoth mountain lodge covered in natural stone and exposed cedar beams greeted us. From the front walkway, we could see completely through the house to the vista below. The entire back of the house was a wall of windows that overlooked what I learned later was West Lake. This was not some out-of-the-way little cottage Beckett had rented for the holiday. It was a mansion with meticulous design and elegant details; it had to have cost a fortune for the weekend.

Landon grabbed our bags from the back and met me at the door. I rang the doorbell, whose chime alone sounded like it sang, 'I am ri-ch, I am ri-ch.'

Beckett answered the door a few seconds later and welcomed us in. 'Glad you could make it, man,' he said, greeting Landon with one of those handshake, back tap things guys do.

'Thanks for inviting us. It'll be so nice to relax.'

'I'd imagine. Life on the road constantly wouldn't be for me, but I watched you pitch on ESPN two nights ago. I don't know much about pitching, but you looked good, man.'

'Thanks.' Landon quickly deflected the compliment. He was always quick to give them, but uncomfortable receiving them. 'This is quite a place.'

It was just as glorious inside as I thought it would be. A massive stone fireplace dominated the open living room. Natural-stained cabinets lined the kitchen that had all the proper finishings for a house of this size.

'Nice, isn't it? A friend of my father owns it, but he only comes up here to ski in the winter, so he was happy to let us use it for the weekend. Here, I'll give you a quick tour.' He led us down one hallway. 'This room is for you two,' he said, gesturing right. Landon entered, placing our bags on the king-size bed. The room was painted a dark green to match the wooded hills surrounding the property. The dark mahogany woodwork matched the plush draperies and bedspread. The door to our private balcony was propped open to let in the warm summer breeze.

He walked further down the hallway to show us the room Jenn and Declan would be staying in. Each bedroom had a private balcony off the back with a lattice screen separating them. At the end of the hallway, he gestured towards a closed door. 'This is where Hannah and I will be. Here, come this way and I'll show you the game room.'

He led us back down the hallway to the main living area. We crossed it and entered a door behind the fireplace. It opened to a gigantic area that wasn't visible from the front of the house. Its large windows overlooked the lake, of course, and the room was decorated in muted burgundy tones. The green felt of the pool table was the lightest color in the room. Four large leather captain chairs sat in front of a large, projection-style screen.

'If you guys need anything, let me know. It's only a five-minute drive into town if you forgot anything. Cell coverage can be spotty up here, and don't go out on a hike at night alone. There have been some bear sightings in the area. Other than that, feel free to roam around. Jenn and Declan should be here sometime after dinner. Oh, one more thing,' he smiled warmly, 'Hannah's in the hot tub out back. Feel free to join her. I doubt she'll get out of that thing even to eat. If you can't find her, you know where to look.'

'Let's get our suits on and join her,' I proposed.

'The hot tub sounds like a great plan,' Landon said, rubbing his shoulder. The three of us walked to the bedrooms, agreeing to meet poolside in ten minutes.

I walked into our bedroom first. Landon followed and closed the door behind us. The instant the door clicked shut, I turned to him as he rushed towards me. We met in the middle of the room, our tongues clashing, battling as Landon's hands gripped my wrists and tugged my hands behind his back. When my hands grasped his lower back and snuck under the waistband of his jeans, his hands cradled my jaw and cheekbones. He controlled the angle of my head, the intensity of the kiss. In every swipe of his tongue, I tasted the pent-up lust accumulated over the month we'd been separated. Like feet of snowfall in the mountains, it was deeper than I'd anticipated, and it all came crashing down, an avalanche of demanding tongues and searching hands.

He tore his mouth away, but kept his hands on my cheeks. Nose to nose, I breathed in his air when he spoke. 'God. I couldn't wait any longer. I don't want to hold back. Please. Not this weekend.' His hands shook, vibrating with need. 'I want you right now. Do you know how much control it's taking to not lay you back on this bed –?'

'Why are you holding back at all?' I interrupted, tugging my shirt over my head. My shorts hit the floor next. I stood in front of him, nearly naked, while his eyes unabashedly roamed over my curves. I stepped up to him, my body yearning to reconnect with him, to kindle the fire that never truly went out. 'What are you waiting for? Fuck me like we both want you to. Cover my body with yours. Remind me how big you are, how much you fill me. Cover my hand with your mouth so the others can't hear me scream your name while I pulse around your dick.'

He'd stripped as I talked. Then he grunted, picked me up, and laid me on the bed, and did everything I'd described and more.

'The end of me, I swear,' he chanted when he came. 'You're going to be the end of me.'

We cleaned up and put on our swimsuits. We walked to the hot tub hand in hand where we found Hannah perched next to Beckett, her eyes closed as she snuggled her cheek into his shoulder.

Beckett's skin had already turned pink from the heat of the water. Hell, he'd beaten us there by a good half hour. He simply took a drink of his beer to hide his knowing smirk.

Jenn and Declan arrived after dinner. They hung out and drank a beer as the stars took over the retreating sun. Around the fire pit, each couple sat hip to hip. A casual peck here, the intertwining of fingertips there, an arm around a waist, fingers twisting through a ponytail. I noticed all of these little details, small gestures that spoke of the intimacy each couple shared.

I saw it in their eyes, too. The knowing glances said more than words could. And maybe it was new or maybe I was simply more aware now, but I couldn't help but notice the attentiveness, the awareness each pair of lovers shared. Beckett would replace Hannah's empty beer bottle before she even realized she needed another. Declan saw Jenn's twentieth yawn, and despite her weak protests, picked her up and carried her to their bedroom. 'To bed with you,' Declan said before he yelled, 'Good night, everybody,' over his shoulder.

'Let's turn in too, Hannah,' Beckett said, holding out his hand as he stood over her. 'We'll be up late tomorrow.'

She took his hand and stood. She attempted to whisper in his ear, but drunk Hannah was always too loud. 'You don't have to ask me twice to come to your bed.'

Beckett blushed as he offered us a shrug and pulled Hannah inside where I heard her screech in laughter.

'I really like your friends,' Landon said after they left. 'They all seem very happy together.'

'They are,' I said, distantly, afraid that he was starting a conversation on the topic of my happiness, one that always made me uncomfortable.

That's why I was ever so relieved when his hands slapped his knees. He stood and held out his hand. 'Wanna go screw?'

My hand couldn't take his fast enough. 'Absolutely.'

On Saturday morning, the six of us ate breakfast standing around the large kitchen island. Armed with cups of coffee and rolls, we chatted about our jobs, catching up on each other's lives. Landon fitted in easily. He carried on conversations without needing my help. He acted casual, and at ease, like he'd known everyone as long as I had.

Each couple decided to do something different on Saturday before meeting up for dinner, drinks, and fireworks on the back porch. Beckett and Hannah went for a hike on the trails in the woods just north of the house. Jenn and Declan left for the climbing gym at the local resort right after breakfast. That left Landon and I to

189

search through the morning paper for something to do. The Copper Mountain 3 Ring Weekend celebration was taking place over the holiday weekend with a lot of activities geared towards families. We nixed the parade, juggling workshops, and face painting quickly, making me wonder if we would be able to find anything to do.

Then Landon's face beamed with a mischievous smile. I recognized that one. It reminded me of the day he took me miniature golfing.

'What?' I asked, slightly dreading his answer. 'You're making your "I can't wait to beat you at this" face.'

He slid the paper over to me wordlessly and tapped his finger on a picture. I let out a breath. I should have known. This man was competitive to the core.

'You're going down,' he trash-talked over his shoulder as he walked down the hall to our room.

I joined him a few minutes later. We both dressed in T-shirts and jeans as he hummed 'Eye of the Tiger'.

The sign above the course read, 'These go-karts have larger engines than most traditional karts. Drive at your own risk. No bumping allowed!'

I strapped on my seatbelt and readjusted the height of the steering wheel as Landon folded his long frame into the small cart next to me. Despite moving the seat all the way back, he still looked comical in the small thing, like his knees were resting just below his ears.

I must have laughed, because he said, 'Just go ahead and laugh now. You won't be laughing in a minute.'

Boy, was he wrong. For some reason, I found it absolutely hilarious when he focused straight ahead, intently staring at the small pylon in front of us that told us when we could take off.

'We bettin' the same thing as always?' I asked as we waited.

'Damn right. Just like miniature golf,' he said, not

bothering to look over at me.

It seemed to take forever for the light to switch from red to green, and when it did, I heard his little engine rev so high that it whined.

His fingers gripped the steering wheel at three and nine, his arms straight and locked like he needed the stability to drive at such high speeds. It couldn't have been more than twenty miles per hour, if that, but you wouldn't have known it by the seriousness of his face. Somebody needed to tell this man this wasn't the Indy 500. He was laser-focused on the first turn. He jerked the wheel to the left in the middle of the turn, punched the gas, and drifted around the corner.

I was already two turns behind him by the end of the first lap, but I didn't care. It was worth it to be behind him, watching him cut corners too close and ram the side of his cart into the rubber barrier. His intensity was paying off, though. He was passing people. Granted, they were little boys and girls who could barely reach the pedals or see over the steering wheel, but he was passing them. Definitely more than me. I didn't have the heart to bump a kid into the wall.

His brake light would flash on at odd times like he was losing control and was trying to save it. One time on the fourth lap, he over steered into the turn, which was easy to do in these contraptions, then overcorrected. He slammed on the brakes, the tires screeching loudly, and I swear I saw a puff of smoke from the back tires. I didn't know you could do that at these speeds. A second later, he rammed into the barrier so hard his head snapped forward. A little boy, not older than ten, laughed at Landon as he passed him. He glared at the kid like he was staring down an opposing batter, and since the cart didn't have a reverse, he had to wait for a track worker to come and push him away from the barrier and in the correct direction.

When I passed him, I was belly-laughing so hard I

couldn't breathe. I tried to suck in air so I could say something funny, but I couldn't make my lungs expand. My stomach hurt from the laughter I couldn't control like somebody had just farted at church.

I frankly wasn't very good at driving the carts, so Landon passed me within a minute of being righted, but I couldn't have cared less.

'God, are you going to cackle the whole way around?' He asked as he passed. He was as serious as could be, which just made me start up laughing again.

'Stop! Stop! Make it stop!' I begged through my breaths. Tears welled in my eyes, making it hard for me to see. I wiped them away with the back of my hand and was more than grateful when the pylon's lights turned yellow, signaling we had to head back to the pits.

I pulled to a stop in the lane next to him since I was one of the last to park. He'd smoked me.

After I unbuckled and met him trackside where he was waiting for me with a scowl, I took a deep breath, willing away the giggles I couldn't seem to get rid of. I bit both of my lips between my teeth like I could somehow pin the laughter in that way. It didn't work. One look at his face, and I was done for.

'What?' He asked with his hands held up at his sides, palms up in a gesture that said he hadn't a clue why I was laughing, which of course made it even funnier.

The laughter burst out of me so fast I think he had to dodge some of my spit. 'You,' I managed, pointing at him. 'You're ... so ... competitive. You'd ram your own kid into the wall before you would lose.'

'Damn right,' he said, pulling me to him with an elbow behind my neck. 'Let's go get some lunch, giggles.'

We were the last couple to return to the house at four in the afternoon; since we spent some time walking around the grounds of the resort after lunch.

We'd also been delayed because I had to pay up as the loser of the bet. We drove up to the house on the winding concrete road with the windows down and Landon leaned back and unhooked the button on his jeans.

I licked my lips, unlatched the seatbelt, and leaned over the console. 'That was a bet worth losing. I haven't laughed that hard in years.'

'Oh, shush, you vixen,' he said pressing my head down. I took his semi-hard erection into my mouth and hummed. I loved when I got to him before he was fully hard. I popped off to say, 'I love feeling you get hard in my mouth. That means I can do this.'

I leaned back down, sucking him to the base. His hips slowly pumped upwards as he grew and expanded into my throat. His rhythm sped, matching the labored breaths I could hear over the rush of wind through the windows. Soon, each quick thrust of his hips communicated his urgency.

His right arm straightened as he leaned over, cupping my ass with his hot palm. His fingers slid to rub my sex over my clothes. Then he slid upwards, pressing the seam of my jeans against the sensitive tissue. I wondered how long it was going to be before he went there.

He rasped, 'Any parts of your body off limits tonight?'

I pulled off my mouth and pumped quickly up and down his shaft with a strong grip. A bead of liquid gathered at his tip. 'It never was.'

'Fuck,' he groaned as his hips stilled. I felt his heated huffs of breath on the back of my neck. 'Why didn't you ever tell me? I could have been taking your ass this whole time.'

My mouth curved around his tip to finish him off, but I before I did, I murmured, 'I wanted you to figure it out for yourself.' My hand moved furiously up and down as I sucked on the reddened tip. The veins along his shaft bulged as he grew harder.

He came silently. No curses. No smacks of my ass. I looked up to him. His eyes were narrow slits. The muscles around his jaw flexed as he clenched his teeth. 'How am I going to make it through tonight? Sitting next to you in the hot tub while you wear that scrap of material you call a bikini already kills me. But knowing that I get to go *there* tonight?' He hummed, unable to find words for his unfulfilled lust.

To play with him, I kissed up his neck to his ear. 'No limits, Landon. No. Limits.'

He grunted some curse. I heard the engine of my car rev as we accelerated around the last curve. Our tires rumbled over the gravel driveway before they screeched to a halt in front of the house. A cloud of dust floated around us as we sat in the car and kissed. Landon reluctantly pulled away minutes later and led us through the front door.

When we walked into the house, it was clear from the laughter floating in through the screen door that everyone was out back. We found everyone in the hot tub, so we got on our suits and joined them in the middle of their conversation.

'She flashed a 5.11b today,' Declan said, putting an arm around Jenn, who beamed at what I guessed was praise. I hadn't a clue what that meant.

Beckett spoke, making me glad I wasn't the only one lost. 'Sounds cool, but what does that even mean?'

'Climbing routes are labeled with certain difficulties based upon the quality of the holds and the moves required. Without going into it too far, a 5.11 is considered expert. And she *flashed* it, no rests on the rope, no falls.'

'Stop,' Jenn said, embarrassed.

'I knew you were strong, but, damn, baby, I couldn't have been prouder.'

Jenn's milky white skin flushed with the praise. She quickly changed the subject. 'How 'bout you guys?' She asked us. 'What did you do?'

I snickered under my breath, and Landon rolled his eyes. 'Don't mind giggles here. She just thinks it's funny to lose so bad at go-karts they called the race two laps early just to put her out of her misery.'

'They did not!' I told the story of Landon's competitiveness, and by the end, everyone was trying to hide their sniggers as Landon pretended to glare.

'How –?' I turned to Hannah to ask her how their hike had gone, but I stopped short. Hannah's right hand covered her mouth as she studied me with narrowed eyes like I was a painting she didn't quite get. I'd never seen that look from her before. I recovered, 'How about you, Hannah? You guys have a good day?'

Beckett climbed out of the hot tub. 'You all want a beer while I'm up?'

'Yep,' the four of us said while Landon said, 'Just a water.'

'The hikes are so different here,' Hannah started. 'The light is so much different. The trees are thinner. Thanks,' she said as Beckett handed her and then everyone else their drinks.

He sat on the side of the hot tub, only dipping his feet and calves in the bubbling water. 'I don't know how you guys stand that. It's too hot for me.'

Hannah slid deeper into the water so only her face was above the top of the water. 'You're crazy. This is lukewarm.'

'Well, this *lukewarm* water is about to burn the boys,' Declan said, pulling at his suit. He sat on the edge next to Beckett.

Hannah sat up and wiped the beads of sweat from her red face. 'Beck, can you start the grill? I'm starving.'

'Sure. Are you girls going to prepare the rest?'

Jenn groaned as she peeled herself out of the water. 'If we have to.'

I helped Jenn and Hannah prepare the burgers and hot dogs and took them out to the guys, who were standing around the grill.

Then we cut vegetables for the salad and slid fruit onto skewers. Hannah had brought some homemade potato salad, so we put that into a bowl and carried the food to the outdoor table.

The purple hues of twilight cast long shadows across the back porch. Photo sensor lights detected the coming darkness and flicked to life around the patio. Lanterns full of candles flickered around the perimeter, filling the air with a lavender scent. Two steps down, the infinity pool, lit by blue lights under the water, seemed to drop off the edge of the earth.

The cobblestone walkway was uneven under my feet, so I walked slowly, careful not to spill the two trays of food I was carrying. Beckett, Declan, and Landon stood around the grill as trails of smoke wafted upwards. Landon's white Dallas Stars T-shirt glowed in the muted light. His tan arms flexed as he gestured. His now dry board shorts clung loosely to his narrow hips. The tendons in his wrist hardened as he unscrewed his bottle of water and brought it to his full lips. He licked a bead of water off his bottom lip as he replaced the cap.

'Almost ready, Beck?' Hannah called from behind me.

Beckett nodded, turned off the grill, and shoveled all the grilled food onto a serving plate.

Steam rose from the burgers and hot dogs when he placed them at the end of the buffet line. Everyone filled their plastic plates with as much food as they could and sat down at the large, hexagon table.

When Landon gently placed his plate next to mine and sat down, I shook my head in amusement. 'What?' He asked.

'You and your condiments.' His bun was bursting with every condiment imaginable. Ketchup dripped down the side. I pointed at the slowly escaping drop. He scraped his index finger along the side, collecting the drop before it hit the potato chips. He sucked his finger into his mouth and shrugged, unembarrassed by his addiction to condiments. I smiled at his nonchalance, his ability to be himself without feeling like he had to impress someone. He never pretended to be something he was not, a lesson I had yet to learn.

The yellow beginnings of a sunset burned the edges of the few wispy clouds. The top of the lake shimmered in the distance as the cicadas began their first chorus of the night. 'Beckett, did you say the fireworks are at nine over the lake?' Declan asked.

Beckett pointed to a dark grove of trees on the horizon. 'Yep. Right out there, I think. I hear the show is usually forty-five minutes long.' He looked at his watch. 'We have about an hour.'

The conversation was light throughout dinner and almost everyone got up at least once for more beer or food. Stuffed, I leaned back in my chair and patted my stomach. 'I think I just ate enough salt to last me a month.'

'Nice work,' Landon said, looking at my empty plate. 'I love a woman who can eat.'

'You've never seen this one eat,' Declan joked with a thumb pointing at Jenn. He leaned over to Landon like he was going to tell a secret he didn't want Jenn to hear. 'Man, she can eat more than me.'

'Dec!' She said, feigning anger. She lifted her hand like she was going to swat him.

He laughed and pretended to duck away from her slap. Jenn wadded her napkin in frustration and threw it onto her plate. 'You done?' He asked.

'Well I am now, if I wasn't before,' she huffed.

'Perfect,' he said as he leapt out of his chair, grabbed her around the waist, and fireman lifted her over his shoulder. He stalked towards the pool.

'Declan! What are you doing? Put me down,' she protested. She kicked her feet and tried to push up her body with her hands on his back like she was desperate to get away. But she was laughing so hard her protests fell on deaf ears.

'No one's going to come to my rescue?' She pleaded.

Everyone at the table laughed and shook their heads as Declan lifted her small body from his shoulder and threw her in the pool. The big splash cut off her loud screech as she sailed through the air.

He dove in after her so that they surfaced at the same time. Jenn pretended to pout, but seconds later her arms were wrapped around his neck as he carried her through the water.

Everyone looked away when their lips tangled in a passionate kiss.

Beckett stood abruptly, pulled out Hannah's chair, and went to pick her up like Declan had Jenn. 'Don't even think about it, lover boy,' she warned.

He kissed her forehead. 'Getting a rise out of you never gets old, babe.' With a wink, he carried the leftover food into the house.

Landon just about fell off his chair next to me as he held his stomach in laughter. 'Nina, you didn't tell me you had a twin,' he said as he pointed at Hannah. Then he motioned to the pool. 'You'd never let me get away with that.'

Hannah reached over the table to high-five me. Our hands met with a loud slap that made my palm sting.

'There are no secrets about who wears the pants in our relationships,' she said. Then she added, 'Speaking of, it's too cold for a swim. I'm going inside to change into warmer clothes.' She gathered the plates and dumped them into a trash bag before she stepped through the sliding glass door.

I had to admit there was a chill in the air when the sun

went behind the peaks, and with the slight breeze, I shivered. When I moved to join Hannah inside to change, Landon's hand wrapped around my elbow. His intense eyes smoldered. 'How much longer until I get you alone? I want you on the balcony tonight, under the stars.'

I wanted to jump this man right now. To hell with the fireworks. I rubbed my hand over the front of his pants that were already tented with his arousal. 'Not soon enough, but we can't bow out now. It'd be rude.'

Another cool breeze blew over the lake, and my skin goosebumped under his hand. He glanced at my arms and rubbed them up and down. 'You're right. Go change. You're freezing. I'll come in and change, too.'

We picked up a few more plates of leftover food and followed Hannah inside. Beckett had already changed into a pair of khaki pants and a collared shirt. With his sleeves rolled up to his elbows, he was washing the few dishes we had used. 'Why are you dressed up, Beck?' Hannah asked.

He jumped when she spoke like he was deep in thought. I heard him force a casual tone into his voice when he spoke. 'Oh, this is just what I brought with me.'

Hannah eyed him suspiciously before she shrugged, grabbed another beer, and walked back outside.

'Go change, babe,' Landon said to me as he grabbed a towel and started drying the dishes Beckett had washed.

I moaned. 'A man who does the dishes. My dream come true.'

Landon and Beckett laughed before Landon said, 'Scoot. Go get changed. The fireworks are going to start soon,' and gestured towards our bedroom.

After changing, I found Hannah outside. We sat next to eat other on the outdoor couch surrounding the fire pit. The big orange flames crackled and spat specks of fire into the air as we sat and stared at the dancing blaze like we were mesmerized by it.

Ten minutes later, all of us were seated around the fire.

Everyone had changed into warmer clothes and Beckett brought out three blankets, one for each couple.

Each pair huddled on a separate couch under the navy blue blankets as light and shadows from the fire twisted and leapt. The once jovial, rolling conversations morphed into whispered, private pillow talk. I nuzzled under Landon's chin and allowed my hands to roam under the cover of the blanket. My nipples peaked as Landon's hand snuck under my shirt and pinched the sensitive nubs.

'I want you now,' he whispered as he squeezed again, and I had to bury my head in his shoulder to hide my squeak.

'You gonna make me come right here in front of everyone?' I dared.

His hand slipped under the waistband of my pants. 'You challenging me? You know how I love challenges.'

'Oh my God! No way!' Hannah suddenly cried out. 'What are you doing?' I'd never heard such urgency in her voice.

I flipped around to see what was happening. And that's when I saw Beckett in front of her.

On one knee.

A velvet box in his hand.

The wide-eyed shock painted across her face turned into waves of tears that slid down her cheeks, uninhibited. Just like her smile.

One of Beckett's hands held the open box, the diamond nestled inside sparkling from the light of the fire. His other hand grabbed both her hands in her lap as he began. 'I wanted to ask you an important question tonight, in front of all our friends since that's where we began. Nearly a year ago, this beautiful, confident woman stood in front of me. I willed her to choose me, door number three, because although I pretended nonchalance, I had been staring at her all night from across the bar. Like opposing magnets, we were drawn to each other for reasons we didn't understand.

But now when I wake up to her every morning and fall asleep with her each night, I *do* understand. It's the little things. The pizzas on Tuesdays. The way she closes her eyes when I brush her hair. How I feel when I sit next to her on a boulder after a hike and eat a bag of Cheetos. Hannah, I want a lifetime of little things with you, a lifetime climb full of peaks and valleys. I promise to be both your cliff and your safety net, your lover and your husband. Hannah Black, will you marry me?'

He barely got the last word out before she launched off the couch and fell into his arms. 'Yes,' I saw her lips say against his, their smiles making it difficult for them to kiss.

Landon's arms wrapped around me from behind as he laid his cheek against mine. My eyes filled with happy tears. When I sniffed, his arms squeezed a little bit tighter.

I looked across the fire to Jenn, whose cheeks were red and stained with paths of tears she didn't bother wiping away. Her eyes met mine and she mouthed, 'Oh my God! Did you know about this?'

'No,' I mouthed, shaking my head emphatically.

'Me neither,' she mouthed.

'Congratulations, you two,' Declan said as Beckett and Hannah unfolded themselves from the concrete floor and sat on the couch. He slid the ring from the box and slipped it onto her finger. He twisted it around twice and squeezed her hand into a fist, clearly happy with how it looked on her finger.

'Thank you,' they both said. Hannah added to Beckett, 'Wow, what a shock.'

'Really? I'm glad. I was so nervous all night. I thought for sure you suspected something.'

Hannah turned her attention to the rest of us as she stood and pulled Beckett off the couch. She started to tug him away from the fire pit. 'I love all you guys, but right now ...' She left unsaid what all of us understood.

Ever the proper gentleman and perfect host, Beckett

tried to slow their retreat, but he soon gave up. Over his shoulder, he said, 'Can you guys take care of yourselves?'

'Go, man. Take care of your fiancée,' Declan yelled.

As the couple neared the screen door, Hannah squealed as Beckett grabbed her from behind in a playful hug. Beckett started, 'If you guys need us –'

'– don't come find us,' Hannah finished as the screen door closed behind them.

'Balcony. Now,' Landon whispered in my ear.

I lifted my legs off his lap and stood. 'Sorry to bail on you guys, too,' I said to Declan and Jenn, 'but we're going to watch the fireworks from the balcony.'

'Sounds good,' Jenn said, distracted, and Declan simply gave a thumbs up. They were already nuzzling under the blanket, cocooned in their own happy ending.

Landon grabbed my hand and tugged me across the patio so quickly I had to jog to keep up with his strides. He slid the screen door aside and pulled me up the stairs and into our bedroom. The first boom of fireworks reverberated off the side of the house. Its explosion filled the room with red slants of light.

Landon drew the comforter and blanket off the bed and carried them to the balcony, which was about the size of a king bed. He spread out the thick comforter on the dark-stained wood decking.

'Lie down.' We were both fully clothed as his body folded over mine and he pulled the heavy blanket over us. As our lips joined in a languid kiss, his hands roamed across my body, reverently, gently, like he was exploring and memorizing at the same time. Soon they were tugging at my clothing.

'Watch the fireworks,' he said, pressing my chin so it rested over my left shoulder. Through the thin wooden balusters, I saw the fireworks ignite. They shot upwards, a small spark with so much potential, so much hidden energy. When they attained maximum height, they burst, raining sparks that sizzled and crackled. Some fluttered peacefully while my favorite left long streaks of glittering light in the sky that looked like a weeping willow tree.

As I watched, he pulled off my shirt and pants. My bra unhooked with a click. He slid my underwear down my legs, his hands caressing the soft skin behind my knees and ankles as he descended. He tugged off his shirt and kicked off his pants under the blanket.

I felt the vibrations of the large fireworks in my chest as his naked body lay on top of mine. He held his upper body up with his elbows under my shoulders. His fingers brushed the hair back and away from my face. The pads of his fingertips brushed along my forehead, across my temples, and around my ears.

'I love how I can see the color of the fireworks as it reflects off your skin.'

I tried to turn my head to him for a kiss. For eye contact. For anything. But his thumb pressed my chin back over my shoulder. 'No. Keep watching.'

Another big firework climbed the peak and tipped over, spilling its sparks.

'Green,' he said, nuzzling my exposed neck.

The next rained flickering sparks that looked like strobe lights.

'Red,' he said as he pressed his lips against my racing pulse.

'Purple,' he said a moment later as one of his hands pressed between my legs and swirled in the need pooling there.

'What are you –?' I asked a moment later, but I stopped myself when I understood. He was guessing the colors of the fireworks as he explored every inch of my skin. I couldn't have felt more adored, more cherished, more precious than in that moment.

He let me turn my head to him. I lifted it off the comforter, reaching for the kiss I so desperately needed.

When our lips locked, two of his fingers penetrated me. My hips rocked into the glorious pressure.

I whimpered against his lips. 'Please. I need more.'

'Me too, baby. Roll onto your side. We're going to watch the fireworks as we make our own.' His warm body nestled behind me. He pulled my right leg up to rest over the top of his as he notched himself at my entrance.

'I don't want to use a con –'

'It's fine. I'm on birth control,' I interrupted, anticipating his request.

'Thank God,' he hissed as the first few inches of his velvet soft skin rubbed against and into me. I felt the weight of him more as he pressed in with nothing between us.

His base pressed against me and he held himself still, fully seated as a rapid series of fireworks spread across the sky from left to right and back like a windshield wiper.

His teeth grazed my shoulder blade before his lips pressed against the sensitive nerve endings. The fingers on his right hand entwined with mine. He bent his arm so that our mess of tangled fingers rested between my breasts.

A thin layer of sweat misted our bodies despite the cool mountain air surrounding us. He slid in and out slowly like this for quite a while, content and happy in our peaceful ascent that kept building, creating tension as it climbed.

His fingers released mine at my breast and trailed down my stomach to my swollen clit. He circled it twice with just enough pressure for me to feel the tightening in my core. I circled my hips, trying to chase more pressure, more friction.

'Wait for it,' he commanded. 'Let it climb.' Another small streak rose in the sky. Its meteoric light went out in a moment of weightlessness just before it exploded. Landon tapped my clit twice before pressing down firmly so that the bundle of nerves was trapped between my pubic bone and his unyielding fingers.

My mouth opened in a silent scream as I exploded from my center. The energy raced through my arms and legs as I soared then floated back down. His hips kept the same rhythm as he let me settle.

'That was a beautiful one,' he said against my neck.

He lifted my leg off his hips and placed it bent in front of me, exposing my backside to him.

'You've done this before?' He asked. 'I don't want to hurt you.'

'Yes.' He brought the first two fingers of his right hand to my mouth. I sucked and licked them before they popped from my mouth. I felt the wetness on my puckered entrance as his fingers circled and pressed.

'Rub your clit for me,' he said as one of his fingertips penetrated me. 'Fuck.' He blew out a breath. 'You're so tight.'

I pressed back into him, wanting more. I felt each knuckle of his fingers as they eventually both worked into me. They circled before they started to pump, matching the rhythm of his hips.

He pulled his fingers and shaft out of me all at once. He took his dick in his hand and lined it up where we both needed it.

The first inch burned, so I circled my clit faster.

He paused, waiting for me, before he asked, 'You good?'

I nodded and he said 'breathe out' before he pushed in further. A sting later, he finally popped through the initial resistance.

'Yes,' he praised. 'You're going to do this for us, aren't you?'

'Yes.'

'You love this when that part is over, don't you?'

'Yes. Yes. Yes,' I chanted my responses. I could feel my stretched muscle spasming around him as I adjusted to his size. 'So full.'

His balls rested against my swollen sex as he filled me. His slow retreat and unhurried thrusts made me arch my back. His hand gripped my wrist and pressed it between my legs.

'I want you to feel me inside of you. Put in two fingers. Hurry. I'm not going to last,' he added as I hesitated. His breaths heating my back were uneven as his muscles strained with control.

I circled my first two fingers at my entrance to gather wetness before I eased them in. I angled them backwards so I could feel his length, how rock hard he was, how he filled me. The thin membrane separating us allowed me to feel everything.

'I can feel you,' he echoed. 'So hot.'

I pressed my shoulder blades back against his chest when he sped up the rhythm. The pace of the fireworks show sped up too as it readied for the finale. His fingers gripped my hips with new intensity, his careful reserve long forgotten. Beyond restraint, he thrusted into me and pulled me back onto him. I pressed my palm against my clit. My muscles contracted in response.

'Do it,' he urged. 'Then I'm going to tell you what you're going to do. After you come, you're going to wait until I say. When I do, you're going to roll over onto your back. You got me?'

'Yes,' I managed.

'No limits, right?'

Something in the commanding rasp of his voice sparked something in me, like the fuse finally met the gunpowder. I felt my orgasm most strongly in my ass where my muscles squeezed and tightened around his length. My clit pulsed against my hand in a shorter, more intense orgasm than the first.

After three harsh strokes, Landon tapped my ass twice. 'Roll over,' he commanded. My sweaty back welcomed the cool comforter as Landon mounted me, straddling my hips. His knees trapped my arms against my body. My chest lifted and fell in heavy breaths as I realized what he planned to do. He could truly come wherever he wanted. On my stomach. On my breasts, my neck, my face, my hair.

His stare was powerful and dominant as he loomed over me, the roar of the finale vibrating the wooden deck under my back. Its sound echoed off the mountains, its light illuminating one side of Landon's body so that each curve of muscle was outlined in reds, greens, and oranges. His eyebrows furrowed in concentration while his hand pumped up and down his shaft furiously.

Then his first forceful spurt landed between my breasts, followed by many other waves. The liquid found multiple paths down my body. It pooled along my collarbone and ran down my ribs.

With his right hand still massaging the remnants of his orgasm, his left moved to my body. With an open palm, he spread out the come. No place on my chest or throat was left uncovered. He brushed his left index finger along the thin layer and brought it to my lips. I opened and sucked his finger clean, tasting his pleasure.

The same finger searched out more of his pleasure from my breast. As he did, his eyes never left mine. Even in the near darkness, the wetness glistened on his finger. This time, his finger traced lower to my sex where he pressed in, claiming that part of me too.

Finally, his finger traced through the wetness covering my ribs. He reached behind him where I feel a single finger penetrate my tight hole.

This part is mine too, he said with his eyes. And, strangely enough, I felt no trepidation, no anger over his possessiveness, his need to mark me. In fact, it made me want him even more.

Then he pursed his lips together and blew cool breaths over my stomach and chest. The liquid dried and tightened on my skin.

He leaned forward and took my lips in a languid, methodical kiss.

Minutes later, his lips pulled away, but his face was still inches from mine. I tilted my head to the side towards where the fireworks had gone off. 'That was some finale.'

He smiled. 'I'll say.'

Chapter Sixteen

'They seem happy,' Landon said as he pulled on to the interstate, heading for the Denver airport.

'Really happy,' I agreed. Hannah and Beckett were the last to arrive for breakfast earlier that morning. They held hands as they fed each other bites of fruit. His hands were always circling her hips, tracing soft lines on her neck or pressing against her lower back. I lost track of how many times she snuggled under his arm, a peaceful smile spread across her lips. We'd all thanked Beckett for the invitation and said our goodbyes as each couple left together.

'Do you want what they have someday?' Landon's question pulled me back to the present.

'Sure. Someday.' I looked out the window, watching the pine trees thicken as we left the higher elevations.

I heard Landon suck in a breath and blow it out. 'We can't pretend to be just friends anymore. The charade is killing me.'

I felt the tension rise in the car like the pressure between tectonic plates before an earthquake. 'What are you suggesting we be if not just friends?'

He took off his sunglasses, folded them together, and laid them on his lap. His eyes met mine when the curving road allowed. 'Are you playing with me? If I have to spell it out, I will. I want us to be *together*.'

'I figured that, and I am truthful when I say I really like you, Landon. You're funny, kind, generous, and you rock my world in bed.'

'And on the balcony,' he added. 'Don't forget that.'

How could I? I let out a defeated sigh. 'But I don't see

how it would work. I'm in Boulder. You're in Dallas, and half the time, you're all over the continent. Unless one of us sacrifices everything we've worked hard for, we're at minimum seven-hundred miles away. How is that good for a relationship, especially one so new?'

He leaned back on the headrest. 'It isn't. Look, this is July. Even if the Stars go deep into the playoffs, the latest I'll be in Dallas full-time is October. That's only four months. Then I'll have the off season. I'll still have some meetings and training, but I could train anywhere, maybe even at the Raptor's facility in Denver. Guys scatter during the winter months anyway. We'd have months to spend together before …'

'Before you go back on the road for seven months,' I finished.

'So what do you want?' He said, anger taking root in his voice. 'You want to drop me off at the airport and pretend we don't have something? You don't want to try to find a way to work this out? I'm trying here, Nina. I really am. Are you?'

My heart fell at his question. Was I simply being practical? Or was I finding excuses to not open myself to him?

'I'm sorry I sound so negative. It's just that … well, let's just say it's been years since I've had anything but a causal relationship with a man. And it scares me that the first one I'm considering is with a man who'll spend months hundreds of miles away. Surely you understand that's not going to be easy.'

His voice softened as he reached across and squeezed my leg. 'I understand where you're coming from. I'm telling you, though, that I'm willing to find ways to get to Boulder whenever I can. Could you do the same? What if I fly you down for a game every other week? Come to think of it, I could fly you to some away games, and we could spend some time exploring cities around the country together.'

His enthusiasm was on a roll, and I had to admit, it was contagious. He continued, 'Hell, maybe this is a blessing in disguise. I don't know the reason why you haven't dated lately, but if it's because you don't want to lose your freedom to a clingy boyfriend, this eliminates the problem. You'll still keep your freedom. Your weekdays and nights will be your own to write and run as you please. Then we'll get to jet off to some really cool places together. San Francisco. New York. Boston.'

That sounded amazing. I'd love that life. Seeing new places. Exploring our relationship with the ability to put distance between us if things were moving too quickly. 'OK. Let's try it,' I said as he pulled into the departure lane at Denver International.

He shoved the gear stick into park and bent towards me. His big hands gripped my neck and pulled me close. Our lips pressed together and his hands tilted my head to deepen the kiss.

Our foreheads rested together as our heavy breaths mixed and joined. 'I guess we're going to get plenty of practice at the airport goodbyes,' he said, lighthearted.

'You sure you want to do this, Landon? You could have a woman in each city.'

His mood sobered. 'I only want one woman in one city.'

A minute later, he turned around one last time, offering me a smile as he disappeared around the corner into the concourse.

That night, a scene popped into my head at midnight and wouldn't stop pestering me until I got out of bed and wrote it.

A month had passed, but Charlotte swore she could still smell the salty sea air when the breeze blew just right as she walked the family's orchard. Life had returned to a semblance of normal since the daily tasks of preparing meals for her siblings and cleaning their small house didn't allow for much else. She found herself daydreaming, though, during those tasks. The hardest days were the ones where it rained. She'd imagine pushing through heavy doors into a garden that smelled of jasmine and roses. She'd remember how the cool raindrops felt on her heated skin and how his lips felt when ...

'Miss Heywood? Would you like a ride into town? It's surely a long walk from here,' the man's voice spoke kindly from the carriage. Charlotte had been walking along the dirt road into town to pick up a bolt of material from Mrs Clayton that her mother had ordered last month. She usually made the trip easily, but today her worn shoes pinched her feet.

'Thank you, Mr Andrews. I appreciate your kindness.' He opened the door to the carriage and waited for her to be seated before he slapped the horses. The carriage jolted forward, rocking her side to side as the wheels bounced on the uneven ground.

He inquired as to where she was going, and when she told him, he said, 'Oh, next to the old Jaspar building. It's been vacant for years, but rumor is that some gentleman not from these parts has bought it, intending to refurbish it and open a business.'

'What type of business?' She hoped it was a new bookstore or a place to buy stationery.

'That I do not know. You'll have to ask Mrs Clayton, as I remember her saying last week, she ran into the fellow. Look, now, wasn't that much faster?' He said, pulling up in front of Mrs Clayton's store.

He offered her his hand as she stepped from the carriage. 'Thank you, sir. I'll be sure to bring some cranberry biscuits by for you and Mrs Andrews.'

'You're more than welcome, Miss.' He tipped his hat

and waited for her to step back before he asked the horses to stride.

The door chimed as Charlotte entered. The plump, red-faced Mrs Clayton greeted her warmly from behind the counter. 'Miss Heywood. I have that bolt right here for you, m'dear.' She leaned down, picked up the folded material, and hoisted it onto the counter. Charlotte paid for the order and made to leave, but as she did, she remembered what Mr Andrews had said.

'Oh, Mrs Clayton. Mr Andrews said that a gentleman bought the vacant building next to you. That must please you very much to have another business so close. Do you know what the business will be?'

Mrs Clayton's eyes lit as she leaned forward as if she was relaying a secret. 'No, I do not, my dear, but I can tell you he was a fine man with even finer taste. He came in one day to introduce himself. He gave me one of his cards,' she rooted around behind the counter, but returned empty. 'I seem to have misplaced it, but while he was here, he bought the most exquisite –'

The door jangled again, signaling another customer. Mrs Clayton leaned away and welcomed Mrs Pilfroy with a nod.

'Thank you, Mrs Andrews,' Charlotte said as she picked up the bolt and left the store. The adjacent building had no signs indicating what business was going to move in, and the front door was locked when she tried the handle.

She started her long journey back to the Heywood home; and just as the shadows were beginning to lengthen, she opened the front door and stepped inside.

'There you are, Charlotte,' her mother called from the small sitting room.

'Is something wrong, mother?' Charlotte walked around the corner and sat next to her mother on the chase.

'No, dear. I've just been beside myself with excitement,

213

waiting for you to come home.'

'Why?'

Her mother reached behind her and pulled out a large white box beautifully adorned with a blue satin bow. On the front was clearly written, 'Miss Charlotte Heywood.'

'While you were gone, this was delivered for you.'

'For me? Who on earth would send me something?' *She tugged the ends of the bow and lifted the box. She pushed aside the tissue to find yards of the most elegant pink brocade. The card inside read,*

Miss Heywood,

We missed that ball. I'll visit you in a fortnight as I have business near you I must attend to. Make something beautiful with this.

Yours, S

Chapter Seventeen

I knew it was going to happen, but it still surprised me with how quickly it did. I'd asked for it, I suppose. Hell, what did I expect when I googled him? Nothing good ever came of that.

It had been two weeks since I dropped Landon off at the airport. We'd talked on the phone every night, but had yet to fit in one of those short vacations we'd talked about. His starts had continued to improve, and I was training harder than ever for the half marathon in just under a month.

I was bored one Sunday night and trying everything I could to avoid writing. I looked up his stats, checked the Stars' league standings, anything I could to postpone work. That's when I saw the picture. Landon's left arm was slung around a blonde's shoulders, his fingers dangling a centimeter away from her tits.

I clicked on it, of course. The link took me to some chick's Facebook page. The photo had been posted yesterday with the caption, 'Landon and I hanging out at Club Allure.'

My blood heated instantly in my veins like I'd been dropped into a boiling pot of water. Just when I'd started to convince myself that I could actually make a go of it with someone, I saw this. Perfect. Fucking perfect.

I copied the photo on to my phone and texted it to Landon, accompanied by three words:

Care to explain?

I knew I wouldn't get an immediate response since his game would last for at least another hour but I still sat by my phone, fuming. This was why I never let anyone close. They had the potential to hurt me like *she* had. As I sat stewing next to my silent phone for hours, I had worked myself up. This time, I vowed, I would be the one leaving, not the one left holding on to the pieces.

When my phone finally rang, I debated whether or not to answer it. The vindictive side of me wanted to make him worry, make him suffer, but my need to vent and yell and scream won out. I picked up on the fourth and last ring.

'Hi, Landon.'

'Nina,' he said out of breath. I heard his car door shut and his engine start. 'I just got out of the post-game meeting. I got your text, and called you right away. You have to understand –'

That wasn't a good way to start, buddy. I don't have to understand anything.

'Really?' I interrupted 'Out of all the women you could have chosen to wrap your arm around, you chose that blonde bimbo? She wasn't even –'

'Stop.' It was his turn to interrupt me. 'I'm not choosing anybody else. That picture was taken months ago.'

'And she just put it up yesterday? That's hard to believe. Why would she do that?'

He huffed, frustrated. 'She works for the Stars, so I've met her quite a few times over the years. She came on to me last night at the after party. She'd had too much to drink, and I reminded her gently that I was committed to you. She didn't take it well, and I'm guessing this is retribution. I think she's just stirring the pot.'

'You have history with her?'

His long pause answered for him. He confirmed with a single word. 'Yes.' Then he continued, 'Look, neither of

216

us were virgins when we met. But I'm with *you* now and no one else. I've already texted her and told her to take the picture down. She said she would.'

I scoffed, unable to let go of my anger.

'Look,' he said gently. 'If this is going to work, we're going to have to trust each other. Because we lead separate lives, we can't be by each other's side, constantly checking to be sure the other person is being faithful.'

'I wouldn't want to do that anyway, even if we weren't trying this long distance thing. I don't want to live like I'm constantly waiting for *it* to happen.'

'I agree. But you have to admit that what you're feeling now is the type of insecurity that distance breeds.' He paused, then ended, 'If you got to see on a daily basis how little I react to the women around me, you'd know I have eyes for no one other than you. I can't stop thinking about you. I wonder what you're doing. How are your runs going? How is your dissertation coming? Hell, on the drive today, I swore I could smell you. There's no one else, Nina. No one else.'

A tear ran down my cheek as he spoke the words I didn't know I needed to hear so badly. 'Thank you.'

Although I didn't think his voice could have spoken anymore gently than it already had, it did. 'Now, tell me the truth. You were planning on leaving me tonight over this, weren't you?'

Yes. 'I'd given it some thought.'

'You want to explain why you jump ship so quickly? Why I'm your first relationship in years?'

'No.'

Unhappy with my answer, he brought out the big guns. 'Does it have to do with your mother?'

I shot off the couch that I'd been sitting on and started pacing like a caged lion. 'What the fuck do you know about my mother?'

'Calm down –'

217

Oh, that was the wrong thing to say to me. 'I'm not calming down. You bring my mother into this and you expect me to do what? Bare my secrets to you?' The muscles in my legs were shaking from anger and the shot of adrenaline.

'Something like that. Don't we owe each other more, especially when whatever happened with her seems to cause problems for us?'

'What the fuck are you talking about?'

'That first night with Laura and now this incident with the picture? I think they're related. You have issues with infidelity.'

'Fuck you,' I yelled, tears prickling behind my eyes. 'Who are you, my therapist?'

He didn't rise to my bait. His voice was tender when he asked, 'Did someone cheat?'

'Of course someone cheated,' I bellowed. 'Everyone cheated. I saw it every day growing up on the road with a bunch of twenty-year-old baseball players. I pretended not to get it, but I did. After Mom and Dad divorced, I lived with my dad, and every summer I traveled with the team and watched as blonde babes in every city would wrap themselves around the players. And they would take them up to their hotel rooms for a night, not even bothering to take off their wedding rings. The wives would visit sometimes and sit in the stands, completely oblivious to their transgressions, or maybe they just acted completely oblivious. I couldn't ever really tell. It happens all the time and you know it.'

'I know, I see it too. Every day. But you didn't really answer my question. This issue is more personal for you, isn't it?'

My whole body was shivering as tears rolled down my cheeks. 'Mom accused Dad of cheating all the time. At nights when it got really bad, I tried to bury my head in the pillow so I didn't have to hear them fight about it. I'd hear her scream at him behind their bedroom door after the team came back from every road trip. Whether or not he did cheat was irrelevant, although he always insisted he was faithful. Cheating didn't break their marriage. The lack of trust did.'

'I'm sorry you had to go through that.'

I nodded but didn't say anything, so he continued. 'It means a lot to me that you told me about this. Now I understand why you have reacted so strongly.'

Feeling wrung out, I breathed a sigh of relief that the inquisition was over. I sat down on the couch to stretch out my trembling legs. Even my hand holding the phone to my ear quivered. It turned out, though, that I let my guard down a question too soon.

'One more thing. You said earlier that after the divorce you lived full-time with your dad. I've seen a lot of players get divorced, and for many fathers, that's not normally how courts decide custody, especially with a job requiring so much travel. Why didn't you live with your mother?'

Thousands of pins pricked the skin on my chest and twisted into my breastbone. They lodged there, content in the pain they were causing. 'She wanted nothing to do with me,' I whispered, unable to cry anymore. 'We were never close. She was a distant mother. I can count on one hand how many times we spent a day at the zoo together. But once she was done with my father, she also decided she was done being a mother. How does a mother do that?' I asked as an aside before I continued.

'I don't know. I couldn't imagine …'

I was on a roll. 'She decided that she wanted to be the one to go off traveling on a whim. Rumor was that she left for California with her new boyfriend when the ink on the divorce decree dried. She craved the freedom my dad had, and a young child certainly put the damper on that. She willingly signed over any responsibility for me, and I never saw her again.'

It was hard to hear Landon's voice drip with compassion. 'I'm so sorry.'

'And all the therapists Dad dragged me to while I was growing up will tell you that my mother's abandonment makes it difficult for me to get close to people. 'Textbook case,' they'd say, like explaining it in those terms would somehow cure me. Hell, sometimes the diagnosis hurt just as bad because it was a disease without a cure. How could I learn to let anyone close when the one person whose love was supposed to be unconditional turned off her love for me like a light switch? How could …' My breath hitched as I sobbed, the hand holding the phone shaking violently.

'So it's easier to just not let anybody in. Saves you reliving that pain all over again. Oh God,' he cursed as I heard his engine rev in the background.

'What are you doing?' I managed.

'I'm driving to the airport. I'm going to get on a flight to Denver. I have to see you.'

'No, Landon. Don't. You have a game tomorrow.'

'I can fly back before the game. It's a late one anyway. We shouldn't have had this conversation over the phone. You're fucking crying, and I can't do anything about it. I have to get to you, to hold you.'

'No, Landon. You could get in –'

'How can I just go home and fall asleep after what you've just told me?'

'I'll be fine. I've lived with these secrets for years.'

He disregarded what I said like I hadn't spoken at all. 'Do you have a hidden key outside your house?'

'Yes.'

'Where is it?'

'Landon. Don't.'

'Where. Is. It?' he repeated, impatiently.

'Under the flower pot with the red geraniums.'

'I'm driving to the airport now. Go to sleep. I'll let myself in.' He disconnected the call.

From the determination in his voice, I knew he would be on a plane to Denver in an hour. I took a shower and fell into my bed with wet hair. I hadn't bothered to turn off any lights or put on anything sexy. On autopilot, I pulled the covers to my chin, numb, anesthetized. I'd always thought that when I told someone the story I'd feel bone-deep pain and relentless worry. But as I lay in bed and stared unseeing at my bedroom door, there was light in all the dark corners. I found it oddly comforting.

Hours later, somewhere between sleep and consciousness, I felt Landon's warm arms wrap around my center as he nestled behind me.

Soft kisses along my neck and shoulders woke me as the soft rays of daybreak peaked through the curtains. It was so peaceful that for a moment I forgot what had happened last night.

'I've got to go,' he said between kisses. 'I hate it, but I do.' He brushed the hair off my face to look me in the eyes. 'There is a plane ticket on the kitchen table for this Thursday. You're going to meet me in San Francisco. I'll have a driver pick you up, you'll come to the game, then we'll explore for a few days.'

I blinked the sleep from my eyes and stretched. My hands stroked through his hair. 'Thank you.'

He smiled. 'You're welcome. We need this.' His lips pecked one last time on my forehead before he peeled himself out of bed. He wore jeans and a Stars T-shirt, which was what he was probably wearing as he left the game last night. He grabbed keys I didn't recognize and his wallet off the bedside table. Before he turned the corner to the hallway, he paused. His fingers gripped the wood casement of my bedroom door like he was fighting the parts of him that wanted him to stay. His face was pained when he said, 'I'll miss you.'

He pried himself from the doorway. To his retreating
back, I murmured, 'I'll miss you too.'

Chapter Seventeen

The rest of the week I spent running, preparing the reading lists for the upcoming classes I'd agreed to teach, and writing my dissertation.

Two weeks had passed for Charlotte and Simon, and she anticipated his arrival in Willingden with each stitch of her new dress. From his letters, she knew it would be tonight. She'd explained to her parents who Simon was. They'd inquired as to why he would buy her such an expensive present, a question she didn't really have an answer for. The Heywoods requested Simon dine with them upon his arrival in Willingden, an invitation he accepted through the post the previous evening. Charlotte knew the invitation was extended by the Heywoods out of common courtesy, but it was also an opportunity for Mr Heywood to gauge the sincerity of the gentleman's attentions for his daughter. Charlotte dressed in the pink brocade dress she'd sewed as Simon instructed.

When his coach arrived, Charlotte's chest fluttered with nervous excitement. She was delighted to see him, of course, but she also wondered how his rich attire and formal manners would be received in her admittedly humble home. His refined tastes seemed more appropriate for Lady Denham's vast estate. In fact, as she stood draped in his expensive tastes, she felt out of place in her modest surroundings. She'd never been embarrassed by her home before, but as his shined boot stepped from the smart carriage, she wondered if it, if she, would ever be enough.

Mercifully, when he entered the home, he didn't examine the room with a critical eye, which was the habit of most people of his class. Instead, he smiled when his eyes landed on the dress she'd made with her own hands.

'Mr Parker. We're thankful for the opportunity to have you visit our home,' Mr Heywood welcomed formally.

'It is I who is most thankful for the invitation,' Simon replied with a courteous bow. He gifted Mrs Heywood a lovely bouquet, which endeared him to her, for she dearly loved flowers. He smiled genuinely at each of the Heywood children as they were introduced, but he saved his warmest smile for Charlotte.

Over dinner, Mr Heywood bridged the topic of Simon's purchase of the old Jaspar building. Simon confirmed the rumors and briefly explained what the building would be used for.

'So, Charlotte tells me that your primary business is located in London, but that you have other locations throughout the country.'

'Yes. She is correct.' He cut another piece of ham into a perfect square.

'Did you have anything in this area before?'

He lifted the fork to his mouth and chewed the meat before he spoke again. 'I didn't before. No.'

Mr Heywood frowned. 'So is this new business venture out of your way for a reason or was it a logical growth of your business?'

Simon shifted in his chair and met eyes with Charlotte who sat still as a mouse. 'We'll just call it an outpost,' he said.

It was because of that comment that Charlotte's heart leapt in joy. It couldn't have been more obvious that he had pursued Willingden for one reason.

And he made that one reason clearer to her as she strolled with him through the family's orchard. 'This is lovely property,' he praised, his strides slow and measured next to hers. The ground was uneven enough that her footsteps sometimes faltered, so he kept a hand on her elbow in the event of a stumble. 'So much different from London. I wouldn't miss the bustle, the noise of London, if I lived in the country. I'd miss some of the culture, though.'

His fingers stroked the texture of the material at her elbows. His eyes darkened. Seeing her wear his dress, something he bought for her, was akin to putting his mark on her. Claiming her. It made him want to do it more.

'How often will your business bring you to Willingden?' Charlotte inquired.

He stopped walking and placed both his hands on her elbows. 'Let's not pretend that I'm coming to Willingden on business. What if we married and moved to London? We could come back here to visit surely ...'

'Let's not pretend that we'd be here all that often.' She closed the inches between them. 'I want to be where my husband is.'

Maybe that's how it ends, I thought. They marry, of course. They spend the majority of their time in London. She would get to experience living in luxury in the bustle of the city, and in the summer, they would retreat to Willingden where her mother and father could spend their old age bestowing love on their growing grandchildren.

I closed the laptop as the plane descended into San Francisco International Airport. As Landon had promised, a chauffeur stood at the arrival gate holding a sign with my name neatly scrolled across it. He promptly took my carry-on luggage from my hands and escorted me to the limousine parked in the passenger loading area. Its hazard lights blinked, casting a yellow glow on my white Dallas Stars jersey as I stepped into the air-conditioned backseat.

'Miss,' the driver said, gesturing to an open drink in the cup holder.

I recognized the green bottle immediately. Heineken. My favorite beer, mainly because it was my dad's favorite. When I turned twenty-one (and a few times before), Dad and I would sit around the ball park before a game. We enjoyed the peacefulness, the quiet before the storm. Before he left me to address the team, he'd always clink his bottle against mine.

I picked up the beer from the holder and took a long, cold drink, touched at Landon's attentiveness. It was these little things that made me feel cherished and adored, and gave me some confidence that we might actually be able to make this work somehow.

The limousine pulled into the ballpark half an hour later. Waves of fans were already pouring into the stadium as the driver opened my door and directed me to the VIP entrance.

I handed the attendant my ticket and the special pass to the suite reserved for the opposing players' wives and girlfriends. 'Do you know where to find the suite, dear?' The attendant asked.

'No. I don't think so, Rita,' I said, reading the attendant's nametag.

Rita called over her shoulder to another employee. 'Hey, Ricky. You got a second to escort Miss ...'

'I'll be happy to escort her,' a male voice said behind us.

Rita looked to me, gauging whether or not I wanted to go with this apparent stranger. Yet he wasn't one. His face looked familiar, but I couldn't quite place him. Then, when he smiled, I knew instantly who he was. My dad's closest friend had more wrinkles than I remembered, and his eyes had lightened as he aged, but I would know that uninhibited smile anywhere. He'd played many games of Go Fish with me as I waited for Dad to finish with practice. It was a sad day for me when I learned that he'd been promoted from his job with the Triple-A Raptors to the Dallas Stars. If I remembered correctly, he had worked himself up in the organization. Now he was vice president of something. That's where my knowledge ended.

'Daniel!' I said, as his arms encircled me in a warm hug.

'I thought that was you, Nina.' He pulled back but held onto my elbows as he looked me up and down. His gaze wasn't creepy; it was more fatherly than anything else. Hell, he'd been more of a parent to me than my own mother. 'Wow. You've grown up. You look great.'

'Thank you.'

He looked behind me. 'Is your dad here or something? No one told me he was coming.'

'No.'

He looked confused. 'You came to see a game? In San Francisco? I mean, it's fine if you did, but I thought you were living in Colorado with your father.'

'I'm ... dating a player,' I said tentatively. This was going to take some getting used to.

'What?' His eyes widened to saucers. 'Which one?'

'Landon Griesen.' I paused, gauging his reaction.

'So *you're* the one who snagged that man. I'd heard about it, but ...' He paused, something dawning on him. 'Wait. Does your dad know?'

I laughed, remembering the day two weeks ago when I'd asked him out to coffee so I could tell him about my relationship. His reaction was more happiness than surprise, more supportive than I anticipated. 'Yes. He was fine with it, actually. Said that Landon was a really great guy when he played for him.'

'He is. He is.' His eyes looked lost in a faraway thought for a moment before he shook his head and came back to the present. 'Well, I'm so glad you're here. Come, I'll show you to the suite.'

'Oh, I don't want to take you away from ... I'm sure you have somewhere else ... where you watch,' I stuttered.

'Nonsense.' He pulled my elbow so that I walked next to him as he continued, 'All the guests of the players use the same suite in San Francisco as the upper management, so we were headed to the same place anyway.'

As we walked, we chatted about what I was doing in Colorado. Then I asked what his role was in the organization, which I learned focused primarily on staffing. As we walked up the steps to the suite, he inquired about Dad's health.

'Good. I'm glad to hear that he's doing better,' he said when I gave him the positive news. 'I'm sorry I couldn't get back to see him when he had that scare. Life on the road, I guess.'

He opened the door to the suite, which was buzzing with women dressed in high heels and short skirts with manicures that matched their handbags.

Only a few of them were dressed like me in jeans and a Stars jersey, and many of those had at least one child in tow. I stood proud with Landon's number on the back of my jersey.

Daniel handed me a beer and gestured towards the door of the suite that led to the stadium seating cordoned off for us. We sat in the first row and sipped our beers. The first inning had already begun, but since the Stars were the away team, Landon hadn't yet taken the mound.

Daniel took a long drink then wiped some foam off his upper lip. 'So when are we ever going to get your dad to the Stars?'

I almost choked on the drink I'd taken. 'What?'

One of his eyebrows lowered. He looked bewildered, and I hadn't a clue why. 'You don't know?'

'Clearly not.' My heart raced. I suspected my dad had been keeping a secret from me for a while.

'We've been trying to get your dad to move up to the Stars. For years, we've been searching for a good bullpen coach, and every time we ask, he declines.'

A part of me had wondered if this was the case. After Daniel had left for the Stars, my little teenage brain always worried that Dad would follow, uprooting us from the only place I'd called home. But as the years passed and Dad didn't move up, I worried less. Then in the last few years, a part of me always wondered if Dad had declined a position in order to stay close to me despite the fact I was an adult. Now I had my proof, and my heart ached for the sacrifice my dad made in his career.

I tried to gather my galloping breath. 'Did he say why he declined?'

Daniel looked over the top of his glasses at me. The corners of his lips turned downward. 'You and I both know why he declined. He wouldn't leave you for anything. And don't you go feeling guilty for it, either,' he added, seeing my grimace. 'That man doesn't regret his choices for a second. He loves you more than anything.'

I took a drink, trying to gather my emotions. 'Thank you.'

His tone turned playful. He sing-songed like he was hatching a plan. 'But if you were to –' He stopped himself. 'Never mind. Now, tell me about this new position of yours.'

I studied his face for a good while, trying to decipher what he had stopped himself from saying. Unable to read him, I decided to move on.

While the Stars continued to bat in the top of the first inning, I told him about the position, what I'd be teaching, and a little about my dissertation, although I could tell he started to zone out on the last part.

'Here's your man,' Daniel said, pointing to the field. The Stars had scored three runs in the top of the first inning, and now it was Landon's turn to pitch. He jogged to the mound and dusted his hand with rosin. Like always, he pointed to the sky and stepped onto the mound.

As he did, I watched his eyes scan the row of suites that

encircled the stadium. I stood and waved to catch his attention. A wide smile stretched across his face when he found me. He mouthed something, but I couldn't tell what it was. He quickly turned away and started throwing his warm-up pitches.

I heard Daniel sigh next to me when I sat back down. 'The father figure in me has to ask. How serious is it?'

'Serious enough that I flew out here to watch him pitch.' It was the answer that made the most sense to me.

He hummed an indecipherable reply as Landon threw a first pitch strike. The catcher's leather popped more loudly than I remembered in Boulder, so I turned to find the radar gun.

95 mph.

'He looks good,' Daniel commented, and I nodded. 'If he stays healthy, he could be great one day. Cy Young great,' he added.

The first batter struck out. I nodded, unable to peel my eyes away from the man dominating the game.

Daniel and I continued to chat throughout the seven innings Landon pitched. The Stars won the game by five runs, and Landon looked like he was able to locate his pitches well with good velocity.

Daniel walked with me towards the visitor's locker room when the game ended. 'It was really nice catching up with you, Nina.'

'You too, Daniel.'

'I have a feeling I'll be seeing a lot more of you,' he said with a wink. 'Make sure to bring your dad next time.'

'I'd like that,' I said sincerely. He gave me a hug and walked into the locker room while I waited in the hallway.

Players slowly trickled out of the locker room after the post-game meeting. Some were on their cell phones already. Some boarded the team bus to go back to the hotel. Some greeted women that were waiting for them in the hallway. As the door swung open and each player emerged, a dose of adrenaline shot through my system, making me jumpy by the time Landon finally emerged.

He jogged over to me in the empty hallway and picked me up by the waist. I squeaked when he twirled around twice before he slid me down his body. My back hit the hard concrete wall as he crushed his lips to mine.

'I like your jersey,' he said when he pulled away. 'I like you wearing my name.'

My cute, possessive man. His need to mark me was something that no longer made me cringe. In fact, it just made me hot. I rubbed my hips against his, reminded of the night on the balcony. 'I like wearing you. All. Over. Me.'

He growled as his hips shoved my pelvis against the wall. 'I'm going to spend all weekend doing just that. Come on. The rental is this way,' he said, tugging my hand so that I followed him down the hallway and out the back entrance. A sleek silver sports car beeped as he pressed the fob.

He opened the passenger door for me and climbed in on his side. The engine hummed when he pulled out of the parking space.

'Where are we going?' I asked.

'You ever been to the Wharf?'

'No. In fact, I've never seen the Golden Gate Bridge.'

'Well, you'll not only see it tonight,' he boasted, 'You'll get to float under it. I was going to keep it a secret, but I can't wait. I've rented a boat for tonight. You'll get to see Alcatraz. We'll go under the bridge. When we get tired, we'll sleep in the boat. We'll have breakfast on it in the morning before I have to be back for the game tomorrow.'

That sounded divine. 'We're not going to be doing much sleeping, I hope.'

His foot pressed harder on the accelerator. 'I'm going

to make love to you until the dawn. I promise you that.'

'Not like I'm complaining, 'cause that sounds amazing, but aren't you tired after pitching? And you have a game tomorrow, too.'

'I'm riding a really good adrenaline high right now. My arm felt good, and my body has yet to come down from all the chemicals racing through it when I compete. I'll crash tomorrow, but the good thing about being a starting pitcher is I don't have to play tomorrow.'

'Just sit on the bench and eat sunflower seeds. Sounds like a rough life,' I deadpanned.

He pulled into a parking stall and shut off the engine. 'It's a lot of hard work, but it also lets me do really cool things like this. Come on,' he said as he opened his door, grabbed our overnight bags from the trunk, and dragged me down a cobblestone path. The man wasn't kidding about his post-game energy.

The salty ocean breeze blew my hair back from my face. I filled my lungs with its scent as our footsteps thumped loudly on the wooden dock. Yachts of different sizes were bobbing on the sizeable waves. We passed three boats before Landon stopped in front of a modern, sleek yacht named 'My Jasmine'. Landon called, 'Hey, Bobby!'

The man who must have been Bobby poked his head out from the enclosed space on the upper deck. 'Hey, Landon!' He called as he climbed down the ladder. 'I hope you guys don't get seasick. The waves are pretty big tonight.'

He gestured behind us to where the breeze was blowing the trees so strongly that the bottom half of the leaves were visible. 'When the leaves shimmer like that, you know it's a strong wind.'

'Crap. I didn't think about that,' Landon said to me. 'You get seasick?'

'I don't think so, but I've never been on a boat in the ocean before.'

'But it's safe, though, right?' Landon asked Bobby.

'Oh yeah. No problem. When we get out a little further, it might actually get better.' He held out his hand to me. 'Nina, right? I'm Bobby, the captain for tonight. It's nice to meet you.'

'You as well,' I said, taking his hand.

He held out his open palm for us to proceed into the main cabin. 'I'll show you around the boat.' We spent the next ten minutes touring the main living area, the small galley kitchen, and the bedroom. The bow of the boat had a large deck with a sizeable sitting area. I walked over to one of the couches.

'You're welcome to stay there if you like, but with this wind, you might get sprayed a bit,' Bobby said.

I plopped down on one of the cushions, not wanting to miss any of the sights by sitting inside. 'Thank you, but I don't mind at all.'

The setting sun made Landon's smile glow as he walked towards me and sat down. His arm rested on the cushion behind me. 'Let's do this, Bobby.'

Bobby made a mock salute. He started to leave, then stopped and said, 'Oh, drinks and food are in the kitchen, Landon.'

'Thank you, Bobby,' Landon called and turned his attention to me.

He bit his bottom lip as he tucked a piece of my hair behind my ear. The wind whipped it in my face in a few short seconds. Landon smiled and tucked it behind my ear again. 'I've been waiting to do something like this with you since we left Copper Mountain. Let's not go this long again.'

As the boat pulled from the dock and picked up speed, his arm pulled me into him so that I lay back against his chest. Soon, salty sea spray covered my face and wet my hair, and the boat rocked considerably.

But I couldn't have been happier.

His arms tightened around me as I nestled into the crook of his shoulder. We sat like that in silence for a while, content as cats sitting on a warm window ledge. He pointed out Alcatraz, the island prison that was closed in the early 60s. Now, it was a historic landmark that people could tour, although from how creepy it looked outside, why anyone would want to do that was beyond me.

After we passed the island, the boat motored further into San Francisco Bay. Landon untangled himself and stood. 'I'm going to grab dinner and bring it out.'

'Hurry. Don't miss the Golden Gate Bridge' I yelled. The iconic reddish-orange structure looked small on the horizon, but as we edged closer, its size was overwhelming. Landon quickly brought back gourmet sandwiches, mine stuffed with meat while his dripped with condiments. I smiled when I saw the green bottle in his hand.

'You don't miss anything,' I joked.

'Only you.' He handed me the warm sandwich. I kept the majority of it hidden in the foil wrapper as I bit pieces off the top. 'Here. Put this on,' he said, holding open a large, oversized coat for me to slip my arms into. It was quite chilly in the breeze, and since the sun was setting and I was damp, I really did need it. He shrugged on a matching one.

'Thank you for all of this,' I gestured around me. 'How do you know Bobby?'

'Personally, I don't. He's a good friend of the Stars' ownership. He likes to do things like this when they are in town. When I knew we'd be coming to San Francisco, I asked around to see if there were any player perks, and when someone mentioned this one, I asked the owner right away. He was happy to oblige.'

'They'll do anything for their up and coming ace. They know you're the future of their team.'

He shrugged, looking troubled. He finished his

sandwich and threw away the wrapper. 'Maybe. I try not to get ahead of myself.'

'I know. That's why you'll be so good.'

I ate my last bite and tossed the wrapper into the bag. He rested his back against the cushioned seat back and stretched his legs out in front of him. He was half-sitting, half-lying as he held out his arms in invitation. I crawled into his lap, my back to his front, and he wrapped his arms around my chest. His chin rested on the crown of my head. I melted into his warmth, my body rising and falling with his slow breaths.

The boat was maybe a hundred yards from the bridge that now seemed bigger than life. We could see the tops of the trucks and cars that were driving across it. From here, they looked like tiny Matchbox cars, certainly nothing a human could fit in. As we edged closer, we could hear the traffic zoom over the top of it, the tires making a whirring sound that sounded like constant, tiny vibrations.

As we passed underneath it, Landon lay back further. Neither of us spoke as we simply took in the size of it. When we came out the other side, we were almost fully reclined, and because my gaze was focused upwards, I noticed the flickering stars that had just started to peak out. The further we drifted out, the darker it got. The only lights on the boat were the small required ones in the front and in the aft that told other boats we were there. A blanket of stars covered the otherwise pitch-black sky.

A few other lights from other boats dotted the horizon, but it felt like we had this vast ocean all to ourselves. With darkness came a calmer ocean, so the yacht was able to cruise comfortably through the water.

Landon patted my shoulders and said, 'Stand up. Let's go to the front.'

He steered me towards the front of the yacht that came to a point. It didn't have any seating area. The three-foot-wide open space let us walk right up to the hip-high railing.

The chilly breeze sprayed tiny droplets of water onto my face. I closed my eyes. 'Like Rose on the *Titanic*,' I yelled. And I felt just like her. The freedom, the serenity, the connection with the man at her back.

'Like what on the what?' Landon asked.

I laughed, the moment perfect despite Landon's lack of knowledge about the best chick flick ever. 'How do you not know the movie *Titanic*?'

'The movie? I've heard of the Titanic, of course. Doesn't it sink?' He asked confused, wondering why I would like to be on a sinking ship.

'Yes, but before it sinks, she gets to stand at the front of it, her love standing behind her as she opens her arms. She feels the wind in her hair –'

Landon cut off my description. 'Ahh. I get it. But does he make love to her there?' His hand crept around the large coat and unbuttoned my jeans. He slid down the zipper and pushed the material down my thighs. I could feel him fumbling with his clothing behind me.

I wanted nothing more for him to push inside me here on the edge of the vast ocean. The salty sea air would forever remind me of this moment. But … 'Landon,' I protested, pointing at the second deck. 'Bobby –'

'Can't see and doesn't care. We both have on large coats, so it will just look like we're standing here together against the railing. Widen your feet.'

I stepped out my right first then my left.

'Hold on to the railing.'

My hands gripped the slippery metal. Landon's fingers dipped into me to test how ready I was.

'I'm ready. I'm ready,' I begged. I knew I was drenched. I *ached* for him to fill me.

'Want you so much,' he whispered as his hot, smooth skin pressed against me. The steel of his erection parted me. I leaned forward against the railing so that I could press myself back onto him.

Inch after glorious inch, he penetrated me slowly. More than once, I contemplated slamming my hips back against his, my body screaming for more. His hands stilled my hips, though, as he took me at his pace.

He grunted when he hit the end of me. His arm wrapped around my chest and pulled me to him. 'Come here. Lean back against me.'

I let go of the railing and pressed my shoulders into his chest. His right hand came around to circle my clit as his hips pushed and pulled in a slow adagio.

His tongue played with the folds of my ear before he lightly bit my ear lobe. 'Can I come inside you here?'

I whimpered. He already knew the answer.

'Can I mark you? Can I fill you? It's something I've never done with anyone, you know.'

I didn't know. But I loved that he hadn't.

'But everything in me wants to do that with you.'

'Do it,' I urged.

His hips sped and his finger used more pressure on my swollen clit.

'You want your thighs dripping with our wetness?'

'Yes. Please. Just …'

'You first.' He thrust his hips forward and pressed back on my clit at the same time. I wiggled up and down on him, gaining just the right friction to let my body leap off the cliff. I felt like I was falling, my hair whipping in the breeze. He held me onto him as I screamed. The intensity of the orgasm was something I'd never felt. It pulsed. It consumed. It suspended time and gravity for a few glorious seconds.

'Now you,' I panted and held still while he used my body the way he needed. I wanted nothing less than for him to feel like I just had. I squeezed my muscles around him, which made him curse and harden.

'Fill you. Fill you,' he chanted as he pressed into me

and held still. I could feel the flex of his stomach muscles as they tightened and spasmed with his release.

When he pulled away minutes later to button up his jeans, his lust left a wet trail down the inside of my thighs. I righted my clothes and joined him in the bedroom as the yacht continued to explore the dark waters.

As he promised, I saw the dawn before I closed my eyes, exhausted and completely happy.

Chapter Eighteen

And so it went for the eighteen days I had until I had to report for mandatory meetings at the university. I flew to so many stadiums across the country I lost track of which day it was. My world revolved around him during those days. We took guided tours around museums in every city. He fed me crawfish gumbo in the French Quarter until I begged for mercy. He bought me a diamond necklace in Chicago. And we got to christen every room in his condo in Dallas. We were so lost in each other every night that we'd wake in the mornings, order hotel room service, eat, and crawl back into bed until Landon had to peel himself away for team meetings.

When he left, I often pulled on my running shoes and found a local trail to run on. My training was going well, a good thing since the date of the half marathon was quickly approaching. But I was so drunk on this new passion that I didn't give much thought to my dissertation. I'd convinced myself that the happy ending was just around the corner for Simon and Charlotte. They'd successfully molded their lives together. They'd learned to overcome the distance between them. With their problem solved, I simply didn't feel like writing, especially when I had Landon offering distractions galore.

And I had zero motivation to put together the class reading lists and syllabi for the courses I'd agreed to teach, something that made me feel mountains of guilt.

No matter what happened later, I knew those days would always be some of the most divinely enjoyable I'd ever experienced. But with the wisdom of hindsight, I could see I was stretched too thin. The continuous travel had pulled me in too many different directions, causing me to sacrifice time with friends, church outings I'd once been committed to, and my career. When my dad called me at ten o'clock on a random Tuesday night and asked if I was OK, I realized I hadn't spoken to him in weeks. I'd never done that.

That had bothered me; and when paired with the guilt over not doing the work for the university I should have been, I chose to stay in Boulder for the weekend to catch up.

I had to fill out forms for the classes so the university could have the correct amount of books on reserve for students to buy. That, along with a dozen other things I had to get done, was on my long to-do list.

But as I sat staring at my computer in the middle of the lonely kitchen, I couldn't make my fingers move over the keys. It was late Friday afternoon, and all I wanted to be doing was flying to Dallas so that I could sleep in Landon's bed. With his arms wrapped around me, he'd whisper dirty thoughts as he took me from behind. I wanted to wake up with him on Saturday morning. I wanted to see him pitch a big game against the Yankees on Saturday night. Everything in me yearned to do that rather than sit here and do all the things I was so unmotivated to do.

'Fuck it,' I said, slamming my laptop closed. I threw clothes into my overnight bag and drove to the airport. My car knew the route by heart. I parked in the long-term parking garage and walked to the ticket counter. The last flight left in an hour, so I booked a ticket, which cost me a small fortune given its last-minute purchase. I put it on my credit card, grabbed some dinner at a fast food place in the terminal, and boarded the plane, excited to surprise Landon in Dallas.

When I'd told him earlier in the week I wasn't coming

this weekend, he sounded disappointed, but he understood. I think he wanted me there given that they were playing a division rival, and the Stars were trailing them in the standings. The game was slated to be televised nationally on ESPN. Needless to say, it was a big start for him.

I slept during the flight, knowing I would need it with the long, gratifying nights ahead of me. The Stars game was in the fifth inning when the plane landed, so I had just enough time to find a rental car and drive to his condo. I wanted to be there waiting for him when he came home.

The doorman in his building recognized me immediately when I walked into the lobby decorated with expensive-looking paintings and a modern, glass chandelier. He turned his key in the lock that allowed the private elevator to ascend to the ninth floor, the entirety of which Landon occupied. When I stepped in, he pushed the button, tipped his imaginary cap, and with a wink and a smile through the closing doors, he said, 'Miss Nina. Have a good night.'

'You too, Martin!' I yelled through the closed doors, punch-drunk on the surprise I was able to pull off for Landon. I didn't regret my decision at all as the elevator doors opened with a ding. I stepped into the small hallway that led to only one door, one that Landon never locked since no one got in the elevator without a key.

The door slid open easily to the empty apartment. The large windows overlooking downtown and the stadium let in the soft rays of twilight that covered the room in an amber glow. I walked to his bedroom and hung up my clothes in his closet. I took a shower and changed into some lingerie that dipped low between my breasts, the kind of neckline that made Landon growl when he saw it. I sprayed his favorite perfume on my neck and chest, and spread lotion all over my body, imagining his gentle breaths against my skin. I grabbed one of the beers from his fridge that he kept in there for me and sat on the chair facing the large windows. I sipped the drink as I watched the sun give way to the stars, a tranquil transition that made me continually check the kitchen clock. Time seemed to slow as I anticipated his arrival.

I heard the elevator ding first. Then I heard his quiet footsteps as he walked to the foyer table and emptied his pockets.

Then silence.

'Nina? Is that you?'

I spun the chair to face him. He stood still in the living room, his hair mussed from the hours it spent in his sweaty baseball cap. There was a smudge of dirt on his jersey and his shoes were untied, but he looked divine.

He reached over and flipped on a table lamp. His smile radiated like a lone star in the dark sky. 'It *is* you.'

He strode over to me and knelt in front of the chair. Each of his hands circled one of my thighs. He pushed upwards, his fingertips disappearing under the lingerie. 'I swore I smelled your perfume when I came in, but I thought it was just wishful thinking.'

'Surprise,' I whispered. 'I couldn't stay away.'

His eyes stared at my chest as he bit his lip. Then his eyes lifted to mine, unembarrassed at being caught ogling me. 'I'm glad you're here, but what about the things you said you had to get done? I don't want to take you away from –'

'Fuck 'em.'

He frowned at my interruption. I didn't miss when he looked down at the beer in my hands, considering whether or not I was drunk. Admittedly, it wasn't like me to shirk responsibilities, so he was trying to figure out what had caused my change of heart.

I took one more sip before I leaned over to the glass table and placed my half-full beer on a cork coaster.

I was completely sober. Well, that wasn't entirely accurate. I hadn't drunk too much alcohol – I was just drunk on him.

His look morphed from inquisitive to hopeful. 'Do you get to stay tomorrow night and watch me pitch?'

'I wouldn't miss it for the world.'

I leaned forward and took his lips in a slow, seductive kiss. My body was already primed for him since I'd been sitting there waiting for him. In those thirty minutes, I had gotten myself worked up thinking about what we'd do when he got home. The kiss poured lighter fluid onto the fire. He hummed when our lips parted.

'I want to take you in my bed.' He stood and plucked me out of the chair. He carried me in long strides to his bedroom. I'd lit a few candles and pulled down the covers, so all he had to do was lay me on the bed and crawl under the blankets with me.

He stripped quickly as I waited for him on the soft sheets where I writhed and squirmed with a need that bordered on painful. Each piece of clothing that left his body revealed another chiseled muscle, another inch of tanned skin.

He climbed in and pulled the sheets over our heads so that we were cocooned in our own tent of lust and need. He slipped into me easily. Both our backs arched at the first glorious penetration. A layer of sweat covered our skin under the blanket, our skin sliding freely as he bucked into me.

'Let's see how flexible my girl is,' he said through gritted teeth.

He pushed his upper body off me and reached behind him to pull both my legs over his shoulders. He leaned forward, bending me in two. In this position, he shoved into me to a depth that made me scream.

'Landon! God! Landon!' I repeated as he used his weight to drive into me. A look of pure, unbridled lust spread across his face. His eyes hooded, and sweat made the hairs at his temples cling to his cheekbones. My nails dug into his elbows as he rode me.

'So deep,' he murmured as his teeth brushed along the insides of my ankles. Somehow, in this chaotic mess of limbs and hands and lips, his thumb found my center. He pressed as he rocked into me, the dual sensations sending me into an orgasm that brought him over with me.

He let my legs fall to the side as he collapsed on top of me. His hot breath panted on my neck as he peppered soft kisses along my collarbone.

'I'd love to come home to this every day,' he whispered.

Every cell in my body wanted to be the one he came home to. 'Let's do it.'

His kiss stilled. 'What?'

'What if I just told the university to find someone else to teach those courses? What if I took an extension on my dissertation? I could live here in Dallas for three months until the playoffs are over.'

I felt his heavy sigh before he lifted his head. His lips feathered against mine as he brushed sweat-soaked hair from my face. His eyes blinked lazily. 'You make me want to be selfish. I want that more than you know, but I'm not sure –'

I anticipated his objection and cut it off. 'Fuck it. I want to do it for us. We're miserable apart. I can't sleep without you next to me. I can't do any of the work I should be doing because I'm thinking about this.' I gestured between our sweaty bodies. 'I'm *addicted* to you.'

He pulled away from me and rolled to the side of the bed so fast I cried out. He pulled on his jeans and sat on the bed with his head in his hands.

'What's wrong? Landon? Look at me.' I tried to crawl up behind him and wrap my arms around him. The muscles in his back tensed and he held his breath.

'Talk to me,' I begged.

His cheeks puffed out when he released his breath. 'I

can't let you do that.'

I pulled away from him and wrapped myself in the sheet. 'Why the hell not? It's my decision to make.'

'Because I can't let you do that to yourself.' I thought that was his simple answer, but he added, more angrily, 'You've worked too hard to throw it all away.'

I scoffed. 'It was just an expression. I meant …'

The tension in the room doubled despite my attempt to play it off. 'That you couldn't help yourself? You couldn't stay away despite your best attempts? How can you be so callous towards the goals and dreams you've had for years? How is it so easy for you to throw it all away?' With each question, his voice grew louder and firmer. 'Sounds like an addiction to me. I'd bet tomorrow night's start that you don't know the first thing about *addiction*. It's ugly. It's a festering wound that never heals. It will eat away at us until we have nothing left, and I won't have that.'

I couldn't help the snide tone that filled my voice. 'And you do know about it, I suppose. Hmm?' I added when he didn't answer as fast as I wanted. 'One of those dark corners you haven't explored with me? You make me share mine, but won't do the same?'

I moved to the edge of the bed, done with him and this conversation. *This* was why I never allowed myself to get involved. With the sheet still wrapped around me, I walked to the closet for a set of decent clothes.

'Stop,' he commanded. Then his voice softened. 'I'll tell you. Just sit down.'

I sat and waited for what felt like an eternity. I tried to calm my breaths that seemed so loud in the quiet room. The silence vibrated around us as his hands gripped fistfuls of his hair. I stared at his back while he spoke looking at the carpet. His swallow was audible before he began. 'I grew up in a two-parent household that was the envy of the neighborhood. My dad was a deacon in the church, my mom a schoolteacher. They doted on me. Dad coached our baseball teams and mom brought the Rice Krispie bars for a treat after the games. What no one saw was that they were both addicts. One drink on a Friday night turned into three on Saturday, and soon they were drinking every night. Even though they were functional at the beginning, by the time I was twelve they were irritable without at least a six pack between them nightly.'

'I'm sorry. I didn't –'

He shook his head for me to stop talking, so I did. I knew as well as anyone that once you were on a roll, it was easier to just keep going. 'The worst part came later when the abuse started, although I didn't have that label for it then.'

I sucked in a breath to say something, but held it in.

He continued, 'It's not what you think. It was verbal and emotional. They never hit me or my sister. I think that my dad knew if he hit my sister I would have ended him. I tried to shield my younger sister Mia from the worst of their abuse when I could tell they'd been drinking for hours. I'd pick a fight so that they'd hurl all of their terrible insults towards me. They called me all the vulgar names they could think of. I was never good enough. Never tried hard enough. Couldn't practice enough. Allowed one more hit than I should have. No matter what I did, I was *never* enough.'

'So that's why you don't drink.'

'That and the fact that my mother died of liver cancer years later. Despite the fact that both of them were in and out of detox more times than I could count, they couldn't give it up. Alcohol made them into hateful, angry people I didn't even recognize. My grandma, who took us in when they went into detox, said she didn't even know her own daughter. She'd help me remember the better times before it got bad, like the trips to Disney World and the ocean. But everything was soured by the fact that they chose the alcohol over our family. And you know the thing that made me the maddest?'

I shook my head even though he couldn't see it.

'I still loved them despite it all. I craved their attention. I craved their praise. I would have forgiven them in a heartbeat had they given it up. And that made me hate myself for the longest time.'

I scooted towards him. 'You have a good heart, Landon. Is that who you point to before you take the mound?'

I saw the wince he tried to hide from me. 'Yes.'

He finally raised his head and looked at me. His eyes were bloodshot, and there were heavy, dark circles under his eyes. 'So now you know why I don't drink. And now you know why I can't let you come here full time.'

'It was just an expression, Landon. I'm not addicted –'

'They swore they weren't either. But I *heard* it in your voice. There was anger in the way you said it, like if you could help it you would. If you could make a different decision, you would. Earlier you even said you "couldn't stay away this weekend".'

He crawled across the bed and sat in front of me, his hands folded in his lap. His teeth grinded together before he said, 'I want you here with me not because you can't stay away, but because you wouldn't want to be anywhere else. As romantic as it sounds to be addicted to someone, I don't want you to be. Because while you need me, you don't *want* to need me. Soon, you'll resent me for needing me. Then what? What are we left with?'

'I won't resent you.' It was a lie. I knew it. I tried to make myself believe it, but the truth burned inside my chest. If I had no career, no PhD I'd worked years for, I wouldn't be proud of who I was.

'You and I know that isn't true. You're making a rash decision you will at some point regret, choosing temporary satisfaction over who you really are.'

Fury bubbled in my blood at what felt like denial. For the first time, I'd wanted more with someone and I'd finally put my neck out to get it. And my offer had been shoved back, rejected immediately. Hurt mixed with anger, which had always made me unreasonable. 'Well, it would make for a really fun three months,' I snipped, trying to protect my emotions.

His brow furrowed as if in pain. 'Is that all you want? A fun three months? I'll tell you right now, I wanted more than that. More than temporary.'

He'd used past tense. Did he no longer want more?

Worry turned to anger. It was so uncomfortable to hear him express his honest emotions when it felt like he was pushing me away. I felt the need to lash out at him, to hurt him. 'Well, Einstein. How do we get long term if we don't start with these three months? I was offering them to you on a silver platter. It was what *you* wanted, what you proposed back in Boulder!' I was screaming now, unable to control my emotions. I shook from the anger and adrenaline.

He fueled it more when he stared at me calmly like I could rage all I wanted and I wouldn't get a reaction out of him. 'Isn't love all about sacrifice?' I spat. 'Well, I was willing to sacrifice so that we could be together.'

He simply looked at me, which irritated me even more. 'Say something!' I yelled.

For a long time, he mulled over what he wanted to say, which made what he ended up saying even worse. 'I appreciate your willingness to sacrifice your career and life to come be with me. I really do. But if the sacrifice makes you give up what you really are, if what accompanies it might turn into resentment and animosity, that will be the end of us.' Then he turned the knife in my already wounded heart. 'And you don't want to end up like your mother.'

I sucked in a breath that actually hurt. 'What the fuck

did you just say?'

He sighed, resigned to sink with the ship. 'Your mother gave up her life to travel with your father. She had no passions of her own. No life outside of him. She had an amazing daughter, and because of her resentfulness, she couldn't even recognize the blessings she had. Her life was clearly filled with regret. I won't let that happen to you. And to us.'

'You asshole!' I screamed, tears dripping down my cheeks as I threw on my clothes and grabbed my purse. I was happy to leave everything else if it meant I could be out of his place a second faster. 'I'm nothing like my mother.'

I ran out of the room on legs made of rubber. I slipped on my shoes, found the rental car keys, and flew to the door. I hated him with almost every cell in my body. The few other rogue ones desperately wanted him to follow me, to run after me, to beg me to forgive him for what he said.

I looked over my shoulder as I opened the door. He leaned against the doorway to his bedroom, one of his forearms propped above his head. He watched me leave with a distant expression that gave away nothing. I recognized it as a defense mechanism he'd probably learned in the face of his raging, alcoholic parents.

And although my mother had taught me very little, one thing I learned from her was how to walk away from someone you cared about without looking back. And I did just that.

Chapter Nineteen

On the plane ride home, I opened my laptop, spurred to write my dissertation for the first time in a long while. On some level, I'd sensed the happy ending I planned for Simon and Charlotte felt too easy, too cheap. Nothing that good was ever so effortless, so simple.

'Are you sure?' Charlotte asked Mrs Andrews. She'd brought over some of her cranberry muffins as promised since Mr Andrews had provided her a ride into town in his carriage a fortnight ago.

Mrs Andrews spread butter onto the warm muffins. Her tea cup clinked against its saucer. 'I'm sure, dear. Mr Andrews saw the sign himself just the other day.'

Charlotte's world tumbled around her. Her ribs strained against the stays in the corset as she fought to take a breath. The Jaspar building had been put up for sale again. No one in town knew why the prospective buyer backed out. In fact, only a handful of people in the town even knew who the prospective buyer was.

Even Mrs Andrews didn't know the implications of the news she'd shared. 'Are you not feeling well, dear? You're awfully pale.'

'Just tired. I think I will need to take leave now. Thank you for your hospitality,' Charlotte said as she made her way to the porch.

'Take care of yourself, Miss Heywood!' Mrs Andrews called from the door as Charlotte walked quickly down the path towards home.

Charlotte's legs gave way under an apple tree. Some of

its ripened fruit had fallen off its branches already. The fallen fruit left bright red stains on her dress as she sat in the shade. She ran and re-ran through her mind the last conversation she'd had with Simon before he left. Surely, she hadn't assumed false interest. He'd clearly intimated he was coming to Willingden for her. He'd spoken of marriage. He'd promised communication within the month, and although that time had not passed in its entirety, she hadn't received any letter. Surely such an event as the non-purchase of the Jaspar building warranted some communication. The lack of it turned her shock to anger.

Confused and jilted, Charlotte found strength to stand and weave between the trees up to the walkway and to her front door. 'Charlotte!' Mrs Heywood cried when she saw the state of her daughter's stained dress. She instantly called for the younger siblings, requiring their help to get Charlotte up to her bed and properly redressed for bed, a necessity given Charlotte's unusually pale complexion.

When the room had cleared, Mrs Heywood dropped a note on her daughter's bedstand. Charlotte stared at the letter. She was thankful for the communication, yet she dreaded what she knew she'd find inside. The letter stared back at her, daring her to open it. Near midnight, she read his words in the flicker of a single candle.

Dearest Charlotte,

I apologize for the time that has passed since you have heard from me. As you probably know, the country has experienced a difficult economic time, which presents new challenges for my business. Thus, my full attention is needed in London for the foreseeable future. I will not be able to visit you in Willingden as I had planned. I want you to know that my interest in our marriage was sincere. I always intended to come for you, to wind our lives together. For a few weeks a year, you would have shown me Willingden, and all the joys of country living, and for the rest of the year I would have shown you London, and all the pleasures of art, music, and culture it has to offer. But it is unfair of me to ask you to wait for me as I do not know when time will allow me to bridge the distance between us. But know in the time that does pass, I will remain fondly

Yours, S

Even though she anticipated the pain that was coming, she hadn't adequately prepared herself for it. It dug under her skin and seared the edges of her heart. It peeled back her nails and poured alcohol on the exposed tissue. This was a sore that would leave life-long scars. She picked up her journal and wrote furiously in it, the pain surprisingly easy to put into words. Then she blew out her candle and waited for the sun to rise.

On Saturday afternoon, I debated for an hour whether or not I was going to turn on ESPN at six o'clock to watch Landon pitch against the Yankees. My simmering anger hoped that I'd turn on the screen to find him down big and looking like hell. Other parts, though, hoped that what happened between us the night before didn't show on the field. Man, if it didn't, wouldn't that hurt too?

I realized it was a lose-lose situation. If he was doing well, I'd be unhappy. If he was doing poorly, I'd also be unhappy. So at four o'clock, I decided to cut my losses and get wasted.

But as luck would have it, I'd just popped open my first beer when my dad called. 'Hey. Just callin' to see what you're up to,' he started. He always had good Dad radar for times when his baby girl needed him.

'Nothing much.' I tried to hide my dour mood, but I

don't think it worked.

'Well, I haven't seen you in a while, and I was hoping you'd come to dinner with me tonight. An old friend of mine, Daniel, is in town tonight, and he said he'd love to see the two of us again. You might not remember him, but –'

'I remember Daniel, Dad. How could I not? He helped raise me. In fact, I ran into him in San Francisco a few weeks ago at a Stars game. Why is he not in Dallas now? They're playing tonight.'

'He said he was doing some scouting here in Colorado. He doesn't have to be with the team every day. In fact, I bet he flies across the country more times than the team does.'

'I had no idea.' I debated whether or not to lie and say I was busy. I didn't really feel like being around people tonight even though it was my dad. And I especially didn't want to be around baseball people because it reminded me of *him*. 'Well, about dinner … I'm not sure …'

'Oh, Nina. Stop it. You're coming on a date with your old man. Now get all dressed up and meet me at seven.' He gave me the name and address of the restaurant and ended the call before I had time to protest.

'Damn,' I cursed into the phone even though the line was dead. I put the full, open beer back in the fridge even though it would taste awful by the time I got home later. 'Fuckin' great. Waste of a good beer.'

I dragged myself into the shower, chose an elegant black dress from the back of my closet, and finished my hair and make-up. My eyes looked tired despite my best efforts. When I reached for the perfume, the unexpected pang in my heart caught me off guard. I wilted to the floor where I sat against the wall and let the tears flow. My mascara ran down my face as I allowed myself to remember the good times. His competitive glare at the go-kart track. The whisper of his breath against my neck distracting me from winning at miniature golf. His humor. His fire. His possessiveness that melted me.

I wasn't ready to let go of my anger, and I still didn't understand why he felt so compelled to turn down my offer, but as I sat curled on the bathroom floor, I gave myself permission to miss him.

And I missed him so acutely that I gave myself license to wear the diamond necklace he'd bought for me in Chicago. I'd worn it every day since he bought it. Without it, the feeling of loss was too much for me to handle tonight. The white gold felt cool against my skin as I latched the necklace behind my neck. I fixed my make-up as best I could and used an extra spray of perfume along my collarbone. Convinced I looked as good as could be expected, I got in my car and drove to Denver.

'Nina, it's so good to see you again,' Daniel said as he stood from the bar stool next to my dad. 'You hungry?'

I nodded more out of obligation than anything.

He smiled. 'Good. Our table's ready.'

We wound our way through the dim main eating area towards a private corner booth that was shielded from most of the noise in the restaurant. A bottle of wine was already breathing on the table next to a glimmering candle that cast random rays of light around the leather, circular booth.

I sat down first. My dad sat to my right, Daniel to my left.

Daniel poured each of us a glass of wine as we opened our menus. I took a sip of the crisp Riesling as I decided between the salmon and the lamb. Thank goodness I'd swallowed it before Daniel said to me, 'I wasn't sure if you'd even be in town tonight.'

'Why wouldn't she be?' Dad asked, and I winced. I'd told him I was dating Landon, but he didn't know I'd basically spent the last two weeks following him around the country. Daniel knew, because I'd seen him at many of the games.

Daniel looked at me wide-eyed. His eyes begged me to bail him out. 'The Stars are playing the Yankees in Dallas tonight, and Landon is pitching. It's a big game, so maybe he thought I would go,' I explained.

My dad's forehead crinkled even more than his usual coach scowl. 'Oh? I didn't know you had traveled to many of his games.'

Whoops. Busted. I looked to Daniel. Thankfully, he thought quickly. 'Just one here or there. Now, what do you say we share an appetizer? What looks good?' My dad's attention turned to the menu, and I met Daniel's eyes over the top of our menus. He winked at me before he read the options aloud.

We agreed on the shrimp and ordered the main course. While we waited for the appetizer, Dad and Daniel caught up on each other's lives. They talked about how the Stars were doing, how the Raptors were faring, and how baseball players just weren't made the same way as they used to be, a comment that made me chuckle under my breath. I remembered how Landon had said that Coach Craig was just too old-school before he knew Coach Craig was my dad.

As I listened, I rolled the diamond necklace between my fingers. Daniel's eyes narrowed on my fingers. I watched as his brain figured out who had given me that necklace. I surely didn't have the money for it, and Dad wouldn't have picked out such an expensive present.

He smiled and lifted his eyes to mine. He folded his hands on the table, a gesture that was more formal than he'd been all night. He cleared his throat, and my sixth sense told me something was up.

I was right.

'So, I have to tell you two the real reason for my visit, although it is nice to catch up,' Daniel said.

'Real reason?' My dad asked, on guard for the first time tonight.

Daniel took a deep breath. 'Ever since I saw Nina in San Francisco, an idea has been bugging me, and I can't let it go without talking to you two about it. I've run it by the upper management, and they are on board.'

'What on earth –' my dad started, and I stilled him by placing my hand on his forearm. His hand quickly squeezed mine as we turned our attention back to Daniel.

Daniel smiled at our held hands. 'I'm glad you two are still so close. That's what gives me hope that maybe you'll agree …' he paused.

'Good Lord, just spit it out,' I said, exasperated, and everyone laughed, thankful for the levity.

'The Stars organization is hoping that both of you will agree to join our family.'

Silence.

'Come again?' I managed to sputter.

'We want to promote Craig to be the bullpen manager for the Stars. We've been looking for an experienced coach for a while now …' My dad dropped his eyes to his lap, and when he did that, I knew he'd been offered this position before. '… and we think Craig would be the perfect fit.'

My dad didn't say anything when Daniel paused. In fact, he didn't even look up. Daniel continued, 'And Nina, we've been trying to hire for a Director of Public Relations forever, but we can't find the right candidate. One candidate knows social media well, but can't write a press release. Another can write, but doesn't know anything about baseball. Many others have young families and aren't willing to travel with the team. Still, others I wouldn't put in front of a camera to save my life. I think that you'd be the perfect fit.'

'Wait, wait, wait.' I held up my hand. 'You're saying you want me to be a Director of Public Relations? I'm so far from a business major it isn't even funny. You do realize my specialty is nineteenth-century literature, right?'

Daniel smiled and leaned back as the waitress brought our food to the table. Even though my salmon smelled divine, I didn't give it a second thought. My mind was too overloaded to process anything.

When the waitress left, Daniel explained, 'I understand there might be a learning curve for you, but you have everything we want. You are obviously a strong writer, one that can spin things with careful language when we need to. You can edit anything that is released to the media. If we sit you down with our lawyers, you won't need to ask what a 'clause' is.'

'What? Someone actually did that?'

Daniel rolled his eyes. 'Yes. He lasted two days. Anyway, you're smart, you're a strong writer, you've grown up around baseball, and ... you have a few reasons to travel with the team.'

I did. Well, more accurately, before last night, I did. I had to make a decision whether to lie and say Landon and I were still together or explain to them we'd parted ways. I opted to let them assume we were still together.

My first instinct was to politely decline the generous offer for multiple reasons. It would be terrible to travel with the team because my path was sure to cross Landon's multiple times a week, and that would be, at first, painful and, later, just awkward. What would it be like to see him wrap his arms around another woman? God forbid, what if I had to write a press release in a few years about his engagement?

That alone was reason enough to decline the position, but I had other reasons too. I also worried if life on the road was a good choice for my dad's health. While I might be able to keep a better eye on him, I still suspected that the added stress of the new job wasn't a good idea.

Most importantly, it was a job I didn't really think I'd

ever want. Up until recently, I never gave a thought to be anything other than a professor. I never thought anything else would fulfill me. Wouldn't taking this job make me feel like I'd wasted years getting a PhD I'd never use? And, of course, there was the little problem that I'd already accepted a temporary position until the end of the year.

I opened my mouth, ready to voice my thoughts. But I paused when Daniel's smile softened and his eyes glistened with unshed tears. I snapped my head to my right where my dad sat. His eyes were still focused on his lap, but the tears coursing down his cheeks couldn't be mistaken.

Dad finally lifted his chin. His red eyes met mine as he tried to wipe away the tears. He smiled at me, regretfully, like he was trying to silently apologize for crying at dinner.

'Oh, Daddy.' I slid over to him and fell into his chest. His arm wrapped around my back as his shoulder shook under me.

'Excuse me,' Daniel said, leaving the table to give us a moment.

I wet my dad's dress shirt with my own tears, overcome by my dad's rare show of emotion. He sniffed a few times before he tilted my chin upwards. My blurry eyes met his red ones.

'I want you to do what's right for you, baby girl, and no one else.'

'Will you accept the job if I don't?'

'Honestly? No. I won't leave you.' He shook his head vehemently. 'But I don't want you to take this offer just because of me. I'm happy where I am too.'

'Oh God.' I buried my cheek into his chest again, overwhelmed with the weight of a decision I hadn't ever contemplated. Dad let me lean against him for a while longer before he lifted his shoulder.

'Your dinner is getting cold,' he said. I sat up and scooted over to my plate. My appetite was gone, but I picked up the fork and knife and attempted to eat under my dad's watchful gaze.

Daniel returned to the table, quickly gauging our mood. He placed his napkin on his lap, and we all ate a few bites in silence.

I knew they were all waiting for me to say something. 'I'll think about it,' I said, before I'd realized it came out of my mouth. Was I really going to consider it? For my dad, I had to.

Daniel nodded. 'That's all I ask. You two would start full-time in January next year. Our current employees are contracted through that time. You would, of course, need to find places to live in Dallas and travel would start with the team in April. All your expenses would be taken care of by the team, naturally. If you're interested, I can forward you the formal job descriptions as well as the salary range, which is negotiable. Is there anything I can add that will sway your minds?'

'No. You've been very kind and generous. I'll let you know in two weeks. Is that OK?'

'That's fine. Dessert?' He asked us.

When we both declined, Daniel requested the bill. He paid for the meal and led us through the restaurant to the front entrance. He turned and shook both of our hands before he walked to his Audi and drove away.

I watched him leave, allowing myself time to gather my thoughts. 'Dad. I don't know ...' was all I was able to come up with.

'Shh, none of that now. We'll talk later.'

He walked me to my car and kissed my forehead. 'Good luck on your race this weekend. I wish more than anything I could be there for you, but you know we have a game.'

'I understand, Dad.'

He closed my door and patted the roof of the car twice. 'Drive safe, my girl.'

Chapter Twenty

Friday night in Idaho springs, I picked up my race packet and my running number. After I went to the pasta feast to gorge myself on guiltless carbs, I returned to my hotel room and curled up in bed at eight o'clock.

Despite the fact I told myself I needed to fall asleep, I couldn't. My mind meandered from one worry to another. Had I trained enough? Had I drunk enough water today? Did I taper off my runs enough in the last week so I could make the 13.1 miles? Did I bring the right clothes for the cool temperatures?

Of course I was worried about other things, too. I hadn't heard from Landon at all, and I didn't bother to contact him. The radio silence spoke volumes. We were clearly over. That was never more evident than the last few days when he didn't call to wish me good luck with the half marathon. He didn't call to ask what hotel he should stay at or what mile marker I wanted to see him at.

'There's nothing that will keep me from being there to support you,' he'd said weeks ago. It turned out there *was* something that would keep him from coming. Today would have been easier if I knew that I'd see him at the finish line. But I knew he wouldn't be there not only because we'd fought, but because he started tonight in Dallas.

And to top it all off, I hadn't been able to come to a conclusion about Daniel's job offer. Had Landon and I still been together, I would have been more likely to accept it. But I didn't want to spend every day tip-toeing around, trying to avoid Landon in the hallways or making sure that

I sat on the other end of the plane or bus. I knew I had to make a decision soon – not only did it affect me, but also my dad.

I'm not sure which worry ended the night for me, but I drifted off into a troubled, restless sleep. I woke before my alarm, thankful that battle was over.

Now it was time for a new one. I wasn't running the half marathon for a medal. Hell, I knew I wouldn't compete in my age bracket. I was more competing against myself, pushing my body to where I'd never pushed it before. Running this distance was as much of a mental challenge as a physical challenge. My body was ready; even though I liked to think of myself as tough, I still had my doubts. Especially with the stress of the last week.

I took a shower, tied my hair back, and clipped up any hairs that might fall into my face as I started to sweat. I taped the back of my heel and the knuckles on my big toes since those were the places I normally got blisters. I dressed in layers. Two sports bras were covered with a short-sleeve shirt. Over the top, I wore a sweat-wicking long-sleeve jacket. Nothing I put on was my favorite since runners in marathons usually strip as they run and discard their unneeded clothes along the course. I laced up my shoes and pulled on my running gloves. My hands always got cold no matter the temperatures. I hydrated with two bottles of water. I managed to choke down half a bagel before my nervous stomach protested anymore.

I boarded the bus outside my hotel that shuttled runners from Idaho Springs up the mountain to Georgetown where the race would begin. Almost the entire course was downhill, thank God, which was one reason why I chose this run. I would run from an elevation of 8500 feet in Georgetown to 7500 feet by the finish line.

The chilly fifty degree weather cooled my heated skin as I stepped off the shuttle. I pinned my yellow racing number to my stomach and stretched the back of my legs. I chatted with a few fellow runners under the inflated arch that marked the starting line. I popped my favorite gum into my mouth like I always did when I ran long distance. My mouth watered with the first chew. I tucked my iPod into the specially-designed pocket of my shorts and turned on the song that always started my runs, 'On Top of the World'.

I was at least seven-hundred people back at eight a.m. when the race started. The more serious runners who were focused on winning were in the front. When the race started, the wave of bobbing heads began at the front and worked its way to me. My legs itched to move, to follow the movement of the crowd.

I could tell from the first hundred strides that I had taken off too quickly. I wasn't striding with the upbeat music in my ear I usually paced myself to. I tried to dial back my strides, to focus on gaining my own rhythm, which was so easy to do when I was by myself. But in the middle of thousands of people, I struggled. While I loved the pace now, I knew it would catch up with me in the last few miles.

The scenery couldn't have been more beautiful, though. The course was iconic, following a frontage road along Clear Creek. It hugged the creek as it wound through the valley between rolling green hills and towering rock walls. I turned the corner with the steep grade at the end of the first mile, completely surprised I had already run that far.

The half mile of gravel in the second mile troubled me. With each footstep, small pieces of rock crunched under my shoes, giving me a different feel than concrete as I pushed off the ball of my foot.

The sun warmed my back as I turned a corner. I smiled as the sun made my shadow appear ahead of me. I welcomed her like an old friend. I imagined she came out today so that she could see the rolling hills dotted with stubborn green trees. She liked hearing the creek trickle beside us. Her footsteps were heavy over the wooden bridge. She kept me company as I hit the first water station at the three mile mark, feeling strong and breathing well.

The throng of runners had spread out by this point, so I could better pace myself and enjoy the scenery without concern for who was going faster or how to pass a runner who slowed to a walk in front of me.

As I started the fourth mile, the sun had burned off the few clouds offering shade, so I stripped off my jacket and threw it on the side of the road. My T-shirt came off a mile later as sweat started to soak through my bras. A cramp in my right calf came and went without much trouble, but it reappeared in the arch of my right foot like a little goblin that was appearing and reappearing in the oddest places.

By the sixth mile, my breath was starting to fall behind my muscles that were screaming for more oxygen. I pulled over to the side and slowed to take in extra water. I knew this was the last stop for portable restrooms before the end of the course, so I peed quickly before jumping back on the course. I didn't like stopping, but I didn't like running with a full bladder more. I knew some runners went to the bathroom in their shorts, but that was where I drew the line.

Back on the course, my body thanked me for the short break. The mile and a half of dirt road that ended at the eight mile mark was the most beautiful of the course. In those isolated and peaceful moments, my body remembered why I loved running. I passed what looked like some abandoned gold mines on my right before I turned back onto the concrete at mile nine.

I hydrated and took in electrolytes one last time and began the run up the only significant hill on the course. My legs had become accustomed to the downhill glide, so when I started uphill, my lungs protested immediately. Had this hill been on mile two, I would have been OK. With my body hollering at me to stop, I tried to focus on the song in my ears or the thump-thump rhythm of my feet. But no matter what I tried, I couldn't control my erratic breath. I resorted to using my last mental trick, the strategy I used when I couldn't make one foot go in the front of the other.

I counted my steps.

Each time my right foot slapped the concrete, I counted. My first goal was thirty. My next goal was one-hundred steps. Breaking down the goal of running the last four miles into shorter, more attainable goals helped me avoid having to stop and walk.

I shook out my arms since my biceps were sore from holding up my pumping arms. I dropped my right arm first and wiggled my fingers for a few seconds to make the blood return to my hands. Then I did my left. I thought I made it through the worst of it when a sharp pain shot through my right hip for twenty consecutive strides, and I lost my concentration. 'Fuck,' I murmured under my breath. 'I might not make this.'

Then this sixth sense passed over me, chilling my sweaty skin until it goosebumped. It was like that creepy feeling when you walk through a spider web.

'You *will* make this,' the voice said beside me.

Landon jogged beside me.

I yelped in surprise. 'What are you doing here?'

'I told you I wouldn't miss it.' He matched his stride to mine. Casual as could be in cotton running shorts, a T-shirt, and his Oakleys wrapped around his eyes, he smiled at me like we hadn't said such horrible things to each other a week ago.

I licked my lips and brushed the sweaty hair from my face. 'But … you … have to … pitch … tonight.'

He maintained his stride as he circled his arm forward and around. 'I could have, but I have this pesky sore muscle right here,' he rubbed his right triceps, 'and my therapist and I agree that I needed an extra day's rest.' A mischievous grin spread across his face.

He'd skipped a start to come see me. When I thought we were clearly over.

Then he added, 'And getting off for one day wasn't as hard as I thought it would be. It seems that a certain Vice President has taken a liking to you. He practically shooed me onto the plane when I asked him for a day off to come see you.'

The idea that Daniel had a part in bringing us back together made me smile. I started to ask Landon if he knew of my job offer, but the question caught in my throat when a shot of pain stole my breath. I whimpered and rubbed my right hip. With each stride forward, I could feel the joint protest. 'This fucking hurts.'

'Mile ten, Nina. You're almost there. You can do it.'

He slowed and started to peel off.

'Wait! Where are you going?'

'I'll see you at the finish line. You need to do this by yourself. Trust your training.'

He spoke the last like an athlete who had to do that very thing. As he slowed and walked back to the parking lot where he must have parked his car with many of the other spectators along the route, he waved at me. I turned my head over my shoulder to watch him as long as I could. Then I turned forward, determined and focused.

Trust my training. I *had* worked hard to be able to run this. I *had* gotten up at six a.m. most Sunday mornings so I'd be ready. I *had* put in the mileage to get me through the next three.

I let my mind wander as my body went on autopilot. I was beyond surprised when my brain instantly went to my dissertation. My muse often came and went at odd times. Sometimes, she'd show up when I was blow-drying my hair or when I was folding laundry. But this was the first time she showed up when I was running. My brain downloaded the next chapter.

Charlotte's days had returned to normal after her sudden illness that was unexplained to everyone but herself and Mrs Heywood. For nearly two weeks, Charlotte had preferred to lie in bed and avoid polite company. Then one sunny Tuesday morning, her mother had thrown open the curtains and commanded her to get dressed. Then she began packing Charlotte's travel chest.

'What are you doing, mother?'

Mrs Heywood continued to carefully fold clothes into the wooden chest. 'Mr Heywood and I both agree that it is high-time that this family takes a holiday.'

'A holiday?' They'd never been able to afford one before.

'Yes. To London.' The very name of the town made her skin pepper with goosebumps.

Despite Charlotte's protests, Mr and Mrs Heywood and the eldest three siblings traveled the distance to London while the youngest siblings were cared for by their grandmother in Westfordshire.

They arrived in the bustle of the city on Thursday where they retired to their lodgings for the evening. In the following days, they attended multiple plays and toured numerous galleries and gardens.

In one such garden that bordered the Thames and was known for its exotic plants and hybrids, Charlotte stood next to her sister Elizabeth as they perused the rock garden. 'Miss Heywood?' His voice asked.

Both of Miss Heywoods turned, but only one knew who she was turning to. 'Mr Parker,' Charlotte said breathily.

He walked cautiously toward her like he was seeing a ghost. 'What are you doing in London?'

'My parents brought my sisters and I on a holiday. You look well,' she added politely.

'As do you,' he returned, although his eyebrows folded downwards. He seemed lost in thought for a moment

*before he recovered. 'I am here with ... my sister ... you
met her in ... Sanditon.' He gestured behind him to where
his sister apparently stood.*

*He stepped forward again and cleared his throat.
'Charlotte, I ...' He stopped himself when he realized
Elizabeth had not retired.*

*'Elizabeth, dear, would you mind fetching me the name
of that amazing purple flower in the next garden over?
You know, the one that smelled so strongly? I want to
plant some at home when we return.'*

*'Yes, Charlotte.' Elizabeth left with a curious glance
over her shoulder.*

*'We don't have much time, Mr Parker. You must hasten
what you have to say.'*

*He gestured for her to sit on a bench under an olive
tree. She perched herself on the edge, her back straight
and proper.*

'Charlotte, I –'

*'Was it really business that kept you away?' She
interrupted, getting to the heart of the matter.*

*His shoulders slumped as his gaze landed on his lap.
'Yes and no.'*

*Charlotte made to stand, the answer neither clear nor
helpful to her wounded heart.*

*'Wait,' he said quickly. The urgency in his voice made
her sit down again. 'I was detained in London on business.
That much was true. But I hesitated for other reasons as
well. I worried that maybe I was asking too much of you to
spend the majority of the year in London or traveling
throughout the country. That's a fine life for a bachelor,
but for a new wife? A family?' He shook his head. 'I
worried that I was taking a fish out of its water and
placing it on dry land. Would you have been happy?'*

'With you? Yes.'

Simon winced. 'Your answer is so quick it scares me.'

'Maybe you were simply taking a fish from a moss-

270

covered pond to a more beautiful one.'

'It might be more beautiful, but the fish was happy with the former. What happens when the luster of the beautiful one burned off? Would it miss the familiar?'

'The familiar can also be prosaic.'

'Could you still? Be happy? With me?' He pinched his eyes closed at the pain he anticipated from her answer.

'I don't know.'

'What has changed?'

'You pushed me away without talking to me. You made a decision you thought was best for both of us without my input. I don't trust you with my heart.'

'What can I do to earn it back?'

Elizabeth turned the corner and started talking before she realized the intimacy she was interrupting. 'Believe it or not, it's a form of a lilac. You would have never known it by looking at it because it looks like a tree, not a bush, but it's called a Miss Kim Lilac.'

Even a side ache in the next mile didn't faze me. I breathed through it, focusing on forcing out large exhales. As I turned the corner on to Colorado Boulevard, the crowds lined the streets. They cheered whoever passed by and held signs, some of which made me laugh for a good half mile. One sign read, "You actually paid to do this!" And the funniest was "Don't trust a fart after mile 11". I swear that sign actually got me through mile twelve.

The crowds lining the streets thickened for the last half mile. I could see the finish line in the distance, and it spurred me to pick up my stride and sprint the last hundred yards. For miles, I'd dreamed of what it would feel like to be done, to not have to put one foot in front of the other, but as I crossed the finish line, I had trouble stopping. My muscles wanted to stride and ached as I tried to pull them back.

When I finally slowed to a gentle walk, the triumph set

in. I'd done it, and I was proud. The feeling of cashing in on all my hard work was more gratifying than I thought it would be.

The volunteers at the finish line handed me a finisher's medal and directed us to the tables of food. Some offered chocolate milk, others oranges, but the table with the most runners surrounding it was what I headed for. This race was known for serving cold slices of watermelon at the finish line, so I headed for that table and grabbed a slice.

The cold juice instantly cooled my mouth as it dripped down my chin. As the sweetness slid down my throat, I closed my eyes and hummed.

Strong, tanned arms wrapped around my neck and shoulders from behind. 'I'm so proud of you,' he whispered in my ear as he rocked me side to side.

I didn't bother to open my eyes. I tilted my head backwards so that it rested on the top of his shoulder. 'Thanks for being there. I really needed it.'

'I'll always be there for you, Nina.'

The vow confused me. Was he talking as a friend? A lover? A boyfriend? I sighed. 'Landon, I –'

'Hush. This moment isn't about us. It's about you. We have a lot of talking to do, but right now, you're going to just enjoy this.'

With Landon by my side, I did.

Chapter Twenty-one

We celebrated the entire day. Landon bought me a beer at a pub in Idaho Springs where competitors gathered after completing the run. He walked with me back to my hotel even though I more crawled than walked. My muscles were already tightening up and I could tell I would be sore tomorrow.

When we got to my hotel room door, Landon shoved his hands in his pockets and looked at the ground. 'You want to come in?' I asked.

I didn't miss the relieved smile even in the dim hallway. 'I was hoping you'd invite me.'

I'd let him in my hotel room, but letting him into my heart would be a lot harder. I sighed and unlocked the door. The air conditioner hummed to life when he stepped in, which made my still damp skin feel like it was tightening around me. 'I need a shower. Turn on the TV and order a pizza. You know what I like.'

As I walked to the bathroom, I heard as he picked up the phone and called the front desk for the number of a local pizza place. I shut and locked the bathroom door before I peeled off my disgusting sports bra and shorts. I stripped off my shoes and socks next. The skin on the top of my feet was rubbed raw, which stung when I stepped into the hot spray.

I stood unmoving for what felt like forever. I had no motivation to lift my arms and wash my hair. I closed my eyes and let the spray beat down on my chest and neck as I remembered what it felt like to cross the finish line. I let my mind soak up that victory before I moved on to the next. My heart thumped in my chest when I recalled the moment I heard Landon's voice beside me.

'Nina? You OK in there? It's been half an hour.' Landon's voice called through the open door. The door handle jiggled as he tested it.

I shut off the water. 'Yeah. Sorry. It felt too good to get out.'

'OK, no problem,' he said, his voice retreating from the doorway. 'Pizza's here!' he yelled.

I dried off and wrapped the towel around me so that I could get clothes from my luggage. Landon was just closing the door, pizza in hand, when I turned the corner. He glanced at the towel covering me. His eyes darkened for a moment before he turned his back and gave me privacy.

While I appreciated his gesture, it also saddened me. How far we'd fallen in such a short time. A big part of me wanted him to stride over to me and rip the towel from my chest. But I knew that wouldn't fix anything; in fact, what would surely follow would probably make it worse.

I chose a T-shirt and cotton lounge pants from my luggage, put them on, and sat on one side of the king bed. He turned back to me when he heard the creak of the bed as it took my weight.

He sat on the other side of the bed and placed the pizza box in the middle. He sat down two bottles of water and Gatorade next to it and opened the box. He must have gone to the lobby when I was in the shower. That detail made the edges of my heart melt. He twisted off the cap of the Gatorade and handed it to me.

'Here, I thought you might want this.' He looked so tentative, so unsettled that I took the bottle from his hand, laid it on the nightstand, and crawled across the bed to him. The need to comfort him, to make things right, was so much stronger than any of the anger I had left.

His face softened further as he saw me come to him. In

slow motion, I saw when a look of absolute agony crossed his face. It gave way to a gracious, grateful smile. I buried my chin in his chest as he hugged me tight to him like he wished he'd never let go.

'Oh, Nina.' His voice sounded like a plea. 'I'm so sorry. I was such a dick to bring up your mother at a time like that. You're nothing like her. You're a gracious, caring person who gives of herself to other people.'

It was my turn, and I felt ready. 'I'm sorry for cursing at you. My anger is something I've never been able to dial back once it gets rolling. You didn't deserve it.'

The kiss to the top of my head told me my apology was accepted.

'What are we going to do, though? I don't understand how we can make this work even though I desperately want us to,' he said. 'But I won't have you giving up –'

I sat up and pressed my finger to his lips. 'Maybe I don't have to,' I whispered.

He didn't blink. 'What are you saying?'

'For the next three months, I'm going to finish my dissertation and get my PhD. I'm going to teach the classes I committed myself to. You're going to pitch the Stars deep into the playoffs. And I'm going to come to as many games as I can without sacrificing the responsibilities I have in Boulder.'

'And after those three months?'

I took a deep breath and jumped off the cliff. 'I'm going to work for the Stars.'

His chin jutted forward in shock. 'What?'

I started by telling him about Daniel, who he was to me as a kid and what he was offering me now. I told him of my dad's reaction and the worries I had over taking the position. 'I'll have to talk to the head of the English Department right away and tell her that I will only be able to do the one semester. If they need someone for the second semester, they'll have to find someone else. And I definitely want to finish my dissertation before I move to Dallas in January.'

'I agree. Absolutely,' he said, shell-shocked. 'But what about leaving Boulder? Your friends. Your church. You love it there.'

'I will miss them, but it doesn't mean I can't visit.'

'Visit,' he repeated with an exhausted smile. 'Fucking perfect.' His head hit the wall behind him. His eyes closed and he shook his head back and forth.

'What's wrong?'

He opened his eyes and stared at me. 'I bought a house in Denver.'

It was my turn to be shocked. We'd broken up. 'Why would you do that?'

'We needed to cool off that night, but I never intended on letting you go. If I had to quit pitching and coach in Colorado somewhere I would have.'

'And I wouldn't have let you.'

'Now you know what I felt in Dallas.'

'Yes,' I whispered. 'I guess I do.'

He let that understanding swirl between us for a full minute.

'Do you want to sell it now I'm moving to Dallas?' I finally asked.

'No. We'll just call that our winter home. We'll go skiing and snowboarding in the winter, and you can be closer to your friends and church.'

'I cannot believe you bought a house.'

He smiled and I swear his chest puffed out an inch. 'I couldn't pass it up. It's a really pretty house,' he joked before his smile sobered and his jaw muscles bunched.

'But Nina, is it work you want to do? What about being a professor?'

I shrugged and opened the box. I picked up a slice and took a bite. It was delicious despite the fact that it was lukewarm. 'That job lost its luster for me a long time ago.

And, if after a year with the Stars I decide I want to teach again, nothing says that I can't pursue that. But taking this job now allows me to be around you and my dad and the game I've always loved. It lets me be a professional with my own career, my own goals, my own successes and failures. It lets me come to you without the resentment you feared.'

I paused, struggling to communicate my feelings. I ended up simply saying, 'I'm excited to start this chapter.'

Chapter Twenty-two

I started the final chapter of my dissertation on the plane ride down to Dallas a month later.

Charlotte smiled and popped the seal on the third letter from Simon this week. He was coming to Willingden to finalize the purchase of the Jaspar building and to ask for Mr Heywood's permission to marry his eldest daughter.

Much to Charlotte's amazement, the anger she felt towards Simon had melted quickly after they met in the garden. When she allowed her anger to fade, she was able to concede that maybe she had been too quick, too eager to agree to move her life to London. The trip had taught her that, although London was a lovely place to visit, she would miss the quiet country life of her childhood; this was still something that had to be ironed out. Simon had been, it turned out, wise to be cautious.

His coach arrived late afternoon on Friday. Dressed in her finest lace, she stood by the door and waited for him to mount the steps to her. The heels of his boots clacked against the wooden steps. His unguarded smile and regal air sent her stomach twisting.

One boot rested on the top step next to her, and with the other a step below, his eyes were level with hers. 'Charlotte, my love, I have something to show you, but first I must talk to your father.'

She nodded as he passed, and just before he entered through the front doorway, he stopped and turned to look at her one more time. 'You look stunning, my dear.'

He entered without hearing her whispered 'thank you.'

Mr Heywood greeted him with a firm handshake and gestured for Simon to precede him into the study. The door shut with a barely audible click.

Thirty minutes later, Charlotte sat next to Simon in his carriage as they drove towards town. Simon hadn't said anything about his meeting with her father, and she desperately wanted to know. 'How –' she started.

He cut her off. 'All is well,' he said simply as his palm patted her leg. He drove them into town where they stopped in front of the Jaspar building. He lifted her down from the carriage, making sure that her dress did not snag on the final step. He produced a rusted key from his pocket. It jangled when he inserted it into the lock, but the door shoved open easily. The dusty interior was desperately in need of cleaning and upkeep since it had been vacant for so long.

'This will be the waiting area for the office,' Simon began. He walked around the room, detailing the various renovations that needed to be made. Then he led them to the back of the room to a narrow staircase. He gestured for her to go up first. Because of the dim lighting, Charlotte could not see clearly enough to dodge the cobwebs that brushed her face.

Simon stood next to her on the second floor landing. The wide open space was empty and dusty. He walked over to the front of the room whose large windows overlooked the street below.

'It needs some work, but I thought this would make a wonderful bedroom someday.'

'A bedroom?'

He didn't answer her question. Instead, he took five long strides to the right. 'And this would be a lovely nursery.'

Charlotte's eyes filled with tears, and although she couldn't see every detail of Simon, she could see his

outline as he walked towards her and bent on to one knee.
'I bought this building so that our business could be
downstairs and we could live above it. We can make it our
own. You can decorate it how you like. It's a blank slate, a
dirty one right now,' he smiled, 'but it's all ours if you'll
have me.'

'What about London?'

He shrugged. 'We can work out the particulars, but I'm
thinking five months in London, five months here.'

'And the other months?'

His smiled deepened. 'I get to show you the world.
Before we start a family, we can spend a fortnight in Rome
or wherever else you want to go. There's so much more to
explore in this world than stuffy English sitting rooms.'

When she didn't say anything more, he asked, 'Would
you do me the honor of being my wife, my traveling
companion, and some day the mother of my children?'

Charlotte knelt by him on the floor and laid her wet
cheek on his shoulder. 'I have only one request.'

'What's that?'

'I want to fill our garden with Miss Kim Lilacs.'

I saved the file, closed down the computer, and looked out
the small, oval window. I hoped I'd done Simon and
Charlotte's story justice by capturing what I think Austen
was trying to write in the fresh, new setting of Sanditon. I
closed my eyes, once again able to envision the ill and
dying Jane madly writing whenever her weakened body
allowed. I envisioned that she had her final hero and
heroine be able to do what she wished she had. She'd
spent her life largely devoid of significant travel. She'd
read about different places but never seen them, and I can
imagine Jane sitting in her drawing room, wishing she'd
traveled more. That's what dying people do, right? They
don't wish they'd bought more stuff. They don't wish
they'd had more parties. They wished they'd seen more of

the world with the time they had. Even now, when people get terminal diagnoses, what do they do? They go see the world with the time they have left. Maybe that's what she wanted for her heroine, to have her see the world when she couldn't – to have her heroine live the life she wished she could have led.

The plane landed softly and taxied to the gate. I grabbed my luggage, found my rental car, and drove to the stadium. I sang along to the radio, tapping the steering wheel to the beat. I was happy, more at peace than I ever thought I could be.

Classes had started, and while I enjoyed what I was teaching, I was reassured every day that I'd made the right decision. Dr Moore understood when I told her I wouldn't be able to teach a second semester, and she added that the professor's cancer treatment was going better than expected, so a fill-in might not be needed at all.

Hannah, Jenn, and Ansley were the most shocked by the news. The day I told them, they all sat around the dinner table and stared at me like I'd grown horns.

'You're moving to Dallas to be with Landon?' Jenn asked.

'And you're going to be doing what?' Hannah added.

I simply laughed and told them I was happy. In the end, that's all they wanted for me, so they got on board quickly.

My dad wasn't as surprised as I thought he would be when I told him we were moving to Dallas. I told him as much, to which he replied, 'Dads always know, Nina.'

Daniel was beyond pleased that my dad and I had accepted the positions. After I'd broken the good news to him, I asked, 'So is this how you thought it would go?'

He paused, contemplating his words. 'When I saw ... those diamonds around your neck ... it gave me hope.'

It did me too – in the worst of times.

But as I turned the corner around the stadium and

parked in the reserved lot, I knew the best of times lay straight ahead. The university was on fall break, which gave me three straight days with Landon. Thankfully, the break coincided with Dallas home games and Landon's turn in the pitching rotation tonight.

Daniel met me at the employee entrance with a wide grin. 'So glad you're here.'

'I'm really happy to be here.'

We walked side by side down the hallway to the owner's box, where much of the upper management and special guests watched the game.

When we stepped inside, it was already buzzing with the pre-game festivities. I recognized a few faces I'd previously met and many that I would meet in the coming months. When I turned to look out the glass windows, something peculiar caught my eye. I excused myself from my dad who was talking with the owner and walked to the box seats reserved for the suite. Standing next to the railing was a woman wearing the same jersey I was, Griesen scrawled across her back. My heart hiccupped with confusion. And then I saw the little boy next to her wearing a matching jersey.

'Jenny! Connor! So nice to see you again!' I welcomed them with a hug. I would know that little boy anywhere, but he'd grown a few inches since I saw him at the batting cages.

'Nina, right?' Jenny asked.

'Yes. Does Landon know you're here?' It was a stupid question. Of course he did, but I was in shock. He hadn't mentioned them at all.

'Oh, for sure. He paid for our flight. He said he felt bad that he didn't get us to a game in Denver before he left. He contacted me two weeks ago and asked if we were free this weekend. Of course we accepted, and he booked us flights, a hotel, a car, and Connor even got to meet the team.'

Landon's generosity knew no bounds. I was proud to

have his name on my back.

Connor's grin under the Stars baseball cap couldn't have been bigger. His left hand disappeared under a glove a few sizes too big for him, one I recognized as one of Landon's old ones. In the other hand, he held a ball, which (Connor made sure I knew) Landon had signed.

We made small talk for the few minutes before the game started. I excused myself to grab a beer and mingle with my future co-workers. Everyone filed out to the stadium seats as the starting line-ups were announced. Landon trotted in from the bullpen and rubbed his hand with rosin. When he pointed to the heavens, my heart panged now that I knew the story behind his gesture. As he walked up the mound, his eyes scanned to the owner's box, and since I stood in the front row, he spotted me easily. His chin flinched upwards as he leveled me with his patented smile. My heart flip-flopped and galloped in my chest when I realized I'd been permanently added to his ritual.

Jenny sucked in a breath next to me. 'You're one lucky woman.'

I took a drink of my beer. 'That I am.'

Landon pitched a complete game shut-out and notched his tenth win of the season, a great mark for any pitcher, but especially for one who started the season rehabbing from Tommy John's. I stood next to Connor and Jenny in the hallway and waited as player after player emerged. Finally, Landon came out, his right elbow wrapped in ice. We closed the distance between us, meeting in the middle of the dim hallway. The cold ice dug into my back when he hugged me.

'So glad you were here,' he sighed into my shoulder. His body sagged into mine like he was looking for a soft place to land.

'Me too. You looked great.' I patted his right arm that

was still holding me tight. 'You OK?'

'Yeah. Just a little sore.' I felt his body tighten. Then, he whispered into my ear, 'Wait here just a sec. I need to say goodbye to Connor.'

I walked to the end of the hallway to allow Connor some time with Landon. I pretended not to pay attention to their interaction, but I couldn't help eavesdropping. Landon knelt down to Connor's level and said something to him that caused a wide-eyed grin to cross Connor's face. He nodded rapidly, and Landon patted him on the shoulder as he stood. I read Jenny's lips when she thanked Landon. They walked down the hallway to the front exit while Landon met me at the back.

He rested his palm behind me on the wall and leaned in like he was telling a secret. 'I have plans for you tonight.' He took me out the back entrance and pushed the unlock button for his car. He stuffed his bag into the back seat and opened the trunk.

'Landon, it's really late. Like eleven, and I'm sure you're tired and hungry.'

'There's only one thing I'm hungry for.'

I rolled my eyes and he laughed. My tone turned earnest. 'No seriously. We have all weekend. You don't have to –'

I stopped when he pulled out a blanket and a picnic basket. He threw the blanket over his shoulder, grabbed my hand, and took me back through the rear entrance with a swipe of his ID card.

'Where are we going?'

'To the field,' was all he said as he marched us through the vacant locker room and out the door to the dugout. He took the dugout steps two at a time and walked to the center of the infield right behind the mound. He looked around the stadium, nodded, and spread out the red blanket.

I stood on the top of the dugout steps, my confused feet

unwilling to move. 'We're having a picnic on the field?'

'Well, yeah, obviously,' he said, gesturing to the food he was unpacking. 'Then we'll fuck.'

I laughed and took off my sandals so that I could feel the perfectly manicured blades of grass between my toes as I walked. When I got to the blanket, I sat down and stretched out my legs in front of me. 'I'm surprised you're going to let all the stadium cleaning crew see your woman.'

'Fuck no. I'm not. They're not here tonight. And even if they were, they wouldn't see anything.' He pointed to the top of the stadium. 'All of these lights will be going off in about fifteen minutes except for the one bank of lights over home plate. Gets pretty dark out here, actually.'

'Bring girls here a lot?' I joked.

'Every night my girlfriend doesn't show up,' he deadpanned. He took a bite of sandwich and chewed it despite his grin. He swallowed before he got this reflective, contemplative look on his face. 'In all seriousness, I like to do this a lot. I like how peaceful and quiet it is. I remember what this feels like and try to imagine it like this when I take the field. It calms me so that my first few pitches don't suffer from too much adrenaline.'

I ate my sandwich too, and bit into the juicy apple. 'Thanks for dinner. I didn't have a chance to eat before,' I said with my mouth full.

'You're welcome.' We finished the meal amid small-talk of my classes and my dissertation. The lights shut off without warning just like he'd predicted. The moon cast long shadows in the shape of the banks of lights that circled the top of the stadium. They surrounded us like we were sitting in the middle of Stonehenge. The stars instantly brightened without the artificial light.

'Congratulations,' he added when I told him I'd finally finished my first draft. He threw our trash in the picnic basket and crawled over to me. 'Now, it's time to celebrate.'

His front pressed against my front so I was laid back on the soft, red blanket. One of his knees spread my legs as his body covered mine. His finger traced the number, his number, on the front of the jersey right above my left breast.

'I love my number on you,' he growled as his other hand unbuttoned the front of the jersey. He sucked in a breath when he parted the material and saw the sexy, black demi-bra I wore underneath. It barely covered my nipples. 'But I think I love this even more.'

His mouth went straight to the lace where he nipped until he could feel my distended nipple through the fabric. I arched my back, begging him to take more into his mouth.

I dug my nails into his scalp and pulled my fingers through his silky hair.

Then his mouth went to my collarbone while his fingers toyed with the necklace I always wore. 'You even wore this during the marathon.'

'Yes,' I hissed as he pulled off my jersey and unzipped my jeans.

'God. Do you know what that did to me? I ran up to you, wondering what you'd say, how you'd react. Then, I saw that, and I ... everything ... everything was OK.'

'Better than OK,' I said, dragging my nails down his back. I grabbed on to the bottom hem of his T-shirt and tugged it over his head.

He grunted and made quick work of my pants and his. His body came over mine again, his head tucked into my neck. He sucked and nipped as he placed himself at my entrance. Over his shoulder, the stars shined and winked, unembarrassed by what they were watching. A few blades of the manicured grass poked through the blanket where they brushed against my back.

He pressed into me slowly and I felt his exhale on my neck. His hands gripped my shoulder and hip so tightly that his knuckles turned white. 'I'm never going to look at this infield the same way.'

I'm never going to look at a lot of things the same way, I thought. The truth of the statement filled me with a sense of harmony and peace. It had taken me a long time to get to this moment, where I didn't have to feel like I had to say something crass to pretend I wasn't feeling anything. I didn't have to make a joke. I could simply trust in the purity of the moment, trust that this rug wasn't going to be pulled out from under me.

Some things are worth waiting for, I remembered Zach saying to Ansley.

This feeling was definitely one of them.

Landon rocked into me, his hands petting and gripping all my most sensitive spots. He ground his pelvis into mine, putting glorious pressure on my clit. Every so often, he held himself still inside me. I could feel the pulse of his member as he fought for control. Then he'd pull out and slam back into me so hard I scooted off the blanket. His hands held each of mine immobile above my head as he took my lips with an intoxicating combination of ferocity and gentleness.

When he pulled away, we both sucked in a desperate breath. 'Landon!' I cried out when I was able to.

His eyes were closed as he did a push up and arched his back. 'Give it to me.'

I wanted to give more. 'I love you, Landon.'

His hips stilled mid-thrust. His eyes popped open as he stared at me. I laughed when his mouth opened and closed, opened and closed.

I thrust my hips up to him, trying to make him resume his rhythm. We were so close to jumping off the cliff together. Finally, his hips started pumping again in small, forceful thrusts.

His arms bent so that our noses were a heated breath away. 'I love you too, Nina.'

I remember that moment not because of what happened but because of what didn't. There was no worry creeping up my spine. No leap of my heart or twist of my stomach. I felt nothing but happiness, and it was glorious.

As he brushed a tear from my cheek, one I didn't bother to hide, he smiled and locked our lips together. I'm not sure what buttons he pushed after that or how quick his body moved over mine. All I know is that his hand was entwined with mine, his breath mixed with mine as we both whispered the love we allowed ourselves to feel.

He stroked my hair from my forehead for a while afterwards, both of us smiling like we'd won the lottery.

'A fitting end to a new beginning,' Landon said.

It was, but then I thought about how far we'd come.

How far I'd allowed myself to come, to grow.

How much I allowed myself to believe in a happily ever after.

'No,' I said. 'A fitting beginning to a new end.'

The Claimed Series
by
Alaina Drake

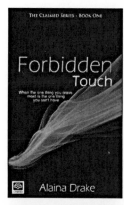

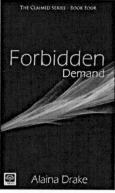

Forbidden Touch
Forbidden Temptation
Forbidden Addiction
Forbidden Demand

For more information about Alaina Drake
and other Accent Press titles
please visit

www.accentpress.co.uk

Lightning Source UK Ltd.
Milton Keynes UK
UKOW02f0836290616

277315UK00001B/3/P

9 781910 939673